The reflection from
with the moonlight flicl
rolling across the blacl
winds, carrying the sweet peach-like scent of plumeria, teased the palm fronds as easily as they tickled the torch lights—clearly a welcomed reprieve from five straight days of stifling temperatures. A catamaran and a couple of small outrigger canoes, their artfully painted fiberglass hulls made to look like the wood of ancient Koa trees, were pulled up along the sandy shoreline. The heavy beat of drums reverberated off the tall palms and set the tempo for a half-dozen pair of grass-skirted hips dancing on the main stage while vacationers laughed, ogled, and stuffed their faces with shredded pork, scoops of lomi salmon, steaming flavored rice wrapped in Ti leaves, thick juicy slices of pineapple, papaya, mango, and freshly roasted macadamia nuts that were all artfully displayed on wide banana-leaf-covered centerpieces. They sat cross-legged in the sand, sipping mai tais from plastic cups made to look like hollowed-out coconut shells, lost in a tropical fantasy that came complete with a souvenir snapshot taken with an authentic hula girl—the perfect paradise as portrayed on the website. The noise from the music, chanting, and laughter drowned out the frantic noise of the nearby kitchen, and it drowned out the desperate pleas and painful cries of Makani Palahia from the far side of the beach at Auntie Lily's Luau Cove and Hawaiian Barbecue.

Praise for Richard I Levine

"As you must know, you have a masterpiece with *To Catch the Setting Sun*. It was amazing, and I liked how you ended it…"

~ Dianne Rich, editor The Wild Rose Press

"Rich, you have a good strong novel that stands to be one of your best works ever. I will be first in line to buy the paperback and the ebook."

~ Lelani Black, Romance Author

To Catch the Setting Sun

by

Richard I Levine

To Catch the Setting Sun

Cover Art by *Jennifer Greeff*

The Wild Rose Press, Inc.
PO Box 708
Adams Basin, NY 14410-0708
Visit us at www.thewildrosepress.com

Publishing History
First Edition, 2022
Trade Paperback ISBN 978-1-5092-4329-7
Digital ISBN 978-1-5092-4330-3

Published in the United States of America

Chapter 1

When the rock is lifted, the light pours in and
the vermin will scurry in panic.
They always do.
The ancestors still come to me in my dreams to caution
that these parasites are as unrepentant and just as
predictable
as they have always been.
Yet we must not become complacent.
Vigilance is the key
or we fall victim to their treachery.
We are close, we are almost there.
Each new day peels away another layer of the façade.
No different than me,
you too can feel the winds of change.
So, take my hand and walk this path with me.
Open your eyes and see it as I do.
When we stand tall, strong, and together,
we will weather any storm.
I take comfort in knowing you also know
the day will be soon that the clouds will part,
and our hands will once again be free
to catch the setting sun.

The reflection from scattered tiki torches competed
with the moonlight flickering off the rhythmic ripples
rolling across the black velvet lagoon. Gentle trade

winds, carrying the sweet peach-like scent of plumeria, teased the palm fronds as easily as they tickled the torch lights—clearly a welcomed reprieve from five straight days of stifling temperatures. A catamaran and a couple of small outrigger canoes, their artfully painted fiberglass hulls made to look like the wood of ancient Koa trees, were pulled up along the sandy shoreline. The heavy beat of drums reverberated off the tall palms and set the tempo for a half-dozen pair of grass-skirted hips dancing on the main stage while vacationers laughed, ogled, and stuffed their faces with shredded pork, scoops of lomi salmon, steaming flavored rice wrapped in Ti leaves, thick juicy slices of pineapple, papaya, mango, and freshly roasted macadamia nuts that were all artfully displayed on wide banana-leaf-covered centerpieces. They sat cross-legged in the sand, sipping mai tais from plastic cups made to look like hollowed-out coconut shells, lost in a tropical fantasy that came complete with a souvenir snapshot taken with an authentic hula girl—the perfect paradise as portrayed on the website. The noise from the music, chanting, and laughter drowned out the frantic noise of the nearby kitchen, and it drowned out the desperate pleas and painful cries of Makani Palahia from the far side of the beach at Auntie Lily's Luau Cove and Hawaiian Barbecue.

****

The hardened steel of the polished blade sparkled when slowly turned a mere few degrees from left to right, back and forth, as if part of an ancient ritual. Makani's teeth clinched against the foul-tasting cloth that had been forced into her mouth and tied tight behind her head, each time the knife circled back

2

toward her face, each time passing closer, each time pausing for effect. When rested alongside her cheek, she arched as far as her restraints would allow—the plastic zip ties cutting deeper into her wrists. She let out a muffled cry, begging for the whole ordeal to stop. A sadistic laugh from the shadows made her pray to Jesus for the long-lost comfort of her mother—a comfort stolen by the alcohol and drugs that flowed through West Oahu as easily as the tides that washed away the sandcastles from its beaches. To watch her struggle not to gag as her eyes pleaded for freedom fueled an adrenaline rush that fed the flames of her assailant—strong and powerful now, like a sovereign over all that was to be ruled and judged. The blade was pulled from Makani's golden-brown skin long enough for her back muscles and her bladder to relax, only to make her arch and plead again when it was returned to her tear-stained cheek.

"This is on you, Princess! Brought this on yourself, yeah? It's a shame, too, because you're so young and pretty. Of all the others, you're the one who looks the most like royalty. The ancients would've been proud of you. But they're not, are they? No, they're not, and you know they're not. You've disappointed all of us with so many of your sins. Are you ready to confess?"

She struggled to reply, but the rag pressed hard on her tongue.

"What's that? You say something? You look like you got something to say."

A faceless phantom-like figure stood tall above her, causing her to squint from the intermittent sparkle of what she thought was a pendant. Makani nodded while she strained to make out the image that seemed so familiar to her.

"I'll loosen the bandana, but I warn you right now, if you scream…" She saw the knife dance again. "But let's not think about that, okay? We calmly talk story a little, yeah?"

Again, she nodded, almost afraid to speak now that her lips could move freely. A rush of fresh air filled her mouth and intensified the pungent taste that covered her tongue. Her stomach muscles tightened as she gagged.

"P-please, let me go. I d-don't know you. I don't know what you want from me."

"Let you go? I think, I think maybe after you confess. I think maybe I can let you go after we finish our business, yeah?"

"C-confess? What business? Who are you? What d-do you want from me? Why are you d-doing this to me?"

"Why am I doing? I didn't pick you, Princess. You made that choice. You made that choice when you picked him and rejected our own."

"P-picked who? Reject you? I d-don't even know you. How did I…"

"You judged us!" A heavy hand landed across her mouth. "You judged me and our bruddahs and sistas when you chose an outsider. Judge not, lest ye be judged, and today is…today is your judgment day."

****

Reece Valentine had a hard time keeping his eyes off the third girl from the left—diverting his attention long enough to down another piña colada or attempt to calm the concerns of his fiancée that he wasn't going to run off into the bush with a native girl. But that didn't stop him from enjoying the fantasy. With constricted pupils locked onto toned abdominal muscles gyrating within grabbing distance of his imagination, he laughed at the memory of frat house Polynesian-style parties that never came close to the evening's entertainment.

"Reece, stop staring. It's embarrassing."

"Come on, Jules, I'm trying to enjoy the show. We're on vakay. Where's your island spirit?"

"I'm trying to enjoy the show, but that's your fifth drink since the luau started, and you're beginning to put on a little show of your own. At least stop howling at those girls. People are starting to look at you."

"Jules, please. I'm just having some fun. It's not every day we get to enjoy something like this, is it? Seriously, when was the last time we saw a show like this back in Portland?"

"Look, I'm not trying be all salty, but when you ran up on stage to do the hula, did you have to grab that dancer's waist? And the way you started rubbing on her…geez!"

"Okay, now you're exaggerating." He grabbed her and nuzzled her neck.

"Really?"

"It was part of the dance."

"Okay, so when the male dancers come out and I go running up there, are you going to get mad when I start rubbing myself all over those well-oiled muscular bodies?" She smiled.

"Now you're the one being silly. Have another drink and chill."

"Chill? You want me to chill? I think I'll go for a swim…a naked swim." She got up and raced down the beach toward the far end of the lagoon.

After a brief moment, as well as a few envious

looks from other revelers, Reece went after her.

"Jules! Julie, wait up!" he called, but the alcohol had hindered his ability to maintain a steady balance over the soft uneven contours of the sand. When he fell, he scraped his knee on a piece of coral buried just below the surface. "Damn it! Jules, wait up. I just…damn, I just cut myself."

Halfway between the luau and the end of the lagoon, about thirty yards from a thicket of Kiawe bushes, she turned to see him sitting on the beach, nursing his knee, and quite possibly his ego. Julie Chow started to head back when she heard some rustling and what she thought was a grunting sound coming from the direction of the bushes. She stopped to listen, only to hear Reece call out again. She tried to listen once more but heard nothing.

"Jules! Come back."

"Why don't you come over here," she said and took several steps toward the bushes. "It's dark and deserted down this way."

"I hurt myself. Come help me."

With a few glances over her shoulder, she slowly made her way back.

"Serves you right. I think the ancient Hawaiian gods were punishing you just now because of your disrespectful thoughts about one of their daughters."

"Stop it, will you? My knee is killing me."

"Such a baby!" she teased. "I'm surprised you can feel anything with all that native juice in you."

"Stop scolding and come help me," he begged. She came close enough for him to grab her arm and pull her down to join him on the sand.

"You're not hurt that bad, you faker!"

"I know, but I had to do something. I couldn't catch up to you." He laughed.

"Because you're drunk, and when you get drunk, you're horny as hell."

"You can say that again."

"I'm being serious."

"Listen, I got carried away, and I'm sorry. But you're right, Jules, I'm horny as hell, and you know I'm not interested in anyone other than you." He leaned in for a kiss, but she pulled away at the last moment. "Hey!"

"There's a lot of bushes down there." She pointed. "Wanna go fool around?"

"What? Get naked here on the beach in the middle of a luau? There's tons of people here."

"It's dark. There's bushes. No one will see us. No one will hear us. Come on, you afraid?"

"They won't see us, but they'll definitely hear us."

"You mean they'll hear you. I'll have you screaming so loud they'll think you're being murdered." She jumped on top of him, and they passionately kissed in a long embrace.

"I've got a better idea." He pushed back to catch his breath. "Let's go back to the hotel, and I'll show you what going native is all about."

"And give up a chance to get my hands on all those sweaty, muscular Hawaiian men? Race you." She took off back to the festivities with Reece in hot pursuit.

****

Makani gagged at the smell of the dirty hand that covered her face—removed only when the couple from the luau got far enough away from the thicket.

"That wouldn't have ended well for those tourists.

Too bad. Would've made the night a little more interesting. So, where were we? Oh yes, about your choice, Princess."

"I d-don't know what you're talking about. What ch-choice did I make?"

"You are one very pretty *wahine*, a very pretty woman, you know that? Yeah, you know you so *nani*, so beautiful, don't you? I'll bet you tease men to get things you want, yeah?"

"If you're g-going, if you're going to rape me, then j-just do it already. Just do it and g-get it over with. I won't tell anyone. Just do it and, and let me go. Please? Please, just let me go."

Save for the low sadistic laugh she had heard before, there was no immediate reply. Her breathing, fast and shallow now, seemed to make the few stars that had been visible through the branches spin wildly and caused her hands, legs, and feet to feel cold—making the hand that inched its way down the outer portion of her thigh feel uncomfortably warm.

For her tormentor, however, there was pleasure in feeling the gentle contours of muscles toned from many hours of hula as rough callused fingers crept over her thigh, past the knee, and down to her ankle. A brief pause to take in the tremble that was felt moving like a wave through her body, watching her lips press together, and her eyes squeeze tight, elicited a child-like giddiness that had long been forgotten.

Makani tightened again from the sandpaper texture of a tongue across her cheek and a heavy breath in her ear. She realized the warm antiseptic scent now lingering on her face was the smell of whiskey. The hand with jagged fingernails carved a return path up the inside of her leg to her knee, then slowed while continuing up the inner portion of her thigh—teasing, threatening. She cried a little harder.

"Did that hurt, Princess? Take it from me, a true warrior princess doesn't cry. She's strong, very strong, and she likes it rough."

"Please, don't…"

"What, make love to you? You make me laugh. I'd never soil myself on a sinner."

She felt the grip tighten around her upper thigh, and in equal response her athletic body tightened just as much.

"I like this. I like how your legs feel. So smooth, so soft. I like how they feel in my hands. It's so…comforting. I bet the boys like touching them too, yeah? I bet you'd really like me to do more, don't you? I can tell the thought excites you. I bet you didn't expect my hands to be this strong and powerful, yeah? Do you feel how strong my hands are? It makes me feel so powerful to hold you like this."

A low-pitched hiss, then a crackled voice momentarily interrupted. "Central to Detective eight-one."

"You almost tricked me, Princess!" The anger was as sudden and sharp as the sting she felt from the three-inch welt created when those hands were quickly withdrawn. "You almost tricked me. You were trying to confuse me. Deceitful women like you do that all the time, but I know better." Again, the blade came into view. "You tried to tempt me with your makeup. I bet you do it to make yourself look young and innocent. But we both know better, don't we? You tried to deceive me, but you're not innocent, not innocent at all.

You do it special for him, don't you? Yes, I think you did it to please him. You make me angry. You make the ancestors angry."

"I d-don't know what you're t-talking about. I don't have a boyfr—"

"Liar!" The voice rose, triggering a shooting glance through the branches, down the beach toward the festivities, afraid they might have been heard. "Don't make me gag you."

Again, a radio transmission crackled. "Central to Detective eight-one, do you copy?"

"Who are you?" she asked, again getting a glimpse of the pendant, focusing on the letters H O N O L U L U across its face. She realized it wasn't a piece of jewelry, but a badge. She tried to narrow her focus— her tears making it difficult to read the number. The radio crackled again.

"Lieutenant Kim to central dispatch, be advised eight-one's radio hasn't been working properly. You can reach him on his cell."

She strained to see the face hidden in the darkness, the voice now mocking the radio call.

"Central to Detective eight-one. Where are you, eight-one? Come save the day, eight-one."

"Dispatch to Kim, copy that, Lieutenant," came the static-filled reply.

"I d-don't know you. I don't know you at all. I don't kn-know what you're talking about. Are you HPD? What do you want from me?"

"You know me," came the whisper, this time placing the sharp edge of the blade across her costume, cutting just enough material on her shoulder to expose her breasts. "Very pretty."

"You said you were g-going to let me go. I should be d-dancing at the show. I should be there. They're going to m-miss me. They're g-going to come looking for me."

"Nobody's going to come looking for you, Princess, nobody."

The blade methodically moved across her flesh— circling, teasing, drawing blood from a shallow incision across her shoulder. At first Makani felt the sting before the warmth of liquid snaked into the creases of her underarm. Her tears flowed freely now. Adding one more indignity to her suffering, the grass skirt she had always worn with pride was ripped aside, and one more time the knife came to rest across her cheek.

"You know who I am, and you know exactly why we're here. We all must face judgment for our sins."

"I don't know...." She stopped mid-sentence—a dirty index finger pressed to her mouth. She gagged at the vile taste—a cross between a lack of hygiene and her own urine. The finger was forced farther into her mouth and pressed against her tongue. She reflexively bit down, drawing blood and a painful slap to her face. "I don't know you," she cried out. "Why are you doing this? P-please let me go! I won't say anything. I won't t-tell anyone, I promise!"

"Let you go?" came the angered reply. A vise-like grip squeezed her cheeks, preventing her from speaking. "Not now, damn you! Not after you bit me! Not after you refuse to confess your sins. Do you see how you've forced my hand? Now you have to be purified." Again, her face was slapped.

"I'm sorry, I am. I didn't mean to bite you. Please? I won't tell anyone, I promise." Her eyes, blurred from tears, tried to follow the figure as it moved about—finally catching a glimpse of a face lit by the glow of a freshly lit cigarette. "Oh my God!" She was repulsed at the sight, gagging as the bandana was forced back into her mouth—arching, straining, and kicking against the nylon cable ties when the cigarette was moved closer to the side of her face.

"I know you don't understand. Nobody does anymore, and that's the problem. In the old days the people needed to make their peace with the gods so they could be blessed and have a harvest, take fish from the sea, and be protected from evil, from the night marchers, from Pele. Those gods and the ancestors are deeply saddened how our way of life, our history, our culture, and our future have all been dishonored. You, and others like you, have dishonored all of us by mixing pure blood, and there's only one way for you to be forgiven. You will serve as a message, a warning to others. And with your purification, with your sacrifice, the gods and the ancestors will grant you redemption."

Makani's heartbeat pounded in her chest and in her head, making the drums, the laughter, and the applause for the fire-eaters disappear. And just as another cold stinging slice was surgically carved across her throat, she thought she heard her killer recite an ancient prayer while she watched the flickering lights of the luau fade away.

Chapter 2

When I was a child
I had a vision.
A man on a horse from a faraway place
crested the hill above my village.
As he made his way past the graves of my memories,
the people took refuge for they did not know him.
Too many times we have been betrayed.
Too many times I have felt that pain.
There was fear,
there was no one to protect us.
How much more could any of us take?
So the people prayed which gave me strength.
It gave me peace.
Death, after all,
is nothing but a pathway to the next manifestation.
So, in this vision, I stood my ground as this was my test.
I was rewarded, a prayer had been answered.
This man had been sent to walk with me on my journey.
He came and captured my trust, my heart, my soul.
And while he did, little did he know,
I would be the one to capture his.
I always knew, when the time was right,
you would come back into my life.

Henry tossed from the images in his head. One moment they flashed with lightning speed. The next they slowed in places and at things he didn't understand or didn't want to see. Some were repetitive, some sequential, and some seemed to have no relevance. The faces danced before him, the voices calling and pleading, hands reaching out beyond his grasp as if they weren't there at all. The pain he felt disturbed him. However, the internal debate to keep from waking was a short one.

He knew these images. He'd seen them before. And as disturbing as they were, he allowed them to play out. Henry searched for more clues, but he innately knew why they've returned. As with the previous dreams, for the most part he was an observer. He found himself behind a barrier and, blind to the detour, cursed its placement. *"I can only do so much by myself, damn it!"* He wondered if this was just another obstacle manufactured to derail his efforts, or if it was his past-life transgressions, manifesting as a karmic bill collector serving a past-due notice. A part of him wondered if this was simply a self-inflicted critique—a review of his analytical skills, his decision-making process, his reluctance to ask for assistance, and his confidence to trust his instincts enough to be able to prevent another senseless killing. And because his self-doubt always lingered just below the surface, this was what he kept questioning to justify his preferred method of seeking refuge—a refuge that was, for now, still based on a need to numb the reality.

As he observed the replay, the faces blended into one, then disappeared altogether. Henry waited. Listening intently, he heard the cries of just one—her face emerging from the blackness. He watched her bleed, and he wanted to break his bonds to get to her, to free her, to save her. He briefly wondered if he was watching himself wield the knife that methodically sliced with surgical precision. *That's what they keep telling me. That's what they want me to believe,* he thought. *They're wrong, I know they are. This can't be me. I can't be the cause of this!*

No matter how many times he told himself he was there to be her savior, no matter how many times he tried, he couldn't break free to do so. And yet, when he looked, he was free. Outside of feeling he didn't have enough knowledge, evidence, understanding, strength—there were no metal shackles. There was no rope, no industrial-grade tape to bind him to his cross. There were no excuses, only guilt, and perhaps, he hesitantly admitted, courage. "*I can stop this!*" His body heavy, his legs immobile and sinking into the darkness that was nothing more than a recurring paralysis of fear, a recurring feeling of doom, a recurring sense of helplessness, a recurring shame that he could have done more if only he had known more. Among the flurry of why, what ifs, and what for—why was this happening, why this girl, why that one, what did they ever do to deserve this—he couldn't stop asking, "*Why me? Why are they being left for me to find? What's the connection to Maya? Maya!*"

In helpless frustration his arms wind-milled against his uncertainties. Landing labored blows against the air, he yelled into the void: "Leave her alone, leave her alone." Again and again, he lashed out, striking at nothing, the effort exasperating. Catching a glimpse of a sneer, he strained to see beyond the nicotine-stained teeth and the cracked lips, which was more than had been revealed in the past. "Who is that? Who are you?"

As his uncertainty weighed upon him, Henry fought to fill his lungs and wondered if he had always been watched. "Who's there?" He shouted at the figure that weaved in and out of the shadows. The smell of decaying flesh repulsed him. He was consumed with anger—unable to make the image any more detailed, unable to make it go away, unable to stop the attack. He observed her struggle to escape—ashamed her efforts to break free seemed to dwarf his response to the assault. He wondered if she knew the tears she shed would be her last. He watched one form, welling up until it spilled over her lash—charting a path across the stains on her cheek, disappearing into a hole that breached the smoothness of her skin. Her chocolate-brown eyes pleaded to him as a knife sliced through the air, but it was her silent cries and look of betrayal that stabbed at his heart. When the knife returned on the downstroke, droplets of blood splattered across his face. As her eyes glazed, "I'm sorry," was all he managed to say. And as if a bolt of lightning shot from the hand held high above their heads, the flash of light pierced the darkness—his eyes widening at the silhouette of a fist poised to strike. And it did strike, over and over. The repetitive impacts pounded away, but save for the remorse of his impotence, he felt nothing.

****

The repetitive pounding on Henry's front door grew louder, forcing him to lurch upright—his sheets soaked with sweat, the blanket twisted in a heap on the floor. He thought his head, feeling far too heavy for his neck, was about to explode. His hands squeezed at his temples, and the pounding made him jump once again. *What fucking time is it? What fucking day is it?* He reached for the aspirin—succeeding only in knocking an empty rocks glass, a tattered paperback, and a small framed photograph to the floor. The steady rhythm and the screeching voice were unmistakable. *Mrs. Coleman!*

"Hank?" she shouted. "What's with all the yelling?"

Not now, for Christ's sake! He wanted to vomit—the images from his nightmare still vivid, the aftertaste of Tennessee sipping whiskey lingered. *You've gotta stop drinking that stuff.*

"Hank, I know you're in there! Are you okay?"

"The house better be on fire," he muttered. He rubbed his eyes to no avail; the grit only irritated them more.

"Hank? Hank, you okay? Tell me you're okay and open the door!" She continued banging. "I hope you didn't break anything."

He glanced down and noticed a small crack in the frame's glass. *It's my fucking picture frame,* he thought. "Yes, yes, Mrs. Coleman, I'm in here! I'm okay!" He reached for the photo and placed it back on the nightstand. "Nothing of yours is broken. Now. Please. Go. Away!" His eyelids pressed tight, he shook his head. *Why me? What did I ever do to deserve...?*

"Hank! I heard you from across—"

"Mrs. Coleman, damn it! I told you I'm okay. I'm all right. Now please leave me the fu...please, leave me alone, already!" He threw his body back into the mattress. "And stop pounding on the door!"

"Hank Benjamin! I can hear you yelling clear across the street to my house. This is the second time this week. What's going on with you?"

This has to be hell. It's gotta be. There's no other

explanation. This woman's never gonna stop, never!

"I'm really okay. Trust me, it…it was just…" he said more calmly, resigned to the fact that his landlady's annoying persistence would not be deterred. "It was just a bad dream."

"Because of that book?"

Probably because of that damn whiskey. He glanced over at his clock radio—staring at it until he realized he had only been asleep for a couple of hours. *Shit! I'm supposed to be covering for Becerra today.*

He had just enough time for a quick shower, jump into a fresh set of clothes, and head back to the bullpen to begin the morning shift.

Henry hated working the four to midnight tour because it always took him several hours to decompress and fall asleep afterward. More than that, he hated working in Waikiki and fielding complaints from tourists, when he could have been working his case.

"Hank? Was it because of the book?"

He glanced down at the paperback. "No, no, it wasn't. I haven't even started reading it."

"I think you have," she insisted.

"And I don't think you can hear me from across the street. I think you were snooping again, Mrs. Coleman. In fact, I've noticed stuff on my kitchen table is out of place again."

"Well, if you're okay, then," she said with a bit of embarrassment, "I'll be going now."

He didn't know how much longer he could stomach the intrusions before completely losing patience with his next-door neighbor and landlord whom he had tolerated fairly well up to now. She went from making the occasional hot meal for him as an excuse to check on the condition of the small plantation-style cottage she owned, to calling him at work or appearing on his doorstep to complain about loud music from a neighbor's house, suspicious cars cruising the street, and, as she claimed, the occasional voyeur. *"She's the eyes and ears of all that is and isn't,"* he once told a colleague. He knew she didn't mean any harm. She was just lonely since her husband had passed away.

For the most part he dismissed her behavior because he knew she had no one to talk to, and accepting her homemade meals, while often giving him indigestion, seemed to give her pleasure. *"She probably takes pleasure because it gives me indigestion,"* he once joked. And that was why he was careful to double wrap and bag the meals he tossed into the trash bin on pick-up day—a practice he started when he noticed her front porch shoe bins came from old bookshelves he had discarded. But then, a few months after he moved into the one-bedroom cottage, she became more persistent and obsessive when Nicky Costa moved onto the street just a few doors away:

****

"This guy gives me the creeps," she had said. "That's the feeling I get when I see him. I can't put my finger on it, but I just feel uneasy when he's out walking that nasty dog of his."

"No offense, Mrs. Coleman, but you said that about Amanda what's-her-face, remember?"

"It's Judy, and yes, this is no different. She turned out to be a junkie and a hooker and…"

"Amanda was not a junkie, she was hypoglycemic, and she was definitely not a hooker. She just had very little fashion sense, wore too much makeup, and had several boyfriends."

"She was a hooker I tell you, and I should know because I'm from New York City, and I know what they look like, and as I said, this feeling I have is no different. He keeps odd hours. I've seen him leave his house at two, sometimes three in the morning. He has visitors come and go except he never lets them in. They come to the door, spend a minute or two, then leave. He's got one of those ugly pit dogs…"

"A pit bull?"

"Yes, a pit bull, and he keeps it chained up in his yard, and it's…"

"Come to think of it, I have heard it barking. But a lot of people in this neighborhood seem to own dogs."

"The thing is, Hank, he always stops in front of my house and lets that beast do its business in my yard. And all the while he's staring into my front windows as if he's daring me to come out and say something."

"Does he pick up after the dog?"

"No, he never does."

"Maybe he leaves it there because he knows you watch his every move and you're making him uncomfortable. He's getting back at you."

"I'd like to get a look inside his windows, but that dog. It's not hard to notice he's hiding something."

"Maybe you can make friends with the dog. Forget I said that. The last thing you need is getting caught on his property."

"Wait a second, I think that's an excellent idea, though. How do I do that?"

"I don't know, maybe throw it some food whenever he's not home. I hear dogs love cheese and chocolate balls."

"You really think that'll work?"

"No, of course not. I'm just kidding. I think I read somewhere that dogs and cheese are not a good combination. And chocolate, oh God no, that'll kill the poor thing. Look, Mrs. Coleman, maybe you should forget about this guy. It's not as if he's living in one of your cottages, right?"

"Yeah, but you know me with my intuition. I'm telling you, this feeling is worse."

"Okay, Mrs. Coleman, if it makes you feel better, I'll go talk to him and see what he's like. What's his name?"

"Call me Judy, and I don't know. There's no name on his mailbox."

"And I don't suppose you might've accidentally bumped into that box, knocked the little door open, and got a peek at his mail…say, for example, one day when you knew he wasn't home?"

"I'm not that kind of person. Besides, it's one of those security boxes, the kind that needs a key."

"I see," he said in disbelief. "Okay, I'll go talk to him."

"Don't just talk to him. Check him out on your computers at work. I'll bet anything he's in your system."

"I'll look into it, and if the guy checks out, I want you to promise you'll stop complaining about him…and stop snooping on him."

****

Although short on time, Henry had kept his word. And it was during that meeting the hairs on the back of his neck stood on edge. Having arrested him ten years prior, he remembered Nicky Costa the minute he laid eyes on him. Costa, however, had acted as if he didn't recognize Henry, but the detective was certain, by the coldness of his stare and the sneering chapped lips, the guy knew exactly what their connection was.

Fucking Nicky Costa! He cried like a little schoolgirl when I busted his fat ass with a teenaged hooker and an ounce of coke, he recalled. *He didn't appreciate being dragged out of his car with his pants around his ankles. I haven't thought about him in years. What the hell is he doing out of jail? And what the hell is he doing living on this street?*

He had to admit Judy Coleman's intuition was right. To say she had him pegged as somebody to keep an eye on was certainly an understatement. And Henry was definitely going to keep an eye on him after confirming that Costa had a reputation as a cold-hearted grifter with a long history of petty crimes and pyramid schemes that left a few dozen people from Oahu to California screaming for his head. But he also recollected the guy had a weakness. Costa wanted people to think he was somebody important— somebody who was well-connected. And while he desperately sought out acknowledgment, admiration, and money from the unsuspecting, he was quick to stalk, bully, and assault those who saw through the façade and threatened to expose him.

Being publicly unmasked had been his Achilles heel. It would send him into an uncontrolled rage. It had been rumored that he ambushed and beat a man to within an inch of his life after it was revealed that Costa had a long list of restraining orders and misdemeanor convictions in California. *First this case that has brass breathing down my neck, then Judy Coleman, and now Nicky Costa. Lord, why? Please tell me why?*

Henry didn't have time for Costa but knew he would be impossible to ignore now that the guy was living a few houses down the street, with Judy Coleman incessantly poking that wasp's nest, and with having once been cryptically warned by the man that "karma had a long memory."

The pounding in his head continued. Again, he glanced at the clock, noted the time, then focused on the bottle of aspirin. *Is this hell? Yes, this has to be hell. Of all the things that I've done in my life to warrant this sort of punishment from the heavens, and I know I've done some bad things, I don't deny it, I don't. I know I'm being punished. But God.* He looked up to the ceiling. *What did I ever do that was so bad to deserve this past year? How much more do you think I can take?* No answer came. It never did. But it made him think of the paperback, and he wondered why he hadn't just thrown it away within minutes of Judy Coleman coming to the Waikiki station to give it to him:

****

"What's up, Mrs. Coleman? What's so important that it couldn't wait until I got off duty?"

"It's Judy, and no, I didn't tell the desk officer that it was important, and I didn't mean to sound like I was insisting on seeing you. Did I take you away from working on a case?" She pointed to the files in his hand. "I didn't stop you from doing something important, did I?"

"Yeah, you did. A tourist at the Royal Palms misplaced her sunscreen," he said with a deadpan look.

"No, really? Oh wait, you're being sarcastic. I get

23

it, I get it." She laughed nervously. "Hey, I got you a coffee, just the way you like it. Black, right? Black with two sugars, right?"

"I've got plenty of coffee here at the station and..." He watched her expression fall. "It's cold and been sitting in the pot all day, so it's probably just a pot of liquid acid. Black with two sugars. Good memory, thank you. So, Judy, I don't mean to be rude, but I really got work I gotta do." He held up his files. "So, what can I do for you?"

"Well, there is one thing." She held out a paperback. "I finished the book. Remember I told you about it? I found it at that used bookstore, the one in Kaimuki."

"No, I don't remember."

"Sure you do. I showed it to you when I brought it home. It was like it jumped out at me. So, I bought it and started reading it, and I noticed it had some similarities to you know who and your case, I mean the case you can't talk about. Divine intervention, right? I told you I'd let you read it as soon as I was done. Well, I'm done! I made plenty of notes for myself, and I underlined some things for you. You'll see some similarities to our neighbor. Here, it's in the book, page eighty-three."

"The book looks like it went through hell."

"You're gonna find this real fascinating, Hank. I'm not kidding. Page eighty-three. I've got it place marked with that newspaper clipping. See it?" she said with more enthusiasm now that he seemed receptive.

"Okay, I'll give it a look." He reluctantly took it.

"And you'll let me know what you think?"

"Give me some time, and I'll try to get to it. But no

promises, okay?"

"Great! That's great. You're gonna thank me. You'll see what I'm talking about."

****

Henry toweled off after a much-needed shower, quickly shaved, dressed, and hit the speed dial on his cell phone.

"Hey, Sarge, Hank Benjamin…I'd call in from the car radio, but it's been giving me problems again…I'm running a little late, but I'm on my way as we speak, so can you log me in? In the meantime, if anything comes up, just call me at this number…yeah, I'm filling in for Freddie…great, you're a pal."

On his way out he noticed Mrs. Coleman's book by the side of his bed. He picked it off the floor, stared at it for a second, then flung it across the room—the placemark at page eighty-three falling out when the paperback hit the wall. He looked over at the photo, apologized for the cracked glass, then carefully picked up the leather-bound journal sitting alongside and held it close to his chest. His fingers caressed the engraved initials on the face of the worn cover and prayed for strength before reading the next entry as he did each morning. *Maya.* The ache gave way to a kinder memory—the voice so clear:

"No matter how many times, no matter how many ways I've asked you, Henry, you've never denied my requests, my desires, my needing you to hold me, love me, protect me."

"Please forgive me, babe."

Chapter 3

I remember the first time I saw you.
The electricity traveled as if a wave over my body.
I felt the heat in my cheeks,
the weakness in my knees,
and my heart ran so fast it hurt.
In an odd way,
I was excited at the thought that others had noticed.
Did they know I was undressing you in my mind,
gliding my fingertips across your chest,
resting my head against your shoulder?
I fantasized you taking me,
until I realized I had caught your attention.
I felt like a schoolgirl in the throes of a summer crush.
Was I that obvious?
Were you reading my thoughts, feeling my lust?
I think you were.
Your eyes bore into me,
and I knew then and there you saw right through me.
And that's when you smiled.
I remember the first time I touched you.
Your confession was every part of the fantasy and more.

In spite of the lot attendant's best effort to block cars from going beyond the makeshift blockade, Detective Henry Benjamin, preoccupied with his recent nightmares, old images that surfaced unsolicited, leads that had gone nowhere, and a myriad of theories, suspicions, and criticisms, was having none of it—not now, not today. He drove his city-issued sedan through the flimsy barriers, yellow warning tape, and past the arm-waving retiree.

"Hey, stop! You can't! Hey, I used to be on the job!" the old guy shouted in vain while frantically pointing to the faded security emblem embroidered on the front of his sweat-stained polo shirt.

As far as Henry was concerned, the shimmering air radiating off the asphalt looked a few degrees shy of a lava pit. With the pleasure of the previous day's trade winds gone, he suffered the late morning temperature as if he had been a recent transplant from the Pacific Northwest.

The attendant was certainly no obstacle as he was determined to park as close to the trees as possible, even if it meant driving right up to the second layer of "crime scene" warning tape, which was now attracting a few tourists hoping to catch a glimpse of a TV star or two.

"I'll bet they're filming a new episode! Look, is that Steve and Danny over there? Quick, I think it's really them, and I gotta get their autographs!" he overheard one say as she rushed past his car.

Tapping the horn a few times, Henry interrupted a patrolman in mid text-chat to get him to pay attention to the growing audience before continuing his drive closer to the beach.

"Well, well, if it isn't Dirty Henry," the patrolman called out in reference to the lone-wolf detective from the classic crime novels.

"Nice to see you too, Kalima. I see you're still

getting assigned the important jobs," he responded while purposely driving over a few traffic cones. "Sorry about that, buddy!"

There were countless palm trees seductively revealing manufactured huts with facades of bamboo, palm fronds, and tropical grasses that lined the crescent moon-shaped lagoon known as Luau Cove. He found a trio of coconut palms that filtered just enough of the sun to help cool what the car's sporadically working air conditioner could never do. He knew he was being jerked around by the motor pool mechanics who claimed it always worked fine for them and suspected this was their payback because he refused to bring them boxes of pastries from Chinatown like other detectives did. *With my luck,* he thought, *one of those friggin' coconuts will fall, break the damn windshield, and those fat fucks won't fix that either.*

From the time he got the message and the forty-five minutes spent weaving in and out of the thick westbound freeway traffic, he hadn't been worried about the irate guest back at the Royal Oahu Hotel who seemed more upset about Henry's attitude than he was about his missing gold watch. He wasn't thinking about the threat of a complaint to the chief of detectives after he turned his attention to the urgent text—forgetting he was in the middle of taking a report of the supposed theft.

"Are you even listening to me, Officer?"

"Hold up a minute, bud...and, uh, it's 'detective.'"

"Hold up a minute? Do you know who you're talking to?" he had barked at Henry who no longer heard him. *"At least my watch, unlike your job, is*

insured." Continuing as Henry turned heel and headed off without so much as an "excuse me, but this is an emergency."

From his point of view, he would have been off-duty hours before, and he would have been had he not agreed to work the day shift as a favor. But he did agree to help out one of the few friends he had at the Waikiki precinct, and now cursed himself for having made that agreement. He couldn't care less about a disgruntled visitor whom he assumed spent more money on his airfare and daily consumption of tropical cocktails than any member of the hotel housekeeping staff got paid in a month. He typically didn't have anything against people of means, but he had no tolerance for the ones who were arrogant about it—always demanding attention and reminding others of their station in life. Henry didn't give the guy a second thought as he made his getaway. He was consumed with the possibilities of what he'd find when he got to Auntie Lily's on the leeward side of the island.

"Detective eight-one to dispatch…eight-one to Central dispatch…" Silence. "Eight-one to dispatch…be advised I'm on lunch," he called but received no reply. "Damn radio!"

He was about to slam the microphone against the dashboard, but the sight of the private security golf cart growing in his rearview mirror preempted the thought.

"I can't let you park here, bruddah," the man shouted in vain as Henry flipped his shield and pushed past him. "Why didn't you say something before, brah?"

"Relax, bruddah, it's probably the most excitement you had today."

"I don't need this kind of excitement, and I don't need your damn disrespect. I still know people downtown, asshole!" he cursed, then drove off in his cart.

"Great," Henry mumbled, "I just made another friend."

Detective Billy Iona took a deep breath at the sight of Henry bulldogging his way past the lot attendant and turned to monitor Lieutenant Mendoza at the far end of the lagoon. When the young lieutenant caught on, Iona motioned to his superior—deep in reporter's questions—that he'd handle it, then hurried to intercept his one-time partner. Still, that didn't stop Mendoza from keying his portable radio to utter a stern, "Iona?"

"Jeez, Hank, I specifically texted you not to come. What the hell are you doing here?" While he displayed frustration with Henry, he knew all along the detective wouldn't be able to help himself. "Didn't the brass order you to stay away from shit outside your district?"

"I thought it was a suggestion," he said with a hint of sarcasm, "and if I'm right, this does concern me."

"You see this, this shit right here? This is the kind of shit that gets you in trouble. At least you could've parked in the lot like everybody else."

"I'm not everybody else, Billy boy. Why should I park a hundred yards away when I have a reserved space right there in the shade?" He wiped the beads of sweat from his forehead before another salty droplet rolled into the corner of his eye. "Tourist, transplant, *Kama'aina*, *Kanaka*, which is it?"

"The area is blocked off for a reason."

"What am I, huh?" He pointed to the gold shield clipped to his belt.

"Somebody who's on really thin ice?" he said. "C'mon, man, you know what I meant."

Henry started surveying the scene, taking mental notes. "Tourist, transplant, Ka—"

"Just stop a sec, or at least slow it down, Hank."

"I am going slow. I'm just asking you to fill me in."

"I told you in the text message that I'd get all the details to you as soon as I could. You should try reading those things from beginning to end. Now please, go back to town."

"I appreciate the heads up, Billy, but please cut the wiseass shit. Look, you knew damn well I wasn't gonna stay away."

"You know, I already got word you walked away from a guy in the middle of taking a report."

"That was fast. Gotta love that coconut wireless, huh? Anyway, it was another one of those things that should've been given to a house dick or a uniform."

"Had I known you were in the middle of something, I would've contacted you later."

"Really? After this was all cleaned up, right?" Henry continued to push forward. "Anyway, Billy, you know it wasn't anything important. The guy's gonna collect on his insurance, and if his precious watch was really stolen, the poor *moke* who pawns it will only get twenty-five cents on the dollar if he's lucky. At least he'll get to keep his family fat on rice and spam for a couple months."

"Or feed his addiction for a week," Iona countered.

Henry nodded, knowing he was probably right.

"So, what do we got, tourist, transplant—"

"*Kanaka*, Hank. She's *Kanaka*, native Hawaiian.

I'm told she lived here on the Westside, on homestead lands up in Nanakuli. Twenty-four years old."

There was no reaction from Henry, at least none that could be seen.

"She got a name?"

"I got here late." Iona shrugged.

"So, you know she's from Nanakuli and she's twenty-four, but you don't have a name? What are you telling me, no license or any other form of identification on her?"

"Not on her, nothing."

"But you know she's twenty-four and she lives on the homestead in—"

"I was just getting filled in when you barreled in here," Iona snapped back.

"I assume, based on what I can see of her outfit, she worked here, right?" he asked, still glued to the lifeless form partially covered with a stained tablecloth.

"Yeah. Danced hula here at Auntie Lily's." Iona motioned toward the large stage at the other end of the beach. Henry nodded and trained his focus across the sand toward the popular tourist attraction before noticing a young Hawaiian girl being interviewed by a reporter.

"Who's the girl?" Henry stared long and hard.

"Stop it, Hank. You're being conspicuous."

"To whom? Mendoza? The reporters? I'm doing my job. Just seeing who's here, who's watching. Billy, make sure someone checks the vic's car and her employee locker for a driver's license. I'd like to get a set of prints too."

After a moment he continued to scan the beach and then the tree line. His mind began to wander. A knot

32

formed in his stomach as images from one of his nightmares played like a motion picture in his head.

"This isn't right, Henry."

"Trust me, we gotta do this. No one will know, no one will be suspicious. She was a loner. She had no family, no friends. She won't be missed. I'll take care of all the paperwork."

"And what do I do in the meantime, disappear?"

"In a manner of speaking, yes, you're gonna disappear."

Iona spoke, but he didn't hear him. His eyes continued to search while he unconsciously searched his pockets for a cigarette.

"Got any smokes? I'm all out."

"Yeah. You're lucky; they're the menthol kind that you like. The kind you got me hooked on, remember?" Iona reached into his pocket. "I thought you quit."

"I did quit, at least up until all this started eight months ago. She a witness, Billy?" He pointed.

"What did I just say to you? I told you she's a coworker. Aren't you listening to me?"

"Yeah, yeah, she's a coworker. I heard you," he lied. "But is she a witness?"

"You weren't listening. No, she's not a witness. She found the vic a couple hours ago when she reported for work. She called us, then grabbed that banquet sheet and threw it over the body. And yes, she had been told not to touch anything that could contaminate the scene."

"And yet she did." Henry lit a cigarette, inhaled, and continued to study the lagoon, the stage area, the huts, and the people. "So let me get this straight…I'm assuming she parked her car at the far end of the beach, way down there, instead of the employee parking lot over at the other end. Then she walks along the beach to get over to Auntie Lily's. On the way she spots the body, has the presence of mind to call nine-one-one, then continues over to the luau area to grab a tablecloth and…" He waited for Billy to respond.

"Come on, Hank, stop it."

"Okay, maybe she did park in the employee lot, and then what? Did she think she saw a beached seal and decided to take a morning stroll to get a better look? Do I have to watch the evening news to find out?"

"Fuck you, damn it, will you calm down?"

"I am calm. Are there any security cameras that might've recorded anything along this stretch of beach or in the parking lots?"

"No, none."

"Okay then, I'll need a list of all her coworkers." His surveillance unrelenting. There were a few on-lookers watching from a distance and, as if on autopilot, he took out his cell phone and began snapping pictures.

"You know those aren't gonna come out clear when you enlarge them, right?"

"Yeah, whatever." He took a few more. "Who are those people way down there?"

"You do know that they're too far away for you to get a clear look at their faces, right?" Billy persisted.

"It's not for the resolution. It's so when I'm going over all this later, I don't have to beat my brain trying to remember if there were five, six, or seven people standing there watching. What do you think, they tourists?"

"Workers at the luau, I guess. Tourist lookie-loos,

maybe."

"Nah, not workers. Tourists most likely. Look how they're dressed, and way too white, whiter than me. Except that one fat guy that's way down there. See him, the slob in the camo pants? He looks local."

"Where? I don't see him."

"Way down there, Billy. Where the hell are your glasses?" Henry motioned. "Never mind, he just stepped back behind the bushes. The employee parking lot is back there as well, right?"

"Yeah."

"There's a uni in the lot over here behind us...Kalima. He's not doing anything. Ask him to get over there and snap some pics of license plates. That is, if he's not too busy texting his girlfriend."

Iona had always resented the way Henry bossed people around, but he called in the request just the same.

"Anything else, General?"

"What about these reporters?" Henry continued to interrogate. "How'd all these reporters get here so quick, and why is one, looks like Kelly Cho from channel four, why is she allowed to talk to the girl? The last thing we need is that kid's face on the news, damn it!"

"They got radio scanners and monitor the calls from dispatch, Hank. You know that." Iona keyed his portable radio and called to the uniformed officer near the reporter. "Todero, who okay'd Kelly Cho to talk to the waitress?"

"I did. Is there a problem?" Mendoza's voice crackled through the speaker.

"Copy that, Lieutenant. Just checking." Iona rolled

his eyes.

Henry grabbed the radio. "Detective eight-one to central, be advised I'm on lunch."

"He does shit like this all the time, Hank. It's part of his goddamn transparency policy."

"It's part of his self-promotion policy. If I was the lead at this scene, I would never allow that kind of shit. And I've seen him do this before, especially with Cho because he wants to get into her pants. The sad thing is, he's so dumb he doesn't realize she's letting him think he's gonna get a piece of that."

"Hell, I'd do her if I had the chance."

"You'd do anybody given the chance."

"C'mon, Hank, you gotta admit she's cute and got a smokin' hot body. What makes you think Mendoza isn't tapping that already?"

"Billy, I'm serious. Put your fucking glasses on and take a good look at him. If you were her, would you do him?"

"I see your point. I see your point."

Billy's portable radio crackled. "Ten-four, eight-one." Then a few seconds later: "Central to Detective eight-one. Be advised Chief Kaneshiro wants you to report when clear."

"Copy that, Central." Henry shook his head, grunted, and tossed the radio back to Iona.

"Not good for you, my friend. Let's get back to business so you can get outta here. You're thinking this is related, aren't you?" Iona half-smiled.

"Not sure yet. I gotta go see the body."

"No, no, you really don't. I know you, and you're already thinking it's related. You're thinking this is number five."

"You don't have to look so happy about it. And for the record, you don't know what I'm thinking, Billy. I gotta see the body."

"Hank, the chief of Ds wants you to report to his office. You were ordered to stay in the Waikiki area because you've—"

"It's been six months since the last one, and I'm on my lunch. I'm on *my* time now!"

"It's been six months, yeah, and the one before that, and the one before that one were only weeks apart, and then there was...well, you know." He watched Henry's face.

"So right away this doesn't fit the pattern. You can't automatically assume this is the same. And that's why I gotta see the body first. So please, get outta my way."

"I'm not trying to stop you," he said, looking down the beach toward the lieutenant.

"Look, I'll handle Mendoza." Henry did a quick sidestep. "Did you get a look yet?"

"Briefly. Her face and upper body were already covered when I got here, but I did get a quick peek. One of the rookies, Taberejo, was first on the scene. He got a good look."

"Taberejo, copy that. Where is he? I wanna talk to him after I—"

"I don't think so. He's...he's not here right now. It's his first body." Iona began to laugh.

"If you're enjoying this, then your sense of humor is worse than when we worked together."

"I was just thinking how he was stuffing his face at the station this morning. Someone had dropped off a big box of malasadas and dim sum. You know, you ought to try giving some to the guys in the motor pool. You might get your air conditioner fixed."

"I like the heat. That's why I moved here."

"Yeah, sure. Anyway, he couldn't help himself." Iona laughed harder. "He took one look at the body and blew chunks all over the beach. We're lucky he didn't mess up the scene."

"Well, from what I see by the tablecloth and the different sets of footprints, it's already been compromised."

"Just the same, Mendoza sent him back to West Oahu station to put on a clean uni and write up his report."

Far from interested in the side stories, Henry followed a partial track through the sand with his eyes.

"Why isn't that clump of Kiawe bushes taped off?"

"What are you talking about? Where?"

"Look at what's left of those drag marks from the bushes over there through the sand to the body." Henry pointed. Again, images flashed through his mind. "A hole in the cheek. Cigarette burning flesh."

"What was that? What hole, what cigarette?"

"What are you talking about, Billy?"

"You mentioned something about a cigarette."

"I just got a whiff of what smelled like burnt flesh. Look here, too much foot traffic through here messing all this up, but you can still see that the body's been dragged over here from that clump of bushes. Didn't anybody check it out?"

"It doesn't look like it was dragged. You're seeing things."

"Sure it does. Look harder. Don't you see it?" Henry stared at Billy in disbelief.

"I'll tell Mendoza."

"Yeah, go ahead and tell the lieutenant," Henry said sarcastically. "This is exactly what I mean about sloppy work."

"Don't look at me, Hank. I'm not the lead detective, I'm not even on this case, and this is not my responsibility."

"Then who's assigned to this? Where is he?"

"Kanakina. Kaelani Kanakina."

"Then can we tell Ms. Kanakina...tell her...oh fuck it." He grabbed a passing CSU investigator. "Get a team, tape off those bushes, and get in there. Tag and bag everything you find."

The investigator looked at Iona who reluctantly nodded his approval.

"And I want an inventory of everything you got so far," he called out, then turned back to the bloodstained tablecloth. "That should not have been missed, Billy. I'm not blaming you, okay? I'm just saying."

"This shit right here, Hank, what you're doing right here is why guys on the job don't like you. This is why we didn't do good as partners. You're not diplomatic."

"This shit right here, Billy, this is why people talk stink about HPD. Not to our faces 'cause everybody's so full aloha, and trowin' down da shakas, bruddah," Henry said, mocking the local dialect, which also angered Iona. "But behind our backs you know they have no respect."

Billy knew he was right and resented that Henry, still an outsider in most people's eyes, was the one pointing it out.

"Forget it, forget I said anything...okay, what about the girl, the coworker who found the body? If she worked last night, we can't rule out she didn't see something, anything." Henry watched her with the reporter, then caught Mendoza's gaze. "I can't believe he's letting her get exposed this way. I wanna talk to her, but not here. Not out in the open. Not with anybody else around to see us."

"You're assuming the lieutenant lets you."

"Well, I'll go talk to him right now." He started down the beach, but Iona grabbed his arm.

"Come on, Hank, don't do this. Not here, not now. Not with news media here. You don't want them swarming you, and you know they will. They still think you had something to do—"

"Something to do with what, Billy? What do they still think, huh?" Henry slowly pulled himself free and took a deep breath. "Okay. Okay, fine…not now."

With Iona continuing to plead for him to leave, Henry walked over to the body, hesitated, then lifted the covering. The knot in his stomach traveled up to his throat—his adrenaline surging. He had no doubt. The scars, the bruises, the burn hole in the right cheek, the cigarette butt neatly placed between the right index and middle fingers. He knew the face, but in that instant, he couldn't remember from where. *Number five.* He swatted at the flies as his thoughts danced.

I know her, but from where…the dream? She was in the dream…I think. No, no, it wasn't in the dream. It was a few months ago she…we… Henry stared at the girl's face. He heard her voice:

****

"I can tell you whatever you wanna know, yeah? But first you gotta buy me a drink." She smiled.

"That's it? Just one drink to ask you questions

about this girl in the picture?"

"Normally"—she laughed—"for someone who looks like you, I'd even ask you to join me. But you're obviously on duty. Maybe you can come back when you get off work, and well, you are kinda cute for your age."

"My age? Never mind my age and focus on the picture, will ya? Do you know this girl, yes or no?"

"She's the one they found all cut up in the alley here in Chinatown?"

"That's right. Just a few yards away from this club."

"I don't think so. I mean…she looks a little familiar, but I don't think she's from the Westside. She does kinda look familiar, but I don't usually come in to town to party, so I can't be sure."

"Well, she didn't usually come in to town to party either. Take another look. Like you, she's a Westside girl."

"Maybe she is, but she's not from my homestead. Let me think about it awhile. Maybe when you get off work, we can talk about it, yeah?"

"Listen to me, missy, there's a nut case out there, and he seems to like girls who look just like you. So this isn't something to be cute about. Take another look at the photo, okay?"

"Yeah, okay…I honestly don't know. I'm not sure. Like I said, I need to think about it."

"Well, you think hard about it. Here's my card. Call me if you remember anything."

"I'm sure I'll remember something, Detective."

****

He closed his eyes, remembered her smile, and

heard her laugh while acting sassy in front of her friends, but when she had come out of the bar searching for him moments after, she had been genuinely scared:

****

"Detective Benjamin, wait up!"

"That was quick," he said.

"You weren't kidding, were you? There's really a stalker around here?"

"A killer, actually. Don't you listen to the news? Forget I asked."

"You got me a little nervous. I'm gonna go home. Could you walk me to my car?"

"No. You obviously had too much to drink. You should have one of your friends drive you home."

"They live here in town, and they're pretty buzzed too."

"I'll call you a ride-share."

"Can you drive me? Please? Maybe I'll remember something on the way home."

****

"Makani!" he whispered, and his heart pounded. "I'm so sorry."

"What did you say? You know her?" Iona studied Henry.

"…what?"

"What did you just say?"

"I…I asked if there was a note. It's connected, Billy. She's number five, and there should be a note, just like the others." He touched her lips, then felt his cheek where she had kissed it the night he had taken her home. His anger was building, and his throat was dry. He felt responsible.

"Hank, you better leave now. Mendoza…"

"I'm gonna take a look behind those Kiawe bushes. You never told me if there were any other witnesses. I mean, besides the waitress who found the body."

"Hank, that's all being checked out. You should really talk to Kanakina."

"I don't know who she is. Point her out, will ya?"

"On the job a few years. She was reassigned to this district just after you got moved to Waikiki. She's good, knows her shit. And unlike you, she plays well with others."

"She's good? She missed the Kiawe bushes."

"Stop it."

"Okay, whatever, fine. Point her out."

"She's over at the luau area talking to the other employees, looking for witnesses, and getting the information you're asking about. And the CSU guys bagged a note which is going to the lab first."

"I'll talk to her later, then." He took one last look at Makani. "I wanna talk to the medical examiner. I wanna know if she was violated like the others were. I wanna know why this poor girl has been lying out here in the sun all these hours." Henry's voice was louder now.

"Nobody from the M.E.'s office has been here yet."

"What the hell?"

"Come on, Hank, you know it's just like every other city agency…understaffed because of the budget cuts. That's why she's been out here this long."

"Understaffed because of poor fiscal management if you ask me." He continued to swat away at the flies. "Okay then, tell me what you think. You've been on the job for eighteen years, Billy. You've seen the others.

What do you think? Was she?"

"I told you I didn't get a detailed look. I didn't examine her. That's not my role here, and you know that. But…from what I just saw, and I really don't wanna speculate…I mean…it's possible, I guess."

"For Christ's sake!"

"You know something? I don't like the way this is going. You're all worked up, you've been barking at me since you got here, and I don't like it, Hank. Take a fucking breath!"

"…okay, okay, you're right, you're absolutely right. I'm treating you like…it's just that I'm…I'm…"

"Too involved. I know, I know. Not to worry, it's all good. We're *pono*, we're good. Now please, go back to town, go see the boss, and I'll…"

Henry started for his car but stopped to intercept the CSU investigator carrying a couple of evidence bags. "I was right, wasn't I?"

"I got some blood that was in the sand and on a few of these leaves and twigs. And I just got the cigarette butt that was between the girl's fingers. Blood looks fresh." The investigator held up the plastic bags. Henry grabbed them. "Hey, man, I gotta catalog that!"

"Hank, you can't take any evidence. Give it back." Iona intervened.

"Relax, you two. I'm on my way back to town now. I'll drop this off at the lab to see if they can get right on it and hopefully pull any DNA. Billy boy, although we butt heads, you know I'm the best one for this case, and you know why."

"Hank, hold up, will ya?" He walked after him. "Hank, stop! Just wait a sec, okay? I'm worried about you. You know how you get with this stuff, and I should've taken that into account before I texted you...but still, man, some people would say you're overreacting on purpose if you know what I mean. You gotta remember I'm on your side."

"Are you?" He was skeptical. "You're on my side? I'm overreacting? Putting on a show?"

"Yes, that's how it looks, but I know it's because you're too emotionally involved. Now before you get in any more trouble, give me the evidence bags. They stay with me."

"With you?"

"With the crime scene guys, Hank!"

"...yeah, okay, I know," Henry said, giving the evidence a last glance before handing them back.

"Look, from your old partner, take a little advice. Go settle down...go have a drink. Then go talk to Kaelani Kanakina. Meet up for coffee or something, but off-duty. You two talk story, get to know one another, share info, and perhaps you guys can, ya know, work together. I'll have her call you. Just remember to play nice."

"What are you worried about? Really, what? Mendoza, or what others are gonna say about me?"

"He doesn't like you, Hank. When he saw you pull up...I know he's gonna...I'm gonna have to tell him I told you about this. He'll be pissed at me."

"I know he hates me," he proudly acknowledged. "And I don't care if he calls the boss, the chief of the department, or the freaking mayor. Look, I'll simply tell him I heard the call on the radio, which by the way, works as well as the air conditioner in that piece-of-shit car."

"Malasadas, Hank. Buy those guys some treats,

and maybe they'll fix your car."

"Screw that!"

"You forget you're the minority on this island."

"I'm reminded of that quite often. Look, man, Mendoza…"

"He knows we worked together a while back. He suspects I still keep you locked in on things out here on the Westside, and he actually warned me that he didn't want you here today or anywhere near this district. Hank, you know you're a troublemaker. The guys out here even have a nickname for you that's not very flattering."

"Yeah, I heard about it from Kalima."

"Can you blame them? You've been living here for just over fourteen years, and you're still acting like a New York wiseass."

"I'm not a troublemaker. It's just that Mendoza's the kind of guy who runs away from trouble, or anything that remotely smells like trouble. He's scared of his own shadow and only advancing in rank because of his family. My work ethic makes him and others like him look bad." He softened his tone. "I'm not a troublemaker. I'm determined. I work hard, and I get results. I know I step on toes. I know I make the homegrown look bad. I know I can be aggressive and obnoxious at times, and I know some people on this job think that I…never mind. But this…this is number five, and therefore, it should still be my case. Billy, we didn't just work together once upon a time. You, dare I say it, were my mentor. You know I appreciate what you taught me."

"Then why don't you ever follow protocol like I taught you?"

"Protocol, even island protocol, has its place. But not for this. Not when this is linked, not when there could be more on the way."

Iona shook his head in frustration. "How much time you got in now, twelve, thirteen years?"

"Yeah, coming up on fourteen."

"You know I got less than two years to go to reach twenty. Nineteen months before I pull my pin, and I don't wanna fuck that up."

"At this point, what are you worried about? It can't get any worse for you, can it? You're working the Leeward Coast, Detective Iona. Everything west of Auntie Lily's is the armpit of the island. You said so yourself. I'm sorry if my saying that now upsets you because you live up in Waianae, but you're up to your ears in drunk drivers, gambling dens, abandoned cars, illegal dumping, drugs, and the occasional gang shooting, am I right?"

"True dat," he reluctantly acknowledged.

"And me? Somebody downtown is throwing roadblocks up and interfering with my investigation. You gotta ask yourself, who at HQ or city hall is getting in my way, and why? Meanwhile, I'm working purse snatchings and hotel room break-ins on the night shift in Waikiki. I'm a fucking glorified hotel dick. I don't know who's got it worse."

"I should've been a sergeant, Hank. Detective sergeant."

"You're still not blaming me for that, are you?"

Iona ignored the question. "Just the same, any time you wanna trade places, just let me know."

Chapter 4

You never ask for much,
you never do.
But like a thief in the night,
you come stealing.
You blend into the shadows.
You take what you want.
How can I blame you when I cannot resist?
I never could, I never try.
Why play that game?
Why waste the time?
Is that what feeds your confidence,
or fuels your bedside bravado?
I know that is what feeds mine.
And without a spoken word
I know it is me whom you desire.
It has always been me.
No matter which lifetime,
I am your aphrodisiac,
and you are surely mine.

From the vantage point of his outdoor table at Hokulani's Oceanside Café, Henry listened to the waves crash along Maili Beach while nursing his coffee. After another restless night of intermittent sleep because of bad dreams, staring at lists of suspects, and pacing the floor, he knew this would be the first of several cups to help him get through the day. He'd had nights like this before, but lately, too many to count. As he looked out at the retreating darkness, he couldn't stop thinking about swatting flies away from Makani's lifeless face. It's not what he had wanted to focus on, but like his nightmares, the image came without consent.

Kaelani Kanakina told him if he had wanted to talk story about the case, she'd meet him at her favorite breakfast place on the Waianae Coast. She picked the time, but he still came well before sunrise. While he too had a fondness for the café, he hadn't come that often nor did he visit any other place on the west side over the previous eight months unless it had something to do with his investigation. And even though the Waianae Coast wasn't the Hawaii found in travel brochures, it hadn't been the absence of pristine beaches and half-naked hula girls that fueled his disappointment about the leeward side of Oahu. He got over that fantasy a long time ago. In spite of how much community leaders had painted over the reality of life on this side of the island, Henry had caused an uproar a few years back when he dared to question the honesty of the community's civic pride:

****

"I've often been asked for explanations regarding the constant crime here on the coast. I've also been challenged about HPD's effectiveness. And every month when I come to this meeting, you reject the official response that I'm allowed to give. And along with your outright rejection, many of you demand I be honest and give you the 'real' answer. We both know what the real answer is. I can give you my opinion

49

based upon personal observations and experience, if that's what you want. But I gotta tell you as I've told you many times before, after working in this district for a decade, I know many of you are not gonna accept what I have to say…either because I'm not one of you, and God knows some of you continue to remind me of that, or you simply don't wanna acknowledge the truth. I believe that both of those choices are valid here. Still, you keep on asking what I think, and you keep getting mad because I don't tell you. Tonight's meeting is different, however. Tonight, one of the most chronic and loudest complainers in this community, who just so happens to be one of the most frequent offenders in this community, stood up and accused HPD of not caring about what goes on here. He accused us of taking our time to respond to emergencies or ignoring them altogether. What's worse, I heard a lot of voices in agreement with him. Okay then, you better hold on to your seats, folks, because the truth is painful, and the truth doesn't care about your feelings. So here it comes. For all this talk of the aloha spirit and your love and respect for the land, the love and respect for the *aina*, or the importance of tradition, many of you continue to blame everybody from city hall, HPD, and even the tourists for the conditions out here while you're the ones who continue to shit in your own backyard," he had said to a shocked audience. "Look at the damn arrest reports. It's not the tourists coming up here from the resorts to dump old refrigerators and mattresses along the Makaha Valley Road, are they? Are they driving all the way up here to rob the convenience stores, or is it a neighbor or someone's relative that you all turn a blind eye to? It's not the folks from windward side either, and you all know it. Let me ask you, how many times are towing services from Waianae gonna haul auto wrecks out here from Honolulu and dump them on these streets in the middle of the night because they don't wanna pay the dump fee? You all know why crime is an issue out here, and you can stop it if you really want to. But do you want to? Stop protecting this community's bad actors. I know some of you are pretty pissed off at me right now, and I suspect by this time tomorrow my comments will be twisted or taken out of context to a point that those not in attendance tonight will be calling for my head. Well...you got my boss' phone number."

****

And while that heated discussion at a neighborhood meeting prompted a local activist-turned-opportunist to print and sell a few thousand tee shirts and bumper stickers proclaiming "Westside Pride," Henry was just as critical when none of the twenty dollars per shirt went to help clean up the illegally dumped cars, washing machines, and construction debris that continued to be an eyesore throughout the district. Not one penny of the proceeds had been donated to the local food bank, and less than a handful of concerned citizens had volunteered to participate in a neighborhood security watch group.

As expected, many people were angry with Henry, but they knew he was right. They knew the burglaries, the drug dealing, and the dumping were coming from bad actors within the community itself. It was a dirty little secret that nobody wanted whispered, let alone shouted by an outsider. He certainly didn't endear himself to the local folks that night, but a few years later, more than a few community leaders, frustrated with the ongoing problems, confided that his candor had been needed, was greatly appreciated, and would be sorely missed after learning of his reassignment to the Waikiki precinct.

When he did have pleasant thoughts of Oahu's West Coast, they were of the lazy Sundays he had spent with Maya lounging on the front lanai of their Nanakuli rental, or helping her friends who worked the local farms in the Waianae and Makaha Valleys. And then there were the early morning breakfasts at Hokulani's—a rustic place that had been family operated for several generations—offering up home-style comfort food served with lots of opinions and a bit of sass to the well-deserving. Henry knew the menu well and was one of the few non-locals who had been treated like *'ohana*, like family—an honor that had been bestowed, at first by way of who he knew, then cemented over time by display of his character. That's how lasting relationships were formed here on a rock in the middle of the Pacific—especially if you're a transplant.

He remembered many mornings sitting there with a fresh cup of coffee watching the night sky capitulate to the sun as it crept over the mountains, the smell of another pot of freshly brewed Kona beans floating by him like a piece of driftwood at the mercy of the currents, and the sound of waves rhythmically crashing along the shore before the weekday rush-hour drowned out the sounds of the sea. The thought was comforting until images of swatting flies returned—only to be chased by a welcomed dose of Hokulani's sass for his recent absence.

"Three fried eggs sunny side up, a little crispy on the edges, whole wheat bread toasted no butter, three slices of bacon well done. A little too well done if you ask me," she said, wagging a finger, "but I don't gotta eat it. And you got your coffee with a little special splash, which, like your taste in women, is hot, dark, and extra spicy, by the way, is just like me. And if I'm not mistaken, the last time you were here, I'm pretty sure it was for a booty call. Am I forgetting anything, Detective?" Hokulani set the plate down and handed him a set of cheap utensils neatly wrapped in a paper napkin. "Now maybe you can focus on your food instead of on my waitresses."

"Just one. She's hot, dark, and she looks rather spicy," Henry said without a hint of shame. "I never did get a menu."

"You never used one before. I guess this is what happens when you stay away so long."

"Tastes change."

"But you still asked for a special splash, so did they change that much since you've been gone?"

"Stop it, will ya. It's just a little nip for this nasty headache…and it hasn't been that long."

She side-eyed him with a smirk. "Eat up. I gotta couple things to do, and then I'll come join you," she said before seeking out another customer to scold.

Henry continued to watch one of the waitresses move effortlessly between tables. She too would glance his way from time to time but kept her distance. In a way, that frustrated him. He wondered if there would ever be a good time, a safe time to approach her. *Not here, too many eyes,* he thought. He studied her curves and admired her body, the natural bronze of her skin, the sparkle of her deep brown eyes, and the hint of a smile. *God, she's toying with me, and she knows it.* He imagined her long black hair pulled back into a ponytail but knew he wouldn't dare suggest it. He continued to imagine the smoothness of her skin, brushing his lips into the small of her back while his hands moved slowly down the outside of her hips and legs and then back up the inside of her thighs, at which point Hokulani broke his concentration.

"Didn't your momma ever tell you no dessert before you finish your meal?"

"Plenty of times."

"Just the same, some woman on the other side of the café asked me if you're a stalker."

"What?" he asked, noticing other patrons staring at him.

"A blind man can see you devouring that poor thing. Do you have her completely undressed yet?"

"I'm sorry. I didn't realize."

"Now that you realize it, you best stop it, Hank, and let her do her job. Don't you give these people anything to gossip about either. The last thing we need out here are more rumors. And keep in mind that most of these folks still remember you and your big mouth."

"I spoke my mind, much of which has been misquoted or just completely distorted with time."

"I know you spoke the truth that night. These people need to hear it now and again, but that's not how they see it. You know how they are, especially with what happened again yesterday." She sat down and folded her arms. "Boy, you never ever change, do you? Nope, you don't, not one bit."

"And you still got attitude, still a *tita*."

"Only when I gotta be. Where you been the past few weeks, Hank? We haven't seen you, we haven't heard from you, but we're hearing plenty about you, though. And not all of it good."

"Not surprised."

"I was thinking maybe we undercooked your eggs or something like that." She touched his hand.

Henry hesitated—at first, he rationalized that he didn't want to give her business a bad reputation if he kept coming. Then he thought Hokulani would've contacted him if there had been any kind of emergency. He did feel guilty for not coming in as much after he had been transferred. Before he knew it, the excuses to avoid the morning drive became easy. One week away soon turned into two, then three. By the time it was a month since he made an appearance, the thought of popping in felt awkward. But she was right that when his physical needs surpassed his hunger for comfort food, he certainly found his way back to the café.

"I don't know what to say. You know, or at least I think you know what—"

"You don't gotta say it. I know what I need to know. And for the record, everything here is *pono*. I never believed what some of those guys were sayin'. I never believed it for one second…so tell me, how are things? Be honest, how you holding up?"

"It's been hard at times. I get the cold shoulder at the job. For the most part it doesn't bother me because I'm busy. I've got a lot on my plate. You already know that I moved. Old news, right? I couldn't stay at the old place. Not after…it just didn't feel right. I never told you, but in the couple weeks after…I'd see things that weren't there, hear noises, and sometimes even feel things. Plus, the neighbors kept giving me the stink eye." He laughed. "But now in this new place…I still come home to an empty house and…"

"You're lonely. I get it."

"It's not that, well, it is…but I got this crazy landlady now who just won't leave me alone. From noises in the night to peeping Toms. She even wants to play detective. Sometimes I just wanna…" Henry made a choking gesture but caught himself before the words of frustration betrayed him. "Anyway, I got this whack job on the loose and—"

"Let's not go there. I mean, there's a lot of bad stuff that goes on up and down this coast, but stuff like this thing. People knew these girls. I knew some of these girls, Hank. We're all uneasy."

"You're right." Henry dug into the pocket of his windbreaker and pulled a pack of cigarettes.

"What's this? I thought you quit a long time ago."

"So did I." He smirked while taking one out of the box. He stared at the brand name, the packaging taking him back to Auntie Lily's, back with Billy Iona.

"Got any smokes? I'm all out."

"Yeah, you're lucky. They're the menthol kind that you like, the kind you got me hooked on, remember? I thought you quit."

Henry rolled a cigarette between his fingers, looked at the green print by the filter end, and thought of the evidence bag. "It's hard to change old habits," he said. "Tell me, what's the latest on your hot little waitress?"

"The one you just ate instead of your breakfast?" She winked at him.

"I assume she's working out fine and all that?" he

asked, watching her serve another table.

"Mary's been working out real fine. I actually hope she stays for the long term."

"She's that good, huh?"

"It's hard to keep good people, and she's been here almost eight months. Never misses a day, everybody loves her, she's hard working, easy on the eyes, and pays her rent on time."

"It's nice to know you appreciate good help." He watched her work the tables.

"You're being creepy, Hank. Stop staring at her."

"I didn't realize I was that obvious."

"Just the same you should know better. You best keep your distance."

Henry gave her a half smile. "You gotta admit it, she is exotic. So, tell me, she, uh…seeing anybody?"

"Okay, enough already. So why the visit today? You just horny, or is it about the girl they found on the beach?"

"I'm meeting somebody from the job to discuss the case."

"Here?" She was slightly annoyed.

"She suggested it. Says it's her favorite place to eat. I figured why the hell not. I've been wanting to stop back in. But my coming here does have me worried about…you know."

"And what about me, Hank? Are you worried about me too?"

"Hell, are you kidding me? That guy wouldn't stand a chance against you," he said to Hokulani's disappointment. "Don't give me that look. Of course, I'm concerned about you too."

"Just concerned?"

"Worried! I'm worried about your safety as well. Now, before she gets here, what can you tell me about Kaelani Kanakina?"

"That's who you're meeting? I should've guessed." She looked around, then lowered her voice. "Local girl. Born and raised here. Family goes way back. Supposedly she can trace her blood line to Queen Liliuokalani. But I don't buy it. Everybody out this way, especially on the homestead, says they have some relation to the royals, ya know? She was a troubled teen. She ran with one of the local gangs before she got busted for jacking cars. A judge gave her a choice, jail or a youth boot camp. She did the camp and then enlisted. It surprised many people because she was known to rebel. Did two tours in Afghanistan with the Hawaii Army National Guard. Military Police of all things. And you know what I heard?" Hokulani leaned in a little closer. "I heard she killed a guy over there, an enlisted man. I don't know if that's true, but I do know she got a quick temper. Some say she once beat up an ex-girlfriend 'cause she was cheating on her. Put her in the hospital. Gay or not, I'm no judge, but maybe that's why a good looking *wahine* like her is still single. Anyway, she got lots of aunties, uncles, cousins up here on the West side. Most are good, some are a little shady, but who isn't, right? I mean, we all got a skeleton or two, yeah? But there's one uncle who's just plain bad, but he's not blood. He married into the family. And get this, the wife, Kaelani's auntie, disappeared one night and hasn't been seen since. Everybody says he did it, but nobody saw it happen. So, who knows? But that guy did time. I just can't remember if it was for drugs, burglary, or what. It's getting so hard to keep track of everything that goes on out here. People tell me he was involved in a lot of weird stuff, so I don't know. But I know he's a bad egg, Hank. Rumor is when he got outta prison, she threatened to kill him if he ever came back to the homestead. He's not even Hawaiian, so he didn't belong there anyway. I wish I could tell you his name or what he looks like now. It's been so long. She don't like to talk about him, though. It gets her very angry, so be careful not to say anything. And if you do, you didn't hear it from me, got it?"

"Yeah, I got it."

"Oh, I forgot to tell you, she came in a couple minutes ago, been sitting in the dining room watching us."

****

"So how long were you gonna sit there watching me?" he asked.

"I didn't wanna interrupt you guys. I suppose you were asking all about me?"

"You suppose incorrectly. Hoku and I are old friends, and we've got plenty of other things to talk about. Have a seat. You have breakfast yet?"

"I see you didn't touch yours. What's wrong with it?"

"Not hungry. Help yourself." He pushed his plate toward her. She waved it off but eyed his cigarettes. She'd seen the brand before. "Go ahead and take one."

She hesitated before allowing herself. "Thanks, left mine in the car. Interesting brand."

"Japanese. I get 'em in town. Bad habit, yes?" he said, watching her use his lighter.

"I ran with the wrong crowd when I was a kid.

59

They all smoked."

"I see you're a southpaw."

"A what?"

"The way you lit your cigarette, the way you hold it. You're left-handed, a southpaw. It's a baseball term. I like baseball."

"Look, I gotta drive in to town, to the CSU to check on a few things. Mind if we skip the pleasantries and get straight to it?"

"Go ahead and shoot, but be careful. I think we're on the same side." He waited for a reaction.

"…you got some reputation, Detective Benjamin."

"Hank," he said, then sipped his coffee. "You gonna sit, or what?"

"For a minute." Kaelani nodded. "Then you don't deny the stories?"

"Depends on which stories you're talking about. Some are true, some are urban legend, and most are just pure bullshit. I'll bet you've got a few of your own that are…myths?"

"Not that I know of. Maybe you can enlighten me."

"None that I know of." He smiled.

"I hear you got yourself suspended again."

"That's true." Henry nodded.

"From what I heard I can't say I'm surprised."

"I didn't know the guy with the missing watch was a friend of the attorney general. He gets his panties all twisted in a wad, calls the AG, the AG calls the mayor, the mayor calls the chief, and voilà!"

"And if you had known?"

"…I wouldn't have changed anything. And you? What would you have done if you were me?"

She ignored the question.

"I hear you think I run a sloppy crime scene."

Fucking Billy! Henry thought. "Iona could never keep anything to himself, but that's just one of several reasons why I couldn't work with him. Yes, in my opinion it was sloppy, and I call it the way I see it."

"I heard that about you. Perhaps that's one of several reasons why a lot of guys on the job don't wanna work with you. Ever think about that?"

"Not for a moment. If given a choice between working with a slacker and having to crack a whip to get them to do their job properly or working alone, I'd rather work a case alone because I'm no freaking babysitter. I'd get better results too. I saw shit the other day that I'd never tolerate."

"Meanwhile you made off with some evidence from my crime scene." She held up his box of cigarettes.

"Evidence that you missed," he countered. "I had to get back to town and was gonna take those bags to the lab so they could get a jump on it. That's what that was about, but no, I didn't take them."

"Then where are they? Nobody can find those two evidence bags. CSU says they don't have them, and I want them back, Detective."

"So, I was right. The scene wasn't managed properly," he charged. "I actually handed both bags back to Detective Iona, and a guy from CSU was standing right there and witnessed it. So, one of you guys lost it."

"Don't look at me. Between Mendoza and Billy meddling, getting in my way, micro-managing everything!" she said in protest. "I'm not the one screwing it up."

"Welcome to my world." Henry tried to find common ground, but Kaelani didn't seem to be receptive. "Why is Billy meddling? He told me he had nothing to do with the investigation."

"Just another senior male detective trying to insert himself with his advice, if you ask me."

"I can empathize." He looked for some indication of acknowledgment.

She maintained her tough persona.

"We've now got five young native Hawaiian women who were brutally tied up, tortured, sliced, diced, and murdered by the same sick bastard, and for almost a year now you've—"

"Eight months, not a year," he corrected. "Although it seems like a few years."

"For eight months now, you've made no headway in your investigation, an investigation you insisted on heading up in spite of a major conflict of interest. Why do you suppose that is?"

"Are you here as a fellow detective to compare notes, or are you a prosecuting attorney?"

"I'm just trying to figure out if I want you anywhere near me or this case. As it is, things got stalled when you got assigned to Waikiki."

"So, you just answered your own question, Detective. I was punished for not playing well with others. Tied up with bullshit work. Denied resources because of supposed budget constraints. And in spite of what you think, I was still investigating and getting almost no cooperation from command, or from many of our colleagues."

"And now because you've been suspended, this entire investigation has been given to me."

"I'll be back soon enough, so I don't think so."

"Well, think again. You're off, I'm on, and I'm gonna need your files...all of your files. Even the information you've been withholding about your wife," Kaelani said to a stone-cold stare.

Henry felt his blood pressure rising. In less than two minutes, she managed to get under his skin faster than Judy Coleman ever could. *She's a hard-driving interrogator, which could be a great asset. Street tough for sure. I bet Hoku was right that she probably did beat up an ex-girlfriend, but is all this just an act for my benefit?*

"Since you smell blood, continue. But tread lightly, because I know what's coming next."

"Okay. I know your wife was the first victim. Yeah, I did my homework. I wouldn't bring this up, but the problem that I have with you, Detective, is that you messed with that first crime scene. Evidence went missing, which some people still believe you have or destroyed. That's why you were suspected of murdering your wife. That's why you had another partner quit on you. Tell me, was that your third or fourth partner since getting your gold shield?"

Henry didn't answer.

"Some people have suggested that maybe you have something to do with the other three girls, and maybe even this latest one. You know, to make us believe there's a serial killer, which, by the way, would then be you. What do you have to say about that?"

Henry gathered his thoughts. He knew he could say something he'd be sorry for if not careful. Out of the corner of his eye, he could tell they were being watched by Hoku and Mary as they continued to service their tables. He reached for his coffee as if it were a pacifier and fingered the porcelain before draining his cup. She caught a whiff of whiskey but didn't say anything as he signaled for a refill.

"...I could tell you to go fuck yourself, but I won't," he calmly said while he locked onto her eyes. "I could tell you to go fuck yourself and go to hell for insulting my integrity as well as my wife's memory, because you just crossed a line with that, Detective. But I'm not gonna do that because I'm not who think I am. I didn't do what you're accusing me of doing. What you said just now...do you know how crazy that is? To think that I murdered my wife and then continue to murder to cover it up is beyond ludicrous. Yeah, there is a serial killer out there, and my wife was the first victim."

"Then help me out. Explain the conditions that CSU reported about the scene."

"I came home from work...to find her lying in a pool of blood...on the floor of our bedroom. As it turns out, the other four vics, similar height, weight, ethnicity, similar cuts, similar bruises, same burn hole in the cheek, same way the killer placed the cigarette butt between the fingers. Similar notes all addressed to me, and I suspect the fifth one, the one I didn't get to see yesterday was also addressed to *me*. So, I may be suspended, but I'm not off this case, not by a longshot. In fact, I'm integral to it. So, no one is gonna stop me from investigating."

Kaelani stood to leave, however, took a moment to observe his mannerisms when he continued on.

"When I found my wife...I've seen my share of murder victims but never somebody who I...never somebody who was…I lost it…vomited all over the place. I should've called it in right away, but I couldn't think straight. I…I sat down next to her body and took her in my arms and cried like a baby. So yeah, I fucked up the crime scene. When HPD and the CSU team finally got there, they found no forced entry and me, sitting there covered in her blood. Sure, I was a suspect, but a thorough investigation cleared me of murdering my wife and of stealing or destroying evidence. If you did your homework properly, you'd know that. If you knew that and you're just trying to provoke me, you're poking at the wrong hornet's nest. Just know this…there hasn't been one day since that happened that people on this job don't look at me without suspicion. Even Billy Iona has said as much behind my back. So that little act you may see him putting on that we're old friends, that's all it is, an act. We can work together on this, or separately, but I'm not off this case."

He nodded to Mary for the refill, added two sugars, and took notice of how Kaelani's attention had shifted onto the waitress. Although she didn't seem impressed with his explanation, he felt pleased with how smooth he'd become reciting that story.

While Henry spoke, memories of having once been accused of murder also ran through Kaelani's mind. Images of drawing her weapon and firing point-blank into her would-be rapist were as clear as if the incident had happened yesterday. She knew firsthand what it was like to be accused, investigated, exonerated, and still a pariah among her peers. She knew what it was like to have her career, in this case her military career, tarnished, even though the shooting was found to be justified. And yet her intuition told her something didn't seem right with Henry's story.

"I've gotta get into town. I'll need to make copies of all your files, and whatever personal notes you've made."

"Copies? Don't you mean the originals?"

"If we're gonna be consulting with each other, and the operative word is consulting, we'll both need a set, right?"

"Yeah. I gotta stop by the precinct tomorrow to turn in my car and pick up a few things. I'll get everything from my desk. I've also got materials at home."

"Great. Can we work outta your place?"

"Why my place?"

"Anything I do with you will have to be off the record while you're on suspension. Your place will be our office. My place is…I rent a room in a friend's house. She's a homebody and plays a lot of loud music and can be nosy if you know what I mean."

Henry thought about it for a moment, smiling at the thought of Judy Coleman staring through her curtains, jaw dropping to the floor every time Kaelani came by. "That'll keep her up to all hours," he muttered.

"What was that?"

"Sure, I said sure, we can work outta my place."

"Where do you live?" she asked, wondering if she just made a bad decision.

"The old plantation cottages where the sugar mill used to be on the Ewa Plain. On Palehua Street."

"I'll call you."

Chapter 5

I wanted this place,
just as much as I wanted you.
I needed this place,
just as much as I needed you.
My heart had cried enough on the plains of my other
life,
and now it hears the call of the soul song of this other
ancient existence.
They are separate, yet one in the same because they live
within me.
They are part and parcel of my heart, my mind, my
soul.
For it is here that we first met,
first danced by the firelight of tribal ritual,
first made love consumed by primal lust.
We were blessed with resilience, and it is good.
And what of now?
How many centuries,
how many lifetimes did it take for us to reunite?
If patience is a virtue, I am far from virtuous.
I wanted this place,
just as much as I wanted you.
And now that you have followed me home,
it is time for us to face unfinished business.
And while those drums have long been silent to my
people,

Richard I Levine

I still hear them.
I still feel them beat within me.
Let me place your hand on my heart,
and you will feel it too.

Henry stood by the wood-framed screen door,
letting the heat from the ceramic cup warm his hands.
He brought it up to his nose to let the steam kiss his
face, savored the aroma, then took another drink. No
different than this morning, the first cup had always
been his favorite and had always been needed. There
had been times when he'd lie awake in bed, well before
sunrise, with Maya safely wrapped around him and
cradled in his arms—her skin smooth as satin, her scent
both seductive and addictive. He'd laugh because of the
brief debate to disturb the moment for the
uncontrollable craving for that first cup. "*My addictions
run deep,*" he once told her. She had never doubted
those addictions; she enabled them. Especially the one
he had for her. That's what co-dependents do. But she
always convinced him that making love was the best
substitute for any craving, the best treatment for any
withdrawal, and the best intervention for hers. In all the
years they had been together, his willpower to resist her
overtures had never been tested—he knew better than to
try. And on mornings like this he would close his eyes
and could easily recall stealing the heat from her body
and getting lost in every essence of her existence:

****

"Where did you come from? How did you find
me?"

"If I'm not mistaken, Henry, I'm pretty sure you've
been following me around campus for the past two

68

weeks."

"Tell me you didn't start coming to the library on purpose to run into me."

"Only if you admit you transferred into Native American studies once you found out I was in that class."

"Let me think about that one over coffee."

"Better yet, why don't you come back to bed, and I'll show you how we Lakota stay warm on cold winter mornings."

****

He smiled at the idea that a sixty-seven-degree morning could cause a shiver and wondered if he'd be able to survive a Northeast winter if he were to ever move back there. He thought of the snow-covered Adirondacks of his youth and the ice-covered northern plains of his Midwest college days. And that made him think about one of the early dates he had had with his wife—open-mic poetry night in a small campus rathskeller, drinking Irish coffees in the middle of a snowstorm.

****

"That was amazing, wasn't it? You see, that's the kind of stuff I write," she said, realizing he hadn't heard a word. "Henry, stop staring at me like that."

"Sorry, I didn't hear, I mean I wasn't aware..."

"You're being rude. These people, these artists, are expressing their innermost thoughts and deepest feelings. You should try to listen, or at least pretend you are."

He nodded, smiled at her, and continued to be captivated by all that he saw, and all that he saw was her.

"You're not paying attention to any of this, are you, Henry?"

"No. I'm sorry but to be perfectly honest, I'm not, not one word. I admit that I'm preoccupied with something more poetic."

"Yeah, and I'm sure I know what with." Maya pulled both sides of her sweater closer together.

"With you, I'm preoccupied with you, all of you, everything about you. Your background, your intelligence…"

"My breasts?"

"I'm interested in the things you like, and dare I say, how beautiful you are," he continued. "In this light, your black hair and eyes…your face…they take on a certain glow. It makes you even more mysterious, sensuous, and so much more voluptuous than you already are. And on top of all that, you're an old soul, Maya."

"That's the glow from the fireplace."

"Maybe, but allow me to go on."

"Now look who's the poet." She laughed. "You certainly have a gift."

"I'll take that as a compliment. You know, I've never met anyone who was half Hawaiian, half Lakota Sioux. What are the chances? What are the chances of someone having, not one, but two oppressed cultures as part of their lineage?"

"In my case, one-hundred percent."

"And you said it was your mother who was Hawaiian?"

"Yes. She met my father when she came to the mainland to go to school. It was at a lecture about how indigenous peoples around the world were raped and pillaged by European conquerors. Apparently, he had the same gift of sweet talk as you do because he swept her off her feet."

"So how am I doing so far?"

"The jury's still out. But if you're anything like my father was, then I better be careful."

"Oh?"

"He worked fast. I was born just before they graduated."

"Oh!" He laughed.

"Mom had hoped for us to eventually move back to Oahu, but she became ill and passed when I was ten. I grew up in South Dakota, on the rez."

"Are you planning on staying? I don't mean going back to the reservation, which I guess wouldn't be too bad, would it? Maybe it would. What I'm trying to ask is…"

"What are my plans after graduation?"

"Yes, that's exactly what I was trying to say."

"Some poet you are! I've lived on the mainland all twenty years of my life. Been to Hawaii once. A year before my mother passed away, she took me to meet some family. We're not close, but I'm pretty sure I'm going to spend some time there when I'm done with school…might do my grad work over there and who knows, I might end up staying to teach. The rez is too depressing. There's far too much poverty, drug use, alcohol. I should go back and help, but I'm torn, though. I feel this inner calling to go and explore the other part of my heritage. There's also a part of me that feels there's some unfinished business I need to address. I don't know, maybe it's a tribal thing, but it's strong. Please don't think I'm crazy, but I have these dreams…visions of what was and what will be. I can't seem to shake it. What about you? Are you planning on going back to New York?"

"I'm not sure, don't think so. After I get my degree in criminal justice, I'm gonna apply to the police academy somewhere. East Coast, maybe on the West Coast…anywhere near the ocean. I just don't know where at this point."

"If you're not attached to any particular place, then come to Hawaii."

"Hawaii! If those television cop shows are accurate, I'd be extremely busy."

"You make me laugh. Hawaii's not like that at all. It's paradise. You'll love it. People have that aloha spirit. It's always warm and sunny. The tropical breezes will gently rock you to sleep at night. Fresh pineapples, mangoes, and other tropical fruits greet you every day…and I'll be there. Come be a cop in Hawaii, and in our free time we can hike, kayak, surf, and run on the beaches. And as the days end, we can paddle out into the ocean and sit together on our surfboards, look out at the horizon, and we can stretch out our hands to catch the setting sun."

****

He watched the silhouettes of the palm trees begin to take shape as the sky turned from black to dark blue. *Almost no movement in the trees. No trade winds again today. It's gonna be freaking hot.* He didn't turn to acknowledge Hokulani's scolding but knew she was right in her assessment.

"Bad mistake, Hank. You shouldn't have spent the night. You shouldn't have even come here."

"Good morning to you too."

"I'm only looking out for you and—"

"You shouldn't have let me in then, and you certainly shouldn't have let me stay."

"Don't you dare put that on me, Hank Benjamin."

"I'm sorry, but I acted on an impulse."

"You acted on your hormones, again!"

"Yeah, that too." He laughed—more from being the successful conqueror than from embarrassment. "I wouldn't worry. It was late. I parked my car down at the café and walked the two miles up the hill. Nobody saw me," he said as he focused on a car sitting forty yards or so down the street—the headlights and engine both off. It was the intermittent orange glow of a cigarette that had caught his eye. *Careless?* he wondered, *or did you want me to know you were there?*

"Lucky for you the county never fixed these streetlights, but still, you can't be sure. Besides, what are my neighbors gonna think if they see you leaving my house?"

"That you're one lucky lady?" he said without shifting his attention.

"Take a good look at my face, and you'll see I'm not laughing. I don't want people talking, and they do talk. I have a reputation, and things like this get around quick."

"Look, I know you're right. I shouldn't have come, but I did. So please, let's not argue about it. I'll leave now before it gets any lighter."

"What the hell is this?" she asked, pulling a pair of lace panties from his back pocket.

Henry didn't act surprised when he reached out for their return.

"I don't know how those got there, honest."

"I've got no words, no words at all. But I'm seeing some pretty creepy stuff from you."

"I know it looks creepy, but I can't keep coming up here, right? Not while this guy is still out there. It wouldn't be safe. I've got nothing at my place, you know, as a reminder…do I really need to explain this?"

"Look, I gotta get down to the café." She placed her hand in the small of his back. "Come, I'll drive you down the hill."

"And what'll the neighbors think?" He smirked, swiping the lingerie from her hand.

"That you're one lucky man."

"And, uh…Mary? She doesn't have to get to work?" he asked, looking toward the door to her room.

"I'm letting her sleep in. She worked a double shift yesterday and needs her rest."

Walking down the driveway to Hokulani's car, Henry kept his eye on the one parked down the street. He heard the engine start and noticed the car begin to creep in their direction. He instinctively reached for his service weapon, forgetting he had surrendered it along with his gold shield during his meeting with the chief of detectives. The car began to accelerate, still no headlights, and Henry knelt to unholster the small automatic strapped to his ankle. As it drove past, continuing down the street without incident, Hokulani turned and accidentally blocked his view. Henry, frustrated with himself because he couldn't make out the driver, caught her gaze.

"What?"

"Are you all right? What are you doing down there?"

"I had to tie my shoe."

****

"Don't look now, Hoku, but I think those fire trucks are at your restaurant," he said as they rounded the curve heading toward Hokulani's Oceanside Café.

Flashing red and blue lights pulsated through a mixture of smoke and steam obscuring just enough of the view to make years of a family tradition pass before her eyes. She momentarily pulled the car to the shoulder, her emotions running the gamut from shock to relief.

"Hank, it's not the café." She let out a sigh. "It's a car."

"Yeah, I see it…drive, and pull up as close as you can." He pointed to the entrance of the parking lot now blocked by a patrolman.

"Sorry, Hokulani, I can't let you through," the young officer said.

"C'mon, Kimo! I used to babysit you, changed your diapers, and I got stories to tell, yeah?"

"I'm sorry, but I got orders."

Henry got out of the car and walked over to the officer.

"You know me, Kimo?"

"I'm sorry, Detective. I didn't see you," he apologized, then moved the traffic cones. "Sorry to hear what happened to you."

"Word gets around fast, doesn't it?"

"Yeah, like a bad virus."

"No worries. It's not the first time, and it won't be my last. Hoku, you better get inside and check on your staff. I'll go see what's left of…my car."

He looked at the charred remains of what was supposed to be turned in to the department motor pool later that morning. And although he knew he'd somehow catch hell for its destruction, his mind bounced back and forth between satisfaction and concern. He thought of the car and driver that sat in darkness on Hokulani's street and realized he couldn't get the make, model, or license plate number. *I'll bet that was the guy who torched that piece of junk.*

"Hey, Hank! Over here!"

Billy Iona was parked about thirty feet behind one of the fire engines.

"Hey! How long have you been here, and why didn't you call me?"

"I didn't know it was yours until just now, but hey, you couldn't have been too far away, right?"

"Unless it had been stolen."

"Was it?"

"No, but I'm just saying it could've been."

"True. The fact is, I got here just a few minutes before you did...on my way to the station."

"I think I might have seen the guy who did this."

"Just now? You sure?"

"No, about five, ten minutes ago, up at...I mean...down the street. I think I saw him drive by me, but it was dark, too dark to get a good look."

"Did you at least get a make, model, plate number?"

"No, damn it. It was way too dark. No working streetlights and, I'll be honest, I was preoccupied and wasn't thinking fast enough."

"No plate number? Not even a partial? That's not like you."

"No, it isn't. I got nothing."

"Hank, not for nothing, but did you just drive down

the hill with Hokulani?"

"What's it to you if I did?"

"No need to get defensive. I happened to see you get out of her car. So it's obvious you weren't inside the café eating breakfast."

"Okay, so you already knew the answer, yes? So why do you have to bust my balls this early in the morning?"

"Bruddah, it's no big deal to me who you sleep with. I'm just trying to figure out what happened here."

"I parked my car here and…and yeah, I spent the night at her house, okay? So what?"

"Like I said, it means nothing to me, but I doubt you saw the guy who did this. This fire was going on for a good while. Shit, man, I saw the smoke way up Farrington Highway as soon as I left my house. My guess? It's just another car break-in. I'll bet they stole the radios and whatever else was in there, and they torched it to cover their tracks. You didn't leave any police equipment in there, did you?"

"The only stuff that had been in there was stolen about a month ago—parked in the motor pool garage, if you can believe that! I never had the chance to get any of it replaced."

"Well, look at the bright side. When you come back from your suspension, you'll get a new car with a new radio and a working air conditioner. Unless they think you did this on purpose. Then you're really gonna get screwed."

"Great, just what I don't freaking need right now," Henry said. He began walking to the café.

"Where you going?"

"It's the on-duty uni's responsibility to write the

report and request that piece of junk be towed. And knowing the city—" He laughed. "—it'll probably still be sitting there two months from now. I'm grabbing breakfast. Wanna join me?" He stopped, half-expecting Billy to follow him.

"No, not me. I never go into her place."

"You're not still boycotting Hoku over that complaint she made about you, are you? That was like seven years ago."

"Six years and three months. I want nothing to do with that woman. Her complaint jammed me up something good. For months I was filling out forms and sitting before the disciplinary board with one hearing after another. And it was total bullshit. I don't know who broke into her restaurant. I don't know who busted up the place, emptied her freezers, and stole her cash register. Yet she claimed I was covering for the pricks who did it."

"C'mon, Billy! You practically accused her of setting it up for the insurance money, and because of that, her policy got canceled. When she did find another company to give her coverage, the premiums were almost double. That's why she filed a complaint against you, and you know it."

"And your character reference on her behalf made me look bad."

"Oh, for Christ's sake, there you go again. We've been over this a hundred damn times. It was a goddamn character reference, for crying out loud!" Their eyes locked until Iona, acting disgusted, turned away. "Anyway, Billy, it was six years ago and—"

"Six years and three—"

"And I can't believe you two haven't made peace!"

he shouted.

"Well don't lose sleep over it. I'm certainly not."

"Anybody who counts the years and months, and knowing you, the days, is probably losing sleep over it. I'll bet every day you drive past this place—"

"Well, if you wanna eat her food and sleep in her bed, that's your business."

"You're damn right it is."

"Oh my God! You guys are like an old married couple," Kaelani Kanakina shouted from the front lanai of the café. "No, I take that back. You're like an old bitter divorced couple who purposely cross paths just so you can keep the fight going."

"Okay fine, Billy, just fine. If you wanna carry a grudge, then that's your business." Henry resumed walking away.

"Hold up a minute, will ya? She's right. Look at us, damn it. Why are we beating each other up all the time, Hank? It's crazy. We gotta stop it, man. It's *pilau*, bruddah."

"You're right, Billy. It does stink. But you're the one holding onto a grudge, man, and neither Hoku nor I are at fault."

"Now who's the one holding a grudge?"

"Come on now, children. Say you're sorry, shake hands, and play nice," Kaelani teased.

"She's right, Hank. Truce?"

He looked at Billy, then over at Kaelani and realized it was pointless to continue.

"I give up."

"Come on, Hank, why don't you jump in, and we'll go have breakfast. There's a place near the station I like. I'll even buy."

"I guess there's a first time for everything…yeah, okay, truce," he said, then turned to Kaelani. "Were we supposed to meet for breakfast?"

"I was just gonna ask you the same thing. You now making this place a habit or what?"

"Something like that. I'll call you later."

Henry walked over to take one last look at the smoldering, charred remains and couldn't help but wonder if it was a sign from the heavens about his future with HPD. Scanning the parking lot and the surrounding area, he noticed a few people at the bus stop across the street—taking note of the homeless woman camped out on the bench.

"Hold up a minute, Billy. I gotta check this out," he said, then jogged across Farrington Highway. "Aloha, Auntie. Howzit today?"

"Could be better, yeah?"

"Yeah, I suppose it could always be better. You have breakfast yet?"

"Not yet, but God will provide."

"Auntie, have you been sleeping out here all night?"

"I sleep here unless the cops come and chase me away. Last night I slept in the park, but some druggies robbed me. Took my money, my cell phone, and they hit me. You see this bruise on my eye? I couldn't call HPD, no phone. But they don't come anyway…not for stuff like that, not to help us homeless, yeah? They only come to do a sweep. The park's too *pilikia*, you know, unsafe? So, I come here couple hours ago."

Henry nodded.

"Auntie, that's my car over there. The one that burned. By any chance did you see what happened?"

"I might." She held out her hand. He pulled a few bills from his pocket, and she laughed. "So, you are God's messenger today, yeah?"

"No, I'm only someone who just bought you breakfast. But what about you? Do you have any messages for me?"

"He was a big guy, you know? Drove up in a big dark car, about an hour before you come."

Henry pointed to the black sedan driven by Billy. "Like that one across the street?"

She stared for a minute, then shook her head. "No, not that one."

"There was more than one that looked like that?"

"Yeah, more than one like that one." She pointed. "Look like same color."

"So, the big guy was driving a car like the one across the street?"

"No, you confused. The big guy was in a fancy car. The girl drove a car like the one you yelling at."

"The girl that went into the café?"

"Yeah. She come down the hill, *mauka* to *makai*, just before you. You know what that means, yeah?"

"From the mountain to the ocean, yeah, I know."

"The guy that burned your car was the fat guy. He drove a fancy car. Pay attention." She laughed. "A car like that, not something you see out here that often."

"And what about this black car over here, it didn't come from *mauka*? What then? Waianae side? Town side?"

"Bruddah, you wearing me down. I'm sure the girl over there come down from the mountain just like you. The fancy car, the car with the fat guy, he come from town side. The car you yelled at come from Waianae side. You got it now?" She held out her hand again.

"Thank you, Auntie, bless you." He smiled and handed her a few more dollars.

Billy pulled up to the bus stop to save Henry from dodging the growing rush hour traffic heading town-bound on the busy thoroughfare.

"I thought you were hungry for breakfast."

"Yeah, I am." Henry jumped into the car. "Let's go."

"Was she any help?"

"Nope. She didn't see a thing...not a thing."

Chapter 6

You thought I didn't notice
all the little things you do.
How could I not,
when you are always with me.
Be it in my heart or in my mind,
you are there.
Even when I sleep,
I feel your energy.
There are nights I lie awake
and watch your chest rise and fall
as if waves upon the sea.
And it is the hint of a white cap,
that I know you dream of me.
But more than when I watch you sleep,
when you do the most ordinary things,
nothing escapes me.
From the happiness that fills your heart,
to the contemplation in your eyes,
you are an open book
and I freely read your pages.
I take in every detail,
so when you are away
all I have to do is think of your story,
and you will always be with me.
When I wear your shirt, your scent engulfs me,
and I pretend you are holding me, comforting me,

protecting me.
Will you?

The moment Peter Mendoza heard Henry was at the Westside precinct with Billy Iona, he saw red. The heat filled his cheeks, beads of sweat formed on his upper lip, and the flood of adrenaline caused a quiver in his legs that forced him to check if it had been visible. Every one of the detectives knew he had disliked Henry Benjamin—from his lack of tolerance for certain members of authority; and his in-your-face New York aggressiveness when questioning suspects, witnesses, and co-workers alike; to the perception that Henry had no respect for the native Hawaiian culture. Ever since their very first meeting, those became the things he grumbled about to any available ear:

****

"Aloha, bruddah...Peter Mendoza," he said with hand extended.

"Yeah, I know." Henry remained focused on his work. "Whaddya need?"

"Excuse me?"

"Whaddya need? How can I help you?"

"Um, nothing...I was just..." Feeling awkward, he slowly lowered his hand.

"You must've wanted something, Bendoza, or you wouldn't have come over here."

"It's Men...doza. Lieutenant...Mendoza."

"Isn't that what I said? No?" Henry gave a sideways glance. "Okay then, Men...doza. Got it."

"Well, I see you're busy"—he pushed aside a stack of folders to sit on the edge of Henry's desk—"so I'll make this quick."

"Please do, because I'm swamped. My partner is out sick for three days now, we're short-handed or haven't you noticed, and so yeah, I'm busy." He stopped scrolling through mug shots and turned to his unwanted guest. "Look, I was in the room when you were introduced. I know who you are, I know you were reassigned from headquarters, by your own request no less, and I know you've just been promoted…what, the second time in the past two years? All right, so you've got connections, and you have rank over me. I get it."

"You have a problem with that, Detective?"

"…nope, no problem at all…Lieutenant."

"Good, because I thought I heard you making comments about me during roll call. And I wanted to hear them straight from you."

"I made a couple comments, as others did. One being that I thought it was a waste of time for detectives to be brought in for roll call when we have the option to phone in when we're out in the field working a case. But I understand now it was a special occasion to introduce you."

"And the other comment, the one about me?"

"All I said was, 'how does someone with so little experience advance so quickly?' "

"And that sounds like the censored version."

"Censored or not, it's still a valid question. But it was rhetorical, and we all know the answer. You got connections. Good for you. Look, I'm sorry if your feelings got hurt."

"You didn't hurt my feelings."

"That's good. Now if it's all the same to you, I don't have time for small talk at the moment. If you're here to help me until my partner gets over his cold, then grab the files you just toppled over, have a seat at your own desk, and help me find out which of the perps in that stack got released from prison within the last few months…and please try to keep them in alphabetical order. The file clerks get pretty anal about that kind of thing."

"This shit is not happening, Detective Benjamin," he muttered as he walked off, looking for the captain.

****

Henry's disdain for the lieutenant arose not just from his strong suspicion that the Mendoza family's political connections were used to expedite an advancement through the ranks, but also because of an anti-competitive agenda that manifested in his being transferred out of West Oahu to the Waikiki district. What angered him more, however, was that he suspected Mendoza was one of several people quietly interfering with his investigation. He just couldn't figure out why.

Mendoza's animus toward Henry was always on full display at the West Oahu precinct house whenever he popped in unexpectedly. But what made his blood boil more than anything was seeing the former partners anywhere near each other. Henry seemed to always be privy to the politics of the precinct, and Mendoza suspected the two still shared information no different than former spouses sharing the latest updates about their kids. The fact that Iona often spoke ill of Henry compounded his confusion about that relationship.

Watching the pair saunter through the maze of desks—with Henry and Billy vigorously disagreeing on something trivial one moment, and then Billy showing off his "prodigal son" the next—he wasn't sure which part was an act, but was concerned Iona might have been betraying his confidences all along. As it was, given his not-so-secret ambitions for advancement, there were only a few people Mendoza felt comfortable talking to. This joint appearance would certainly remove Billy Iona from his inner circle until he was able to put those suspicions to rest.

Still, he also saw Henry's unexpected visit as an opportunity to give the detective the public tongue-lashing he wasn't confident enough to do privately. *I don't care if he is on suspension. He can't do anything to me here, not with everyone watching.* By making a scene in front of the officers and detectives milling around the bullpen, he hoped to accomplish two things: to continue to create further distrust of Henry, and to hopefully build his own reputation as a badass worthy of the respect that continued to elude him.

Mendoza's charge across the squad room turned into an ungainly stroll when Captain Tanaka stepped from his office to greet Henry and Billy with an act of annoyance that fooled no one. Nonetheless, it was at that moment he got the message there'd be no public flogging.

It wasn't the first time Tanaka had run interference for Henry, who never fully understood why the captain had been so generous with his influence. He reasoned that Peter Mendoza was no different than the obnoxious blabber-mouthed kid on the school playground—the troublemaker responsible for everyone else being disciplined while escaping reprimand for his own mischievous behavior. He also knew Tanaka had once been called on the carpet for a minor procedural issue that had been blown way out of proportion in an unsolicited report from the lieutenant to their superiors. Whether or not that was the reason for Tanaka's support, Henry didn't care. He was grateful all the same.

"In my office, you two," the captain said without turning to see Mendoza break stride like an inexperienced jockey aborting a neck-and-neck photo finish at the race track.

"Hey, Cap, I can explain about the car," Henry said, grinning for the lieutenant's disappointment.

Tanaka, Iona, and Henry disappeared into the captain's glass-framed cubicle, but not before Mendoza signaled to both detectives that he'd be waiting for them. Tanaka lowered the window shades, and the men took their seats.

"Did you see the look on his face?" Billy started.

"Coitus interruptus." Henry smirked.

"Coi...what?" Billy's confusion had Tanaka shaking his head.

"Coffee?" The captain offered up a half-empty pot to his visitors.

"Black," Henry replied, then turned to Iona. "And for the record, who I sleep with, and when I sleep with whomever I choose to sleep with, is really none of your goddamn business."

"Are we on that again? Man, you really hold on to stuff, don't you?"

"You just brought it up in the elevator, Billy. You're the one who can't let it go."

"Enough, ladies, enough!" Tanaka stared at the two, then focused on Henry. "I wouldn't worry about explaining the car to anyone. You've got bigger problems."

"Who, what, Mendoza? I can handle him."

"He does want your pretty ass for some reason, but no, not just him. That reporter, what's her name, Cho?"

"Kelly Cho. What about her?" The bitterness of the coffee made Henry wince. "You got any sugar?"

"Once the call went out that your car was the star attraction at this morning's bonfire, she was waiting in the lobby with a camera crew within twenty minutes…waiting for you, Hank. I guess you didn't see her. I don't know how she knew you were going to be here this morning, but she was asking for you." He looked at Billy who shrugged. "Maybe it's a coincidence, but the media seems to have finally woken up. They've gone beyond reporting these killings. Now they're jumping all over the investigation. They're doing in-depth bios on those girls and speculating to no end. They've been asking for interviews with the chief, the mayor, you name it. They're raising a lot of questions about you and why you're not making any progress. The head of the hotel and tourism association is also making noise with the local press, and she's also breathing down the mayor's neck, and you know what that means, right?"

"Look, Cap, in my defense…"

"No need to defend yourself, not to me, anyway. I know you've been hitting roadblocks since this thing started. I've been keeping tabs on you. I know you've been getting bogged down with bullshit assignments. I know you haven't been given a support team."

"And that support team thing, that's gotta be socio-economic, right? If this were happening to daughters of wealthy families or to tourists…"

"You're partly right, Hank. I'll let you in on a little

dirt that, if the media ever got wind of, the shit will really hit the fan. You're not the only one in this department who's pulling crap assignments on top of what all of us really need to be doing. As you know, the department is short by roughly three hundred personnel—mostly because of attrition over the past few years. In this precinct, we've only got a third of the patrol cars out on the streets during any given shift. The bulk of the department's manpower is kept in the wealthy neighborhoods like Kahala, Aina Haina, Hawaii Kai, and for the hotels in Waikiki of course."

"Hell, Cap, that's what I've been saying, and everyone on the job knows that," said Henry. "I wouldn't wanna be the uni up in Waianae going on a domestic or a late-night burglary when the nearest backup is thirty minutes away or completely tied up on another call."

"That's how everybody on the job feels, and that's why response times have gotten longer."

"So, what's up with that? Why aren't we bringing on new people?"

"It's not just HPD; it's island wide. The mayor has tightened the screws on every department and agency to freeze all hiring. Word is he wants to run for governor. Keeping vacancies unfilled shows up as a big surplus in the budget, and a big surplus increases the city's bond rating. The mayor takes credit for running an efficient administration. Oh, and then we got that whacko councilwoman who wants the mayor's job. So, while she's publicly blaming him for everything under the sun, she's privately fighting the rest of the council to get them to hold off forcing the mayor to release any funding."

"The mayor comes off as a fiscal hero saving the taxpayers' money," Henry added, "and she comes off as fighting for increased services and police protection. A real champion of the people."

"And as long as the business district, the resorts, and the high-end neighborhoods are protected, they'll both get the votes they need."

"Meanwhile, crime is up everywhere else, the roads are falling apart, the parks are filled with homeless, and we catch the blame for incompetent service. By the way, your coffee tastes like shit." Henry carefully placed the foam cup into the wastebasket.

"Yeah, it sat overnight. Sorry about that. Look, the way I see it, Hank, even though you're suspended, the politicians are going to make you look bad about this killing spree. Cho, if she decides to dog you, will also be a pain in your ass because she'll keep your name and face in the headlines. But for right now, I think your biggest obstacle is waiting for you outside my office."

"Copy that," Henry and Billy said simultaneously. Tanaka nodded in agreement.

"What the hell is his problem, Cap?" Henry asked while pointing to Billy's top pocket and motioning for a cigarette.

"Where the hell are yours?" Iona protested but relented.

"You mean besides his ugly face?" Tanaka said, referring to the lieutenant's acne condition. Henry imagined Mendoza fuming when laughter erupted in response to the captain's uncharacteristic remark.

"I don't have hard proof, Hank, but I'm almost certain he's been purposely getting in the way of your investigation since the beginning."

"I kind of thought that as well, but I guess it's Kanakina who'll have to deal with him now."

"I knew it!" Billy said. "Excuse me, Cap, but I've noticed quite a while ago that something wasn't right about him. Hank, back me up on this because I know you've experienced his meddling, and he's given interviews that made you look bad. If I didn't know any better...I mean I just get the feeling...I'll bet anything..."

"Spit it out, already!" Tanaka commanded.

"I almost hate to say it, but do you think, just maybe...I know it sounds crazy, but do you think he might be the guy doing..."

"That he's the one? No, Bill, that's crazy," Tanaka said. "Why would you even think that?"

"I'm telling you guys I've been watching him for some time now, and well, just look at him. Cap, he's always on edge whenever Hank's around, and you're the one who says he's been throwing roadblocks in his way."

"Supposedly. It's just a gut feeling. But his uneasiness around Hank?"

"It's true Hank never shows him any respect," Iona continued, "but let's look at the facts. The guy still runs home to be with his mother whenever she calls. He has no girlfriends. I don't know. Maybe he's gay."

"First off, those are hardly facts, Billy," Henry dismissed. "And what if he is gay? What a dumb comment."

"The *point*," Iona stressed, then turned to Tanaka, "he couldn't get laid by a hooker in Waikiki if he were waving a stack of hundreds. Maybe, and it's just a wild theory, maybe he's taking out his frustrations on them, no?"

"Yeah, it's a wild theory! It's a stupid theory since the girls walking the streets or working in the strip clubs come in all shapes, sizes, and colors. They're not just Hawaiians. And none of the vics were hookers, damn it!" Henry's volume startled both men who immediately remembered Maya.

"Sorry, Hank, I didn't mean...but not for nothing, I wouldn't rule it out completely. What I meant to say is, maybe this guy, the killer that is, maybe he sees these girls in that way, and we've all known one or two guys on the job who seemed perfectly normal and ended up being more than a little psycho," Billy added.

"Billy, you better stop while you're ahead. Look, Mendoza wants to be chief someday." Tanaka also rejected Iona's theory. "Thanks to his father, the family name opens doors we'd never get close enough to knock on. His mother is well connected politically and socially. He's one hundred percent Native Hawaiian..."

"Native Hawaiian?" Hank interrupted. "With a last name like Mendoza, I thought he was Filipino."

"He took his stepfather's name when he was a kid. He's definitely full-blooded Hawaiian. Anyway, my theory is he's tripping you up because he wants to be the hero in the Hawaiian community, which means he wants to be the one who solves this case...or at least wait until the mayor and HPD brass have had enough bad press so he can jump in and save the day—making you, Hank, a transplant who's on record bad-mouthing this community, so radioactive you wouldn't even be allowed to be a meter maid. So, if this thing continues to drag on, and a few more local girls end up..." Tanaka took a plastic bag from his desk drawer and tossed it to Henry.

"I found this on Mendoza's desk."

"This is the cigarette butt and blood samples Kanakina accused me of taking." He looked at Billy. "I gave this back to you. What the hell?"

"I gave it to CSU, I swear. I don't know how the lieutenant got hold of it," Iona protested. "You see, Hank? This is what I've been saying about him. I can't believe you're always quick to blame me."

"Like I mentioned," Tanaka quickly interjected, "I'm just guessing at this point. So, with that being said, I think you getting suspended screws with his plan. Now he's got to try and make Kaelani look bad, and that's going to be hard for him to do." He looked at Henry.

"Because she's *kanaka* and a woman, right?"

"Exactly. Does Mendoza know you're consulting with her on this?"

"I haven't said anything to anybody, and I know she won't. She even wants to keep our meetings on the down-low. As far as I know, you and Billy are the only ones who know."

"Let's keep it that way." Tanaka reached out for the evidence bag. "You've got a place to work?"

"We'll be meeting at...yeah, we got a place. What about Kelly Cho?" Henry asked while focusing on Billy.

"You could hang here until she gives up waiting."

"I don't think so." He laughed. "I gotta get in to town and retrieve my stuff. Billy, do me a favor and drop me at my place without commenting on my personal life?"

"This right here, you sarcastic fuck. This is why we

can't work together," Iona countered, and Tanaka rolled his eyes.

"I'll take that as a yes."

"Hank, it's time to go to the mattresses. You and Kaelani do everything you can to wrap this case up as quick as possible," Tanaka counseled. "Work around the clock if you have to. Knock down whatever doors, pull out all the stops. I'll do what I can to help you two, but for your own sake, if this killer adds to his list, the two of you will be fed to the sharks."

As the two men headed for the elevator, Henry watched Mendoza from the corner of his eye, surprised he wasn't in pursuit. And for a brief second, he thought about excusing himself to grab a private moment with the captain—to relay his own suspicions about Billy—but his gut was churning not knowing who, if anyone, could be trusted at this point. Meanwhile, as he debated with himself, Billy awkwardly walked back to Tanaka's office claiming he had left his cigarettes. While he waited for his return, Henry locked eyes with the lieutenant—almost daring him to start a confrontation.

"If looks could kill," Iona said when he returned.

"Hey, what the hell was that act you were pulling in Tanaka's office? 'I almost hate to say it, but do you think, just maybe, I know it sounds crazy, but do you think he might be the guy doing,' " Henry mocked.

"Screw you, I was being serious."

"Look, I know you've got a bug up your ass about Hokulani and me being the reason you've yet to make sergeant, but maybe, 'I almost hate to say it,' " he mocked again. "Maybe you should consider that guy right there is why you didn't get promoted." He pointed directly at Billy's chest.

"Why can't you just admit you jammed me up?" Iona raised his voice, causing heads to turn their way.

"Given some of the things I've seen you do…" He too now spoke so everyone in the room could hear. "If I wanted to jam you up, you'd probably be out of a job by now. But I'm not that kind of a guy. I don't spy on fellow cops, and I don't rat on fellow cops like some people I know. I would think you'd have known that about me, right?"

"You sonofabitch! Are you accusing me of being a rat?"

"I didn't say that. If I thought you were a rat, I'd say it to your face."

"I hope you're not referring to little shit like free plate lunches and stuff like that! C'mon, man, half the guys on the job get things on the arm," Iona defended.

"Not me, pal. No free plate lunches"—Henry then lowered his voice to just above a whisper—"and no stuffed envelopes from the guys running the illegal gambling rooms up on the coast. Yeah, Billy, I've known about that for quite some time. The question you need to ask is, who else in this room knows?"

"Oh, man, did you really just bring that up? What the fuck is wrong with you?" he whispered through clenched teeth.

"You're just pissing me off…again!"

"And you just stepped over the line, Mr. Walk-On-Water. Damn, this elevator is slow!"

Both men briefly abandoned the back-and-forth, then Henry felt the need to push it.

"If I'm not mistaken, I almost hate to say it, but do you think, just maybe, I know it sounds crazy," again he mocked Iona, "but you've been living with your uncle since your divorce, what, about five, six years now, right?"

"Yeah, what about it?"

"Just pointing out something you brought up in Tanaka's office, that's all." He waited for that to register. "And you haven't been dating anyone, have you?"

"What the hell are you getting at?" Iona demanded as they walked into the elevator.

"Oh, nothing. I was just wondering. It must be frustrating, right? There's a lot of good-looking stuff out there, and from what I hear you don't seem to be able to get any of it. I mean, it must get pretty lonely at night. Just you and your hand…unless you're going down to Waikiki and paying for it."

Chapter 7

The warmth of the sun washes over my body
just as the waves wash over trampled sands,
smoothing out the imperfections created
by time and intrusion.
Much like those waves,
the warmth of your hands
glide over me as a sculptor
smooths the clay of his creation.
My contours speak to your eager fingertips,
discovering new worlds that are as old as time.
But you've been here before,
and I know you'll be here again
because your work is never finished,
your curiosity never satisfied,
your journey far from complete.
Allow me to be your guide.

Henry nursed a black eye while he stared at the
five eight-by-ten glossy photos pinned in succession
along the living room wall of his one-bedroom rental—
a wall he kept covered with shoji screens when not at
home. And while anything that seemed out of place was
minor and chalked up to occasional inattentiveness, he
suspected that when he was working, Judy Coleman
had used her spare key from time to time and knew
exactly what was behind the partitions. He suspected

that her recent offers to have the cottage interior repainted were only made to see how he'd react to her proposed intrusion. Through his poker face, he politely declined and said he'd be happy to take care of it himself:

****

"I've got the best painters, Hank. They'll be in and out of the cottage before you know it."

"That's okay, Mrs. Coleman. I don't mind taking care of it."

"It's Judy! And I'd be here the whole time to supervise."

"Judy, yes, of course."

"I'm not trying to be pushy, but the guys I use are professionals. Everything will be done quickly, efficiently, and most of all, neatly."

"Are these the same guys who painted the cottage before I moved in?"

"Yes, of course they were. I always use them."

"And these professionals, they're the ones who left chip marks on the back door and paint that bled from the window moldings onto the glass?"

"Chip marks on the back door? I didn't see any chip marks?"

"Around the door latch. They're real small. It's no big deal; however, you can't miss the over-paint on the windows."

"It was just a small amount of paint. You can scrape it off with a razorblade if it bothers you that much."

"Mrs. Cole…Judy, I worked my way through college painting houses and apartments. You just leave the paint by the front door, and I'm happy to take care of the rest. This way you'll get a professional job for free, and I won't even ask for a reduction in rent."

****

Above each photo he had printed a name. Below each, lists with pertinent information such as age, height, weight, where each victim worked, lived, cause of death, and where each body was found. Close-up photos of cuts, bruises, and other relevant findings were appropriately connected to each woman by colored lengths of yarn. Lists pinned along the sides of each picture had color-coded words highlighting possible connections between each: victim number five, Makani Palahia, had graduated from the same private high school as victim number two, Pua Kahale, who once dated the brother of Kianui Hale—victim number three. The women ranged in age from mid-twenties to late thirties. However, only numbers two through five had innocently crossed paths at different points in their lives—having had the same grade school or middle school teachers, they had learned hula as members of the same *hui*, the same club, and bought morning coffee at the same strip mall. All were full blooded native Hawaiian—all but Maya who was half Lakota Sioux— but somehow, he thought, the killer didn't know that about her. The only connection the others had to her, the only connection not written on any list, was Henry.

At one time or another during his almost fourteen years on the job, he had interacted with the other four women. One waited on tables at a local Vietnamese restaurant and always had his favorite *bánh mi* sandwich waiting for him to pick up every Thursday. On slow days she'd convince him to sit with her at a sidewalk table where they'd talk about life. He had thought she did it to make the place look busy, but indulged her nonetheless. It didn't matter to her that he was married. She was attracted to him and enjoyed his company. To her, he was not only good-looking. He was educated, had a good paying job, and never talked down to her. In her mind, if Henry was to ever become available, he could have been the escape from a life she felt trapped in. Another had gotten to know him when he was still a patrolman—rescuing her on several occasions from an abusive boyfriend. Whenever he stopped by to check up on her at work, he would always be met with a warm embrace and an assurance that her "ex" had still been in jail. The day he got word that her former abuser had been found dead in the prison machine shop with a shiv sticking out of his chest, Henry personally delivered the news. She had worked at a local florist and had gotten to know him better when he began coming in every Friday to pick up a lei for his date nights with Maya. Because he had always tipped so well, she made an extra effort to use the freshest, most fragrant plumeria for him. On more than one occasion he'd buy a floral halo that he placed on her head as a special thank you for her over-and-above customer service. Victim number four was the legislative assistant for the councilwoman of the district where all the women had lived—the same district Henry had originally been assigned to. She had gotten to know him during the monthly community meetings held in Waianae and Nanakuli. As the liaison, she was tasked with representing her boss at the gatherings—reporting the councilwoman's latest accomplishments and listening to a long list of constituent concerns, which in reality were mostly complaints about the lack of city services. Henry was the HPD representative who presented the latest crime statistics while being subjected to many of the same grievances. They often sat together at the back of the meeting rooms where she would pass along eye-opening stories about the councilwoman. And then there was Makani. She was different. A one-time meeting that came about during the investigation, her murder confused him. He knew the killer had been taunting him, and strongly suspected he was being watched. *But is he frustrated with me because I haven't figured out who he is? Or is he switching things up because he thinks I'm getting close? Maybe too close? I don't get it.* He stared at her photo—the one he took the other day at the beach—somewhat fuzzy from enlarging and printing it off his cell phone. The face an ashen color, her once painted lips void of blood now a cold, dark blue. He closed his eyes and thought back to the conversation they had that night in Chinatown and later at her apartment:

****

"Here you go, home safe and sound."

"No, wait, don't go so fast. I'm…I'm afraid."

"You'll be safe, Makani, I promise. I doubt very much he's been watching you or that he even knows we've been talking. Just to be safe, lock your door and don't let any strangers in. You have my card. If anybody tries to break in, you call me right away, or better yet, call 911 first."

"But what if he's already waiting for me inside?"

"Highly unlikely. Do you trust me?"

"…yes, but could you just come in to check…please?"

"…sure. Just stay behind me, and we'll check it all

out."

"Okay, but make sure you check everything. Even under the bed."

"Even under the bed, got it."

"I can't tell you how much I appreciate this."

"No worries. It's all good."

"Yes. Can I get you something to drink? I mean like water or something like that?"

"No. I'm fine. Everything looks good."

"Don't forget the bed...underneath."

"Right!"

"I really do appreciate this, you know? I've been living alone lately, and there's a lot of bad things that happen here on the homestead. But you'd know about that, wouldn't you?"

"Yup! Sadly, it's not just here on the homestead. Don't you have a boyfriend who could protect you?"

"No, we broke up, and he moved out about a year ago."

"And you haven't seen him since? Not a call, hasn't shown up at your work or bumped into him at the grocery store?"

"He's in the military, deployed overseas...I'm not seeing anybody...you?"

"What?"

"Seeing anybody. You got a girl, you married?"

He smiled at her puppy-dog eyes. "Look at that, nobody here. No one hiding in the closets, no one under the bed. You're safe and sound."

"I appreciate that, but I'm really spooked. Do you think maybe...do you think you could stay a little while?"

"...I don't think that's a good..."

"We can watch a movie. I can make us some coffee and maybe a little something to eat, yeah?"

"That's kind of you, but I really gotta go. I've gotta lot to do. It's this case, you know?"

"I guess. But it's okay to call you if anything…"

"It's actually better to call 911. You see, I'm working in town, in Waikiki, which is over twenty-five miles away. The emergency dispatcher can get a patrol car here much quicker."

"Well, okay, I understand…I'll walk you to your car."

"If you think of anything about this girl they found in Chinatown, anything at all…"

"I'll call you, I promise. What was her name again?"

"Kianui. Kianui Hale."

****

Before opening his eyes, he remembered how they had stopped in front of his car where she surprised him with a long trembling embrace. The strong scent of perfume and the softness of her lips made her kiss seem like rose petals brushing across his cheek.

He opened a folder containing copies of the notes found with each of the first four victims—each one addressed specifically to him. He set aside the first one from the other three as it was hurried and brief as if an afterthought. The others, while rambling, all contained personal taunts: "You call yourself a detective? How easy do I have to make it for you? You're not even close to catching me." A fifth and separate note, which had been mailed to the Waikiki station, was more chilling: "The other day I was standing just a few feet from you, watching how lost and confused you were.

You really are incompetent. I'm trying to help you. Don't be fooled by copycats. They'll mislead you. I'll stay close and, if you feel me watching you, it could be me, or it could be the guilt you feel for your own sins." He kept going back to the fourth note. It grabbed his attention not just because it blamed Henry outright for the "work" that needed to be done, but because of the handwriting. It was almost as if the killer had an injury: "Don't you get it that you force my hand? All because you soiled the daughters of Kamehameha. This is on you, it's on your head. Transplants like you continue to invade our sacred home and oppress our people and pollute our air and our land. You strip our oceans of the food that sustains us, and you soil our virgin daughters who must never be allowed to thin out the bloodline. You white people are a dirty and inferior race, and you will never breed us out of existence. Who's next on my list? You figure it out."

A shiver ran down his spine, and he reached for his phone.

"Hoku? It's Hank."

"Don't tell me you're looking for a return visit already."

"Are you two home?"

"Oh, so you are!" She laughed.

"No, I'm not calling about that. Are you two at home?"

"You sound serious. What's up?"

"Where are you?"

"I just closed the café. We're heading up the hill now. What's going on?"

"...nothing. I'm just checking on you."

"So, you *are* worried about us. The question is,

should I be worried about us?"

"I'm just checking…I mean, yeah, I'm worried about the both of you. Listen, does it look like anybody's following you up the hill?"

"No, I don't see anybody behind us. Hank, what's going on?"

"I'm just reviewing the notes the killer left for me. He knows things that…I've just been thinking a lot. I'm just being cautious, is all. I'm gonna check on you two more frequently until I nail this sonofabitch. I want you calling me as well. I want you checking in regularly. You don't have a problem with that, do you?"

"No, of course not."

"Good. Now do me a favor. I know this may sound crazy, but just do as I ask, okay?"

"I'm listening."

"When you get to the top of the hill, drive past your house and go around the block one time. No need to rush either. Check the street for any cars or anything at all that seems out of place. If there's anything unusual, you call me and then head back down to the café. If everything seems normal, when you get home, you back into your driveway, kill the lights and the engine. Sit there for several minutes and watch the street. Watch your mirrors too. Watch everything and take note of anything out of the norm, got it?"

"You're scaring me."

"Tell me you understand. Tell me you're gonna do this."

"Yeah, of course, I got it."

"If you see anything that seems outta place, anything that doesn't seem right, you drive back down the hill, and you call me."

"I know, you already told me."

"Okay, okay. If everything looks good, then get into the house and make sure your doors and windows are locked tight."

"But, Hank—"

"No buts. Got it?"

"Yeah, I got it. Anything else?"

"Yeah, you make this a daily routine, understand?"

"Understood. Anything else?"

"Yes...do you own a gun?"

****

Henry stood up from the table, stretched, gathered the empty bottles and paper plates, and headed off to the kitchen to refresh his ice bag.

"Are you sure you don't wanna tell me about that shiner?"

"I already told you. I tripped over my garden hose and did a face-plant into the mailbox. You want another beer?"

"I hear something similar happened to Billy Iona, except he broke his nose. Funny how those things happen," she called back.

"Do you want another beer or not?"

"No, not unless you're having one," Kaelani replied while continuing to read through one of the many files that had been neatly stacked in a cardboard box.

"The way I see it, I'm already home, so I don't have to drive anywhere. And I don't have to punch a clock in the morning. You, on the other hand, have to do both."

"Maybe not. Maybe I don't have to drive anywhere." Kaelani continued to study the materials.

"Maybe I shouldn't go home, then. Got an extra pillow?"

"If that's not the alcohol talking, I gotta tell you I don't think it's a good idea. Either way, I'm withdrawing the offer. The bar is now closed."

"God no! That wasn't what I was talking about. Not only do you not know me, you think way too much of yourself, Hank." She laughed. "I'm looking at your notes, which are very detailed and organized. I'm impressed. Very impressed. But I'm thinking there's really a ton of stuff I gotta get up to speed on. Plus, I have an idea."

"Oh, okay…well, you sleep on the futon, then, because it's just too hard for my back. How much longer you wanna go?"

"Another hour or two?"

"You're worse than me…another hour or two? Seriously?"

"Listen, we've both had a long day, and sure, we've been at this for several hours. It's late, but check it out. Every one of these women have one thing in common."

"Me." He returned with two waters and a bag of ice.

"Exactly. That's another reason why I think I should spend the night. Let this guy think I'm your new girl. If what I think is true, he'll come after me. I'll be his next target."

"I don't know."

"Look at the notes this guy left for you. Not only is he blaming you for his actions, but this latest one, the one found with Makani. This is the first one that had a photo attached to it, a photo of you and her hugging in front of her apartment."

"Go on, make your point." He sighed.

"Tell me how he knew you were in Chinatown questioning her? How did he know you'd be driving her home? No way this was a coincidence. This guy's been following you, Hank."

"I suspected that. I mean, he practically said as much in his notes, and this photo...this photo confirms it. I also think he was among the onlookers at Auntie Lily's the other day," he said as he studied one of the photos taken with his phone. "I know it's fuzzy, but do you see that fat guy there?"

"I can't tell from that, but we agree, he's not stalking the women. He's stalking you and going after them *after* he's seen them with you. Don't you get it? He's doing this to torment you. You're the target. He's either got a score to settle with you, or you're standing in his way somehow."

"He definitely has a hard-on for me. I get it. So, to be clear, you're telling me this isn't about a pent-up frustration over native Hawaiian purity? Because I think it's still part of it."

"Hell, there's countless numbers of interracial relationships on this island, right? Are there any other Hawaiian girls not connected to you in the slightest way being butchered? No, there aren't."

"Not yet. My gut tells me this is more than him wanting to torment me. If I crossed this guy somehow, why is he singling out women he thinks are full-blooded Hawaiian? Why not go after my massage therapist who's Japanese, or my chiropractor who's black? Why doesn't he just try to kill me?"

"He's not going after you directly for two reasons.

One, because you carry a gun and he's a coward. He doesn't have the balls to face you directly. And two, he wants you to lose sleep over this. He wants you to suffer. But make no mistake, he is going after you. I think he torched your car."

"The department's car. And you were at Hoku's when it happened. Did you see anything?"

"…no." She hesitated. "I was inside having breakfast. But it doesn't matter that it was the department's car. It was the car he saw you in all the time. Torturing you in this way is what's giving him pleasure, and it's giving him power over you."

"He doesn't have power over me."

"Oh no? Just look at how much his actions have controlled your life over the past eight months."

"So why not vandalize my personal car, throw rocks through my windows, or cut the wires to my internet every few weeks? Look, I'm not saying I disagree with you, but if you're right…"

"I took the liberty of talking with a psych friend of mine. I know I'm right."

"And this friend of yours…he thinks this coward who's afraid to go toe to toe has power over me?"

"Yes, *she* does. Have your eating habits changed? Are you drinking more than you used to? Losing sleep, having any nightmares? What about the way…"

"Okay, I get it, I get it." Henry walked over to a stack of files. "We have to expand the list of possible suspects. This could be some white guy, or a Filipino, or even a woman. I've busted so many people over the years. Who knows, maybe it is a white guy who's blaming me for totally screwing up his life. Maybe he's also got some sort of warped colonist type of domination fantasy, and he's gone ballistic after being rejected by the local girls. Yeah, that's it. He's gone ballistic because I connect so easily with them."

"My God, you do think highly of yourself."

"Perhaps"—he ignored the comment—"perhaps it is a woman who's gone off the deep end because she's so sexually frustrated. Think about that one for a minute. Maybe she knows me. Maybe she sees what she thinks is my having multiple relationships while ignoring her completely."

"Now you're mocking me."

"Not at all. I'm throwing these ideas out there because they need to be considered. Maybe this woman is a lesbian, and she thinks I stole her girlfriend. While we're at it, let's not rule out that it could be my sleazebag neighbor. Or maybe, just maybe it's a cop who went off the reservation because he blames me for making him look incompetent or derailing his career. A cop who just happens to be Hawaiian."

"Who's that, Billy?"

"Yup, Billy Iona. Maybe it's Pete Mendoza. He fucking hates me. What about you?"

"Me? Go fuck yourself. If I had a beef with you, you'd have more than a black eye."

"I believe it. Look, I'm just putting it out there. Billy did lose his temper this morning. Mendoza? It's not hard to make him look bad, and he's had a stick up his ass for me since we met. And you...I was just trying to get a rise outta you."

"You can come up with all the what-ifs you want, but you're still the common denominator. Have you made a list of everybody who could have a revenge motive?"

"I've been making lists since day one. I've been making lists and checking out every person I've busted one by one, even the ones who are still behind bars because they could have someone on the outside willing to help. It's amazing how many people would love the chance to kill me. I've got a bunch more I still need to look into, but so far everyone has checked out except..." He thought about Costa.

"Except what, except who?"

"I guess now I gotta put together a list of everyone else who knows me...everyone that I've interacted with, on and off the job. I know someone at the FBI who could help us, a profiler. I'll give him a call. I want him to take a look at those notes. Especially the handwriting on the fourth one."

"You're just thinking about that now? I got it covered...sent the originals off to the department's handwriting expert this morning."

"Yeah, well, you work a case like this without support and see all the things that you overlook."

"At least now, I'm pretty confident it's not you."

"Are you sure about that?"

"I had serious doubts at first, but looking at all the research you've put into this...the files, the number of interviews you've done, all the hours you've invested on your own, and all without anybody else on the job knowing the time you've put in. You haven't been showboating. That's why I'm sure it's not you. I'm convinced of that now. But tell me one thing: why haven't you told anyone?"

"Who'll listen? Let me know as soon as you hear anything about the handwriting. Now, let's get back to your idea. You wanna spend the night to make yourself a target?"

"He's following you, yeah? What's to say he isn't watching the house right now? The only catch is, if he's a cop, or if he knows that I'm one, he probably won't come after me." She patted the nine-millimeter automatic secured on her hip. "But if he's really one of these whacko separatists, the kind who goes to those secret sovereignty meetings up at the bunkers, he'll think you did spoil another pure blood, and worse, a direct descendant of the queen."

Henry stared at Kaelani, but for a moment he only saw the homeless woman at the bus stop across from the Oceanside Café:

****

"Auntie, that's my car over there. The one that burned. By any chance did you see what happened?"

"I might." She held out her hand. He pulled a few bills from his pocket, and she laughed. "So, you are God's messenger today, yeah?"

"No, I'm only someone who just bought you breakfast. But what about you? Do you have any messages for me?"

"He was a big guy, you know? Drove up in a big dark car, about an hour before you come."

Henry pointed to the black sedan driven by Billy. "Like that one across the street?"

She stared for a minute, then shook her head. "No, not that one."

"There was more than one that looked like that?"

"Yeah, more than one like that one." She pointed. "Look like same color."

"Okay, I got it. So, the big guy was driving a car like the one across the street, yeah?"

"No, you confused. The big guy was in a fancy car. The girl drove a car like the one you yelling at."

"The girl that went into the café?"

"Yeah. She come down the hill, *mauka* to *makai*, just before you. You know what that means, yeah?"

"From the mountain to the ocean, yeah, I know."

"The guy that burned your car was the fat guy. He drove a fancy car. Pay attention." She laughed. "A car like that, not something you see out here that often."

"And what about this black car over here, it didn't come from *mauka*? What then? Waianae side? Town side?"

"Bruddah, you wearing me down. I'm sure the girl over there come down from the mountain just like you. The fancy car, the car with the fat guy, he come from town side. The car you yelled at come from Waianae side. You got it now?" She held out her hand again.

"Thank you, Auntie, bless you."

****

"Where are you, Hank? What are thinking?"

"There was a suspicious car the other night," he muttered almost under his breath.

"Where, here?"

"No." He wanted to ask if she had been parked up at Hokulani's. "I mean yes, here, up the street," he lied. "Turned out to be nothing. Just this guy I busted a few years back. A guy named Costa. You know him?"

"…I know a number of Costas."

"Nicky Costa…a big heavy-set guy who's got a decent rap sheet with a wide range of stuff from harassment, DUIs, assault, drug possession, restraining orders, and then some. The thing that gets me is how he's always getting off on technicalities, a slap on the wrist, or a reduced sentence. Sound familiar?"

"…no." She broke eye contact to study the photo of Henry and Makani.

"Anyway, he moved onto the street several months ago. He's the sleazebag neighbor I mentioned, and he's creeping out some of the folks on the street. I ran his name through the database about a month ago, and the last thing he got nailed for was doing ninety-one in a fifty-five, driving with a suspended, and no insurance. That was a little over a year ago. Doesn't mean he hasn't been doing anything else, though. He's habitual, can't help himself. Anyway, I promised the neighbors I'd keep an eye on him."

"What else do you know about him?"

"He likes to draw attention to himself, big man on campus kind of stuff. A few of the neighbors were saying that he claimed he had been a cop in California. Placerville if I remember correctly. I didn't believe it for a minute, not with his history. So, I called them up to check."

"Let me guess. They never heard of him."

"Oh, they heard of him, but not as a cop or any city employee, but as a civilian volunteer who did bicycle safety patrols in the community parks. He got busted for impersonating a cop. Had a shield and a uniform that he bought from a Halloween costume shop. The guy was crazy enough to shake down people on the hiking trails, demanding money if he found any weed on them during a backpack search. An undercover cop was walking the trail with her dog when he appeared out of nowhere and claimed she was trespassing on government property. She nailed his ass when he demanded sex to let her go without a citation."

"He sounds like a real pig. Let me stay here tonight, and let's see if anything happens with that."

"...all right, we can try it. The futon is all yours." Henry looked at his watch. "Look, I gotta make a phone call. I gotta check up on someone."

"Go ahead. I need to go pee. Where's your bathroom?"

"It's through the bedroom."

During Kaelani's time at the police academy, the instructor who had the greatest impact on her had a favorite quote: "trust but verify." She didn't know it was a favorite saying of a former president who had passed a few years before she was born. Even if she had, it wouldn't have been any more or any less her personal mantra when she carried out her job, or her justification for carefully inspecting every item in Henry's medicine cabinet. "Typical guy stuff. Nothing unusual here, except...everything is so clean and orderly," she concluded. A casual scan of the bedroom also impressed her for the tidiness, which was why two items caught her attention—a yellowed newspaper clipping sticking out from under a dresser, and on the nightstand, a neatly folded pair of women's laced panties placed between a picture frame and a writing journal. Her eyes darted through the article highlighting Henry's arrest of Nicky Costa. A brief paragraph about Costa having once been a suspect in his wife's disappearance caught her eye. She carefully returned it so only a small corner of the aged paper was visible as before.

"Hey, you okay in there?" Henry called from the living room.

"Just girl stuff. I'm almost done," Kaelani said,

moving toward the nightstand.

"No tampons down the toilet, okay? My landlady will kill me if it clogs and overflows."

"Copy that!" She smiled and shook her head.

She flipped through a few pages of the journal, then took a closer look at the framed photo. It was old, but she knew the face. "What the fuck?"

When she returned to the living room, Henry immediately noticed a change in her demeanor.

"You look like you saw a night marcher."

She didn't hear him. She was glued to the eight-by-ten photo of Maya Benjamin. "What the fuck is going on here? They're not...who the hell is..." She had a dozen questions and summoned up all her energy to keep them to herself—for now.

"Hey, what's up? You have an epiphany on the toilet, or what?"

"Something like that. I gotta go." She scooped up her phone and keys.

"What are you talking about? What happened?"

"I just thought of something and need to go to the station. I need to access the database."

"Hold on a minute. Let me go take a leak, and I'll join you. We can talk about it in the car."

"No!" she snapped, which caught Henry off guard. "I mean no, you can't come. We're not supposed to be seen at the station together, remember? Don't worry, Hank, I'll call you tomorrow."

And before he could ask her anything else, he was watching her drive away—and so was Judy Coleman.

Henry dragged himself to bed a few hours and a few beers later. Physically exhausted and physiologically impaired, he collapsed face-first into his pillow—never noticing the laced underwear was no longer there.

Chapter 8

There's a hole that burns deep within my heart.
A hole that carries a burden I do not wish to lay at your
feet.
Because I know you so well,
I know you will make it your own.
I do not wish that upon you,
and yet I feel that I must,
and I know that I already did.
I am filled with the pain
once carried by my mother.
She comes to me in my sleep,
filled with the shame she carried in this life.
She was violated as no woman should be.
I now carry her pain so that she may sleep.
But she is still restless.
Betrayed by someone so trusted among us.
Burned into my memory,
I see his face in my dreams.
I will never forget.
If there will ever be justice for her,
and her memory no longer forsaken by her people,
they must see her face again,
they must hear her name again.
With you at my side
I will stand up, I will stand tall, and I will bear witness.

The Makaha Valley, no different than her sister communities along the Waianae Coast, had long demonstrated a unique dichotomy filled with legends of conquering warriors and the reality of poverty and health crisis. It was a hiker's special place of beautiful breathtaking vistas looking out across the deep blue Pacific once they got past the rusting skeletons of abandoned washing machines, refrigerators, and stripped cars dumped along the dirt roads and trails leading up into the mountains. A tropical treasure where the tranquility of the rhythmic waves easily lulled one to sleep under the comforting blanket of the trade winds that often competed against the wails of sirens responding to another arson fire or a domestic violence complaint. It was a place where many of those who were employed enjoyed the protections and benefits of their civil service jobs, and who made up the growing ranks of Hawaiian nationalists who attached bumper stickers and flags to their gas-guzzling, exhaust-belching pickup trucks demanding "keep the country, country," or denouncing American colonialism and the 1893 overthrow of their kingdom.

But the Valley was also a place that Henry had a love-hate relationship with. It was a place that had filled his professional days with victims of crimes and the perpetrators of those crimes—from a body found in a drainage ditch to shoplifters who struggled to feed a family. From wannabe drug lords publicly battling over a street corner to the wasted life of an addict whose bankrupted soul was the dividend of a successful score. And although it was Maya who had had her own suppressed nightmare of this place cryptically written in a journal, the pages of which Henry now selectively read every morning, she was the one who had helped him see the hidden gems she had so often uncovered. She had an innate ability to always see the goodness of the Waianae Coast and its people, which was why she never had to ask Henry twice to help out with a community beach cleanup, a food drive, or spending a Sunday volunteering at one of the organic farms—the sweat equity filling their pantry with the freshest produce. The good that she helped him see in most of the people subsidized the commitment he had for his job, but also contributed to his frustrations. "How can a group of people, filled with so much pride for their heritage, so giving of themselves to others, also allow themselves to be repeatedly victimized by their own?" He had wondered on more than one occasion. The answers he received never helped him reconcile the disparity.

It didn't matter to those he reached out to because he was, and would always be considered, an outsider. "There are some things you'll never understand about us, bruddah," Billy Iona once told him. "It's best you just leave it alone. The people don't tell you because it's not your *kuleana*. It's not your responsibility. At the end of the day, all you have to know is that when it gets bad enough, it gets taken care of the Waianae way. In-house so to speak. That's when that specific problem disappears…forever. Just one less dog shitting in your yard, yeah? The cops are never called, but guaranteed we still know. It's a well-guarded community secret, and nobody is the wiser."

And the valley did have its secrets. Like the meeting place at the end of a long winding dirt road that coursed through the thick overgrowth, past the illegal dump sites, and up the mountainside to an old bunker that had been one of several built by the army shortly after the attack on Pearl Harbor in 1941. Originally intended as last-ditch storage facilities that had been filled with weapons, ammunition, and food to supply surviving troops-turned-guerilla-fighters in case the island had fallen to the Japanese, these long abandoned concrete caves had, in recent years, been utilized by veterans unable to assimilate back into society because of PTSD and other problems. Their issues, as with their existence, had fallen through the cracks of government bureaucracy, and like the bunkers, they'd been forgotten. But one bunker had become the meeting place of the growing number of *Kanaka Ma'oli*, the native born, dedicated to seeing Hawaii's independence and monarchy restored one day.

A chain-smoking Nicky Costa sat in his car and checked both his gun and the rearview mirrors at the sound of every creaking branch while watching the entrance to this hidden meeting place.

He hated going up there at night as much as he hated not being allowed into the cave. Except for the stars that filled the skies, it was pitch black. And because he hated not knowing what could be lurking in the darkness, it was one of the few places on the island he felt vulnerable. There were many ways to die up in the mountains—be it a misstep that would send the most experienced hiker falling hundreds of feet into a rocky ravine, the vicious wild boars that freely attacked a perceived threat, or even from the careless aim of an anxious hunter hoping to bag the main course for the weekend luau. But the threat of dying at the vengeful hands of drunk separatists who had known and hated him for all the scams he'd played over the years worried him the most. But he, as well as others, still made the occasional trip up any one of the dirt roads that snaked their way through these Western Oahu mountains to add to the many secrets that would never be revealed.

Even if there hadn't been a long list of people waiting for an opportunity to exact their pound of flesh, he would never be allowed inside the bunker because he was of Portuguese blood—something Costa could never understand or accept as the reason for his exclusion from this covert group. After an attempt to join their ranks ended in one more public humiliation, he harbored a deep-seated resentment for the people he wanted so much to be accepted by.

He sat in the darkness, smoked, fidgeted, and sipped cheap whiskey purchased from an all-night convenience store as the fiery rhetoric and roaring cheers echoed into the night. The boredom and the alcohol weighing heavily on his eyelids, the meeting seemed to drag on forever. His head began to bob, but the fear of centipedes crawling through his opened window jolted him upright each time until Mendoza snuck up from behind, brushed the back of his ear with a twig, laughing while he watched Costa suffer in pain from hitting his head on the ceiling liner of the car.

"What the…? You fucking crazy?" he screamed.

"Lower your voice! You want these guys to see you here?"

"Why the hell you do that? I almost pissed myself, goddamn it! What's wrong with you?"

"Relax, damn it. Can't you take a little joke?"

"I've been waiting here two hours. I think maybe

next time I just call you, yeah? Better yet, I'll come visit you at your work, or maybe I join you at your mother's house for dinner."

"Don't you fucking dare. I told you to never ever call me, never come to the station, and don't you even think about getting anywhere near my mother, or I'll kill you."

"You don't have the balls. Anyway, we gotta talk, and it gotta be right now!"

"You're outta your mind. We've got nothing to talk about. Our business is long done. Do you realize how risky it is for us to be seen together?"

"Risky for us? You mean risky for you. I think somebody's worried about his future."

"I think you're the one who needs to be worried." Mendoza drew his off-duty pistol. "I can pop you right here, and not one of these guys will ever say a word. In fact, they might get pissed off because they didn't get a chance to do it themselves."

"Do it! I dare you. But take this to bed with you tonight, brah. I've got everything we ever discussed on one of those flash-drive things," he said to Mendoza's surprise. "In fact, I got every one of our talks on several of them, neatly packed in envelopes and ready to be delivered. If anything happens to me, a friend will deliver them to the press, attorney general, the FBI, and many others. Whaddya think that'll do to your father's reputation, huh? The dead can't come back to defend themselves, yeah? And then there's your poor mother. How you think this will hurt her? You think she'll still be invited to all those fancy charity events? Not when she goes to jail."

"You're bluffing. A slimy lowlife like you doesn't

have any friends, let alone anyone who'll willingly do a favor for you."

"What, you don't think I got friends from being in prison? You don't think they owe me? You willing to gamble your future or Momma's social status? You ready to throw away your parents' dream of you being head of all HPD? Or does your *makuahine* still think her little boy got what it takes to be mayor?" He watched the blood drain from Mendoza's face. "Now put that fucking gun away before you hurt someone. I've got a problem I gotta take care of."

"You've got a lot of problems that you need to take care of, you sick bastard. How many more girls are you gonna carve up, huh?"

"Why so quick to blame me, bruddah? Could be a copycat, yeah?"

"Just the same, you and me, we have no more business. You got your money, and you're not getting any more."

"This ain't about money."

"Then what?"

"I got this old *haole* woman live a few doors down from me. She's up in my business, always watching me, always talking stink and telling anyone who'll listen to her."

"So, why is that a problem?"

"I come home the other night, caught her snooping around the back of my house, digging through my trash. Not the first time, yeah?"

"I thought you kept a dog tied up in your yard."

"I do, but I had to take him to the vet. I think the old bitch poisoned him."

"So why are you coming to me with this? You

need me to tell you how to take care of your business? You need me for what, permission?"

"I don't need your permission for anything. I'm coming to you because she's a problem for me, which means she's a problem for you. I'm coming to you because she lives across the street from the guy you hate, the guy who busted my ass ten years ago. She's his goddamn landlady."

"You moved across the street from him? You're fucking nuts!"

"You think?" Costa's chapped lips spread wide, revealing his nicotine-stained teeth, his foul breath causing Mendoza to gag.

"My God, what the hell were you thinking? He'll be all over you like flies on shit!"

"You best pray that don't happen. You best pray he never finds out that you hired me to—"

"What are you planning to do?"

"Don't worry about what I'm gonna do, but I'm gonna need him off that street for a few hours. I need you to get him away from his house, away from that street."

"And how am I supposed to do that?"

"I'm told you a smart boy, Mendoza. I'm sure you can think of something," he said, enjoying the upper hand. "Use your connections if you gotta. God knows your mother's got plenty. I'm giving you two days. Come up with something."

"This isn't gonna end well for you."

"Two days, brah, two days…I see you got someone waiting up the path. Better get back up there before he come down here. Anyway, time for me to get out this godforsaken place. The smell gonna make me throw up."

Mendoza watched him drive off before heading back up to the bunker.

"You okay, Lieutenant? You look like you saw a ghost."

"I'm fine, just exhausted from a long day." He looked over his shoulder to make sure Costa was gone. "I'm glad you were able to join me tonight, Billy. I'm glad you got to see firsthand what this group is all about." Mendoza patted his shoulder.

"I have to admit I was hesitant. But you're right. These guys are passionate and make a ton of sense. They definitely seem organized too. I'm impressed with what they did on the big island to oppose that new telescope on Mauna Kea. It's really inspiring."

"Small steps on the greater path. So, you're onboard with us? You're ready to join the struggle?"

"Not quite yet. Don't get me wrong. I hear what they're saying. I get the message, and of course I'm proud of my heritage."

"But?"

"I'll be honest, Lieutenant…"

"Pika! It's my Hawaiian name."

"Nice, it means 'the Rock.' It fits you well."

"When we're on the job, it's Lieutenant, but when you're here, when you join the fight, we're all brothers."

"I'll be honest, Pika. I gotta take some time to think this through. It's not that I don't wanna, it's just that I got less than two years before I put in my papers, and I don't wanna jeopardize my pension."

"What are you worried about, Billy? You saw how many guys from the job were here, right? You saw many familiar faces, didn't you? Guys we know from the fire department, sanitation, heck, from every city and state agency. We're not just a bunch of disgruntled *mokes*, but a growing movement made up of bruddahs and sistas, yeah? We don't turn on each other. And with my family's connections…"

"I know, I hear what you're saying, but…"

"Look, I'll be straight with you. I asked you up here tonight because I'm concerned about you. I needed to be sure we're on the same side. I needed to be sure about your loyalty. I've confided in you before, but lately…lately I've been having my doubts. There's a lot more things that I'm gonna need your help with. There's a lot more stuff that I wanna be able to trust you with. Being in this group with your brothers and sisters is important to all of us and our sovereignty, but your relationship with Hank Benjamin worries me."

"You see this broken nose, yeah? He did this to me! You really think we're friends or that I'm telling him anything that you and I discuss? Hell, I couldn't stand working with him when we were partners because he's the one who's untrustworthy."

"Then take the oath and join up with us." Mendoza peered into Iona's eyes. "Why so hesitant?"

"Give me a day. I just need a day to wrap my head around all of this."

"…fair enough, Billy, but remember, one day we *will* have our kingdom restored and, if you're with us, you'll be able to leave a legacy for your descendants to be proud of."

"I hear you, Lieutenant, I mean, Pika."

"Okay then. I'll expect your answer tomorrow," he stressed. And as Iona headed off to his car, Mendoza thought about Costa. "Billy, hold up, one more thing I almost forgot. Given everything that's been going on, I still need assurances. I need to be able to fully trust you."

"You *can* trust me."

"Good, because I'm gonna need for you to prove it."

"Prove it? Like how? I mean, what do I have to do, kill someone?"

"A loyal brother doesn't ask what or why. A loyal brother asks how soon."

Iona swallowed hard.

"...sure. Just tell me what you want."

"...are you familiar with a local con named Nicky Costa?"

Chapter 9

For many years,
unrelenting and persistent,
my dreams had disturbed me.
For many years,
I did not fully understand the
messages from my spirit guides
who have brought me back to this place
to seek the justice that will set me free.
A justice that will bring a lasting peace to my heart.
My ignorance and confusion became enlightenment
the day you came back to me.
I saw it in your eyes the day we reunited.
I felt it in my soul the first time we touched.
You are here now, and you are my strength.
You knew your journey here was
far from random chance.
A past-life obligation?
A lover's commitment?
Does it even matter?
You came searching for me
and in spite of my desire to spare you this weight,
you always knew you were destined to be the instrument
to fulfill this deed for me.
I am blessed that you have come home.

Kaelani's car had been parked in front of Henry's

cottage for approximately fifteen minutes by the time he noticed it. "What the fuck? How did I not hear that?" On his way down the front walk to look for her, he caught sight of Judy Coleman peering out from the curtains covering her living room windows. *Not now, Judy, please not now,* he silently prayed while scanning the empty street.

"She's twenty minutes late. Where the hell is she?" he mumbled, then checked his phone. "No messages. I wonder if…" Before he realized it, his landlady had him targeted and was closing in.

"Hank! Hank, are you looking for that girl?" Her voice like nails on a chalkboard.

"What girl, Mrs. Coleman?"

"Judy! I keep telling you to call me Judy."

"What girl, Judy?" he said without looking at her. *Why can't you just tell her to get lost, damn it? You would to anyone else. Tell her to get lost, or she'll never leave you alone.*

"Who do you think? The girl that parked right here in front of the house. The same girl who was here the other night. She sure left in a hurry, didn't she? She actually looked quite mad too."

"You don't miss a thing, do you? Even in the dark." He walked over to Kaelani's car to feel the hood. *Still warm.*

"Well, if you're going to take that attitude," she huffed and folded her arms. "I don't know what's gotten into you lately."

"I'm sorry, it's just that…well, yeah, okay, if you must know, she's a friend and—"

"If she's your friend, then you've got bad judgment. And that's all I've got to say about that!"

"What the hell are you talking about?" He zeroed in on Costa's house as Hoku's words came back to him:

"But there's one uncle who's just plain bad, but he's not blood. He married into the family. And get this, the wife, Kaelani's auntie, disappeared one night and hasn't been seen since. Everybody says he did it, but nobody saw it happen. So, who knows? But that guy did time. I just can't remember if it was for drugs, burglary, or what. It's getting so hard to keep track of everything that goes on out here. People tell me he was involved in a lot of weird stuff, so I don't know. But I know he's a bad egg, Hank. Rumor is when he got outta prison, she threatened to kill him if he ever came back to the homestead. He's not even Hawaiian, so he didn't belong there anyway. I wish I could tell you his name or what he looks like now. It's been so long. She don't like to talk about him, though. It gets her very angry, so be careful not to say anything. And if you do, you didn't hear it from me, got it?"

"Hank, are you listening to me? I said she pulled up nearly twenty minutes ago."

"And I'm sure you saw where she disappeared to, Detective Coleman." He now glared at her.

And again, his tone and body language disturbed her.

"...shortly after she parked, that goniff Nicky Costa came out of his house and drove off. Maybe it's a coincidence, but it was as if he saw her and took off on purpose. So then, she gets out of her car, and get this, she flips a lit cigarette into the street! You know it's been hot and dry, and that could start a fire, right? What am I supposed to do if my house catches on fire?"

"Judy, please!"

"You young people shouldn't be smoking to begin with."

"Judy, would you stop!"

"Anyway, she goes running over there and starts sneaking around the outside of his house, looking in his windows, going through the bushes like she's some sort of cop. Is she a cop, Hank? She is, isn't she!"

"Where is she now?"

"She went around back a few minutes ago. Lucky for her I'd been feeding his dog cheese balls filled with chocolate, and it had to be taken to the vet. Otherwise, she'd have been mauled by that beast."

"What!? Are you crazy!?"

"Well, it's your fault, you told me to do it! But look who's talking. Look at the kind of girl you're hanging around with, Hank."

"Judy, for Christ sakes, goddamn it!" he exploded. "Would you please just stop already? You're driving me nuts!"

Taken aback, she gave him the stink eye before storming away. "...from now on, it's 'Mrs. Coleman' to you!"

"Judy, I'm sorry...I didn't mean...aw, fuck it!"

****

Kaelani walked through Henry's front door and straight into the bathroom as if she had done so dozens of times before.

"Make yourself at home," he called after her.

From the living room he could hear water splashing into the sink.

"There's clean towels in the closet."

"First aid kit?"

"Under the sink, the red canvass duffle to the

right…anything serious?"

"Just a small finger cut I got a couple days ago. I snagged it on something just now, and it's bleeding again. I'll survive. I heard some yelling before. Anything I should know about?"

"That was my landlady. She was going on and on, saying that she was disappointed that I was seeing a girl like you. Wanna tell me what you were doing at Costa's?"

"No. She thinks we're seeing each other? What gave her that idea?"

"I can assure you it wasn't me. Want me to take a look at your finger?"

"No, I got it…and what kind of girl does she think I am?"

"She came running over here to tell me you were sneaking around Costa's house, so I guess she thinks you're the wrong kind. Are you sure you've got nothing to share with me?"

"It's nothing."

"The other day you told me you didn't know Nicky Costa. The other day when I asked you, you told me that you know many people with the name of Costa but you didn't know him, and today you're—"

"I told you it's nothing, so leave it alone, okay?"

"I think you should know that I got a call earlier from Freddie Becerra."

"Don't know him."

"We were in the academy together…good detective over at the Waikiki station. Anyway, got some interesting stuff on Costa that I never knew. He's got a son by the same name. They're estranged, haven't talked in years. Get this, the bastard used the kid's social security number to secure a home loan. Not only that, he's already in default. He hasn't made one mortgage payment since he moved in, and the bank just started proceedings against him. You can check it out. It's actually on the judiciary website."

"Why are you wasting precious time on trivial stuff like that?"

"Because I busted him a number of years ago. You knew that, right? He's *opala*. He's garbage! I don't like him. Not that I like people who break the law, but this sleazebag is different, and I don't think it's trivial. That's why Freddie's helping me out by looking into his history."

"I hope you didn't tell him you're working on this investigation with me."

"He knows what he needs to know, so don't worry, Freddie can be trusted."

"You guys are wasting your time, damn it, so try staying focused."

"What the hell has gotten into you all of a sudden? Here, let me see that finger." He reached out, but she walked past him into the kitchen for a beer. "So that's how it's gonna be?"

"And what's that supposed to mean?"

"We're supposed to be helping each other, and it's obvious you're keeping something from me."

When she slammed the bottle onto the table, beer foam poured out over the opening. Henry ran for a hand towel.

"Keeping something from you? What am I keeping from you?"

"Why were you staking out Hoku's house the other morning? Yeah, I saw you. I saw your car parked at the end of the street. Are you following me around?"

"You've got to be kidding me. The house where I live is down the next street, which is all torn up by the water department. There was a water main break, and the street is blocked off. I couldn't get to my driveway, so that's why I parked there the night before. I didn't know you were at Hokulani's until the two of you came out together."

"Oh." Henry felt awkward.

"Look, I sat there for a few minutes, okay? I didn't want you to think I was doing what you're now accusing me of. But you wanna talk about keeping secrets? You wanna talk about withholding information that could be important to this case?" She walked over to the photos pinned to the living room wall and poked a finger at the first picture. "Who is she, Hank? Who's the vic?"

"Is this a joke? Because it's not funny."

"It's no joke. You wanna tell me who she is and what it is *you're* trying to hide?"

Henry studied the photo as he had done countless times before, but he didn't answer. Kaelani walked into the bedroom, returned with the small framed picture from his nightstand, and shoved it into his chest without letting go.

"Okay then, unless my eyes are playing tricks on me, the woman on the wall and the one in this frame are not the same person, and don't try to tell me otherwise."

He pulled the frame from her hand, looked at the photo, then looked at the one on the wall.

"…you're right, they're not the same."

"I know the woman in the picture on the wall is not your wife."

"And how do you know that?"

"The other night I noticed the picture by your bed...and the underwear."

"And you didn't consider that maybe I started dating again? That maybe I was actually seeing someone?"

"I considered it, but you have a history of playing by your own rules. And because my gut said something wasn't right, I took the underwear and brought it to the CSU lab to get a DNA sample."

"And the test results from the sample you got came back as what?"

"The lab is overworked and understaffed. I was told it would take a little time. But I don't need those results, do I? No, I don't, because I went to the medical examiner's office to look at the body and go over the coroner's report. Hank, your wife is half Sioux Indian and half Hawaiian. The woman on that slab in the morgue was full-blooded, one hundred percent blood quantum, *Kanaka Ma'oli*. That woman, the same woman in the photo on your wall labeled 'Maya'...who is she?"

With a head nod, Henry acknowledged he'd let her in on a story he had kept to himself for the past eight months.

"It's complicated."

"Who is she, Hank?"

"I'll set up a meeting at Hoku's house. It's best if we discuss this up there."

"Why not right here and now?"

"Because Hoku is sort of involved."

"...fine, but it better be tomorrow."

"It will. I'm telling you right now, though, I'm

137

expecting a little quid pro quo."

After she left, he stared at the folders on the table. He picked one up, then another, and another one after that. Henry flipped through the pages but didn't focus on the words. Then he looked at the photos pinned in neat order on the wall—his eyes darting between the five women before finally settling on the first one. Again, that night returned to him, as did the guilt that had been there since the beginning, the guilt he struggled to suppress to maintain his sanity:

****

"This isn't right, Henry."

"Trust me, we gotta do this. No one will know, no one will be suspicious. She was a loner. She had no family, no friends. She won't be missed. I'll take care of all the paperwork."

"And what do I do in the meantime, disappear?"

"In a manner of speaking, yes, you're gonna disappear."

****

He walked into the kitchen, let out a sigh, and stared at the bottle of whiskey. *Just a short one. You're stressed, you need this,* he justified, then filled a tumbler with ice.

Chapter 10

When I think of home,
I am torn between the plains of my youth
and the windswept sands of my past.
A part of me wonders if I belong to either.
A part of me feels as if I belong to neither.
I am torn between the life that I once lived,
and the new one that I have been given.
It is hard sometimes, and yes,
it would be easy to walk away.
Still, I see what is and dream of what could be.
It is a reminder of why I must go back.
It is a reminder of why I must stay.
Forgive my confusion.
Like you, I anger at the complacency,
and the ease with which both my worlds
surrender to their own despair.
My heart is heavy,
But I will still dream for them
as I will dream for you,
as I will pray for all of us.
I declare my gratitude,
for you are one with your word.
We are one in the same.
In that we have always been as one.
You love this place as I do,
and the injustice hurts you just as much.

Richard I Levine

It is hard sometimes, and yes,
it would be easy to walk away.
Patience.

Honolulu City Hall had always been a busy place
for official hearings, ceremonies, and news interviews,
and where most of the real business had been conducted
away from public view—be it after hours during a
private fund-raiser at the Queen Emma Polo Club, in a
seedy roach-infested tiki bar on Sand Island, a back
room at a Chinatown pastry shop, and even the back
seat of a union boss' limo parked behind a cold-storage
warehouse in Kalihi. Money, drugs, women, and
campaign endorsements were the common currency
exchanged for the sleight-of-hand deals that were
quietly made. As such, regulations were frequently
ignored, and questionable bills were often introduced
with little to no time for scrutiny from the electorate.
That's how it had always been, and how it would
probably always be in this island paradise. So, to many
who'd grown weary of the business-as-usual governing,
city hall wasn't just the one-hundred-year-old Spanish-
Colonial style building that housed the executive and
legislative offices where the people's work was
supposed to get done. It was, however, understanding
that the intricate stonework of this artisan-crafted
masterpiece was merely a façade to please the eye
while concealing what went on "behind closed doors."
It was an irony that wasn't lost on Henry as he enjoyed
the ornate carvings, frescos, and massive chandeliers
that graced the interior courtyard of this monument to
corruption.

With each new administration's empty promises of

reform and transparency, Henry saw residents' automatic dismissal of the pandering as one more example of how this malignancy was tolerated on the island. "Perhaps these people feel helpless to do something, so they don't do anything," he once remarked to Captain Tanaka while discussing a new round of administrative pay increases that survived the latest budget cuts to the department. But with all the vocal protests over cronyism, increasing taxes, user fees, mismanaged public works projects, and increasing crime raised at every city council meeting, in the op-ed pages of the local newspapers, and over the airwaves of local talk radio, it baffled him that island residents predictably voted for the same bad actors. "I've been living here my whole life, Hank," Tanaka had replied. "I can tell you it's been like this for ever. It'll never change. If it wasn't for tourist dollars and taxpayer-funded government jobs, this place would be just one more banana republic."

The last time Henry had come to city hall was when he had been summoned by Councilwoman Carmen Ramos-Brown after Malia Opunui's body had been found in a dumpster behind the Waianae Community Center. Malia had worked for Ramos-Brown and was the staffer who had provided Henry with more intimate details about the councilwoman than he had ever cared to know—from an extra-marital affair that led to the birth of her son, to her belief that she was the reincarnated Princess Ka'iulani, sent back from the afterlife to deliver the Hawaiian people from oppression and poverty. They were in near hysterics after Malia confirmed that the half-Irish half-Filipino Ramos-Brown refused to attend those community meetings or subjugate herself to "those people" as it was beneath her to have to do so. "She's supposed to be our savior? If she didn't hate being around us Hawaiians so much, I wouldn't have a job. How ironic is that?" She had laughed.

It was well known throughout the political community that Ramos-Brown went through staff faster than a bucket full of holes ran out of water, so it was a surprise to Henry when she had used him as a prop in front of the local news media to declare that she would not rest until her beloved Malia's killer was brought to justice. It wasn't a surprise, however, that neither he, nor the local media, hadn't heard her utter another word about the murdered woman since—that was, until she phoned him earlier that morning, insisting they meet as soon as possible for an important briefing.

On his drive into town, he reminisced about Malia—their conversations, her laughter, and her desire to work for anyone other than Ramos-Brown. "I'm telling you, Hank, the Carmen Ramos-Brown that the public sees, all the smiles and talk of love and peace and protecting the *'aina*, protecting the land…that's pure bull. That is not the person that exists in private. Wanna talk about your psycho bitch? She once threw a muffin at me because it had raisins in it. She eats raisins all the time, and not just any raisins, oh no! It had to be white raisins, organic white raisins. Who knew she hated eating raisins baked into a muffin? And God forbid if a raisin ever got stuck in her new dental work before a full council meeting! I've been on her shit list ever since. She called me incompetent every day for two weeks after that. Told me I should go be a greeter at one of those big-box stores because that's all I could handle. She's a Jekyll and Hyde, and we never know which one is going to show up to the office. All she cares about is becoming mayor and then governor, and she'd sell out her own family to get there. I gotta find myself a new job because this one is killing me."

****

Palehua Street in the Ewa Villages neighborhood between Kapolei and Ewa Beach was one of a few dozen streets lined with the classic plantation-style cottages originally built for the laborers who had worked at the old sugar plantation. Though the cane fields and mill had been bulldozed many decades before, a few structures from the 1891-built processing plant remained as a reminder of Oahu's agricultural past. The small one- and two-bedroom cottages still standing had been purchased and renovated by a number of people who recognized the fixer-uppers were a great bargain and easy to maintain. Judy Coleman and her late husband were no exception—purchasing three of them before others caught on to a craze that drove prices of the average nine-hundred square foot cottages above five-hundred thousand dollars—much higher if they had been updated with the latest amenities.

Built with plywood, two-by-fours, and single pane windows, Henry doubted they'd withstand a category three hurricane or the forceful break-in of a home invasion. But Palehua Street, much like the surrounding neighborhood, was relatively quiet—save for the feral roosters that woke him each morning, the stray cats that howled through the night, and the pit bulls and rottweilers that served as sentries in yards of many of the homes. And then there was the watchful eye of Jodi Chung who had headed up the neighborhood security watch team. Two weeks after Henry had moved onto the block, Jodi had brought him a week's worth of homemade dim sum as a thank you because Judy Coleman stopped calling her in the middle of the night with her suspicions.

Even with her pride still smarting from Henry's scalding words of the other day, it wasn't Jodi or the neighborhood security watch team whom Judy immediately thought about when Nicky Costa unexpectedly began banging on her kitchen door. One moment she was sitting at her breakfast table, enjoying a cup of coffee and clipping grocery coupons, and the next she was frozen in place, trying to process the wide eyes and clenched teeth that filled the small window pane in the middle of her back door.

When she gathered her thoughts, she knew the iron security bar wedged under the doorknob would give her a minute, maybe two, to get to her phone and hit the speed dial for Henry—if she could only start moving.

Costa began thrusting his shoulder into the door to the point where the small window shattered. He jammed his arm through the opening, his now bleeding hand spastically searching for a lock or a doorknob. Judy knocked the half-filled coffee cup onto her lap when she jumped from her chair. She didn't feel the hot liquid soaking through her nightgown. Costa continued to pound his large frame into the door—cracks now visibly spreading through the aging wooden frame. She grabbed a butcher's knife and stumbled from the kitchen. The tightness in her chest had her gasping for air and unable to scream. As adrenaline pumped through her veins faster than caffeine flowed at the local coffee shop, her trembling legs began to give way, and every step became a physical effort she was unaccustomed to. Still, she continued to search the living room for her phone—finding it on the couch, she pressed the buttons and prayed for Henry's voice.

****

From the interior courtyard of city hall, Henry tried to stay out of view as he watched Carmen Ramos-Brown finishing up an interview with Kelly Cho. In spite of his effort, she still noticed him and waved like an excited spouse greeting a naval vessel returning to home port. Just as Cho spotted him, his cell phone began to buzz. "Judy Coleman! I should have known," he grumbled under his breath, then ignored the call.

Cho had her cameraman zoom in while she announced, "And finally, while fear continues to grip the island, we'll get to hear from the elusive and controversial detective who's been suspended for his failure to make any headway on catching a serial killer, a killer who's been stalking and brutally killing young native Hawaiian women for the past eight months."

With her statement echoing through the cavernous lobby, all eyes suddenly turned in Henry's direction as he raced up the stairs to the second-floor landing where Ramos-Brown and Cho held court. In one brisk motion, he pushed the camera out of his face, pulled the microphone from the reporter's hand, and pointed it back toward her, causing her eyes to momentarily cross.

"What the fuck?" he demanded, then ripped the wire from the mic. "What the fuck did you just do? Are you crazy? Do you know what kind of panic you're going to create if this shit airs?"

"I'm doing my job, Detective! Now give back that mic!"

"Your job? You're doing your job? You're being irresponsible!" he yelled, then turned to the cameraman coming to his colleague's defense. "Back off, sparky, or I'll shove this thing down your throat! The last thing we need is for this fucking whack job to have publicity. If this goes out on the air tonight, Ms. Cho, this will empower him. He *wants* people to know he's out there. He *wants* people to be terrified, and he *wants* people to think he's winning, damn it! Don't you people ever think?"

"The people need to know this killer is out there," Cho defended. "The people need to know what their police department is doing about it. They deserve to know what *you're* doing about it, Detective! And obviously it hasn't been enough! Is that why you've been suspended?"

"And that's another thing, lady. Why don't you ever give people the facts instead of passing along opinions, rumors, and inuendoes? There's some serious shit going on here, and the last thing the people on this island need is this tabloid crap. You're supposed to be reporting the news, not making it up as you go along. And for the record, I wasn't suspended because of a lack of progress." Henry tossed the microphone back to her. "Learn how to handle a stick this big before you put your mouth to it!"

"Okay, you two, I think we've heard enough," a smiling Ramos-Brown broke in. "Kelly, I'm so sorry for this rude interruption, and I'm just as appalled as you are. Why don't I have my office manager call you to reschedule this interview? Perhaps if you're free tomorrow?"

****

The back door leading into Judy Coleman's kitchen splintered into dozens of pieces as Nicky Costa exploded through it like a fullback bowling over a defensive goal-line stand for the winning touchdown. From the living room, she summoned enough air to scream into her phone, begging Henry to answer. Again, she pressed the speed dial and again the call went straight to voicemail. Save for Henry's pre-recorded message, she noticed an abrupt silence that seemed to suck the oxygen out of the room. Judy hesitated, looked up to see Costa standing in the entryway, and watched his plus-sized torso struggling to breathe as if he had just completed a hundred-yard dash.

"Come on, you fat sonofabitch," she dared, holding up the knife.

"Bring it, you battered old hag!"

Frantically swinging, she lunged straight for him. He grabbed her arm in mid-stroke, shook her like a rag doll, then snapped the brittle bone as if it were a dried-out twig. She cried out, but he wasn't finished. He lifted her by the neck, squeezed until she gasped for air, then threw her onto the couch. Wheezing, and with one arm now dangling and useless, Judy continued to resist by kicking her legs for dear life. She nailed her attacker in the groin, briefly sending him to his knees. Managing to sit herself upright, she struggled to stand, but the pain was more than she could bear. She had no doubt her existence would soon be over, but she was still determined to make him work for it. While he struggled, she retrieved her knife and continued to taunt him.

"Look at you, big man. You get off by beating up

old ladies?" she baited. "I'll bet you watch me from your bedroom and pleasure yourself, you disgusting pig."

"I was gonna make this quick, bitch, but now I'm gonna take my time." Costa's pain etched into his face as he returned to his feet.

"What's the matter, fat boy? Did I kick you in your vagina?" She raised the knife. "Come on, tubby, it's time for your hysterectomy."

He grabbed onto her ankle and jerked as hard as he could. The knife flew from her hand, and she cried out from the ripping sound as a lightning bolt of heat shot through her hip. Costa pulled at her ankle again. As her body elevated off the couch, she managed to get a couple of fingers onto a curtain and pulled. He yanked her leg a third time, dropping her onto the floor, her forehead hitting the corner of an end table. He fell backward when blood spurted from just above her left eye and splashed across his shirt. With the room now seeming to spin, Judy crumbled and thought how proud Henry would have been to see how tough she could be. She saw Costa moving toward her, and with the largest breath she could manage, she tried to curse him one last time.

"Go ahead and scream, you filthy sinner, because today is judgment day." His eyes protruded as if he were possessed. "That's right, you're a sinner, and you must pay for those sins." He was seething like a rabid dog and began wildly landing punches on her head, her neck, and her chest. Her rib cage caved with a crunch that startled even him. He didn't care that she had lost consciousness or that the furniture, the carpet, and his clothing were now covered in blood. "Poison my dog?

Well, how do you like your payback, you nosy bitch, huh? This is what you get for getting all up in my fucking business." His chest heaving, he drooled all over her and continued to land blows across her broken body.

****

Henry sat watching the councilwoman move about her office, spreading essential oil vapors from a diffuser.

"I must say, that was some hostile display." She shook her head. "You carry a lot of anger inside of you. I don't suppose you use essential oils at home, Detective, do you?"

"No, should I?"

"Well, you're clearly not at peace with yourself. These oils are great for cleansing your space and protecting one's spirit by repelling dark energy. And they also create a sense of tranquility."

"Interesting. Did you learn that at that new-age enlightenment center you go to?" His comment took her by surprise, but she still managed a smile.

"…you don't believe in that kind of thing either, do you?" She carefully set the diffuser on the credenza. "No, you don't. I can tell. Maybe if you did, you wouldn't attract so much dark, evil energy into your life. What happened out there between you and Ms. Cho is simply a small example."

"Is this meeting another one of those examples? I'm only asking because I do seem to be attracting a good deal of that dark energy these days."

"You don't like me very much, do you?"

"Given our previous encounters, can you blame me for not being a fan?"

"If you're referring to that news interview…"

"You mean that media stunt several months back? Just the latest of several of your little ambushes on me and HPD over the past four years. Why do you despise us so much?"

"Despise you? Oh, Detective, I don't despise you or HPD. But I can see you know very little about politics."

"I know enough. And I do know that you have little appreciation for how serious this situation is. The news media is gonna destroy every chance the department has to catch this guy. Please stop helping them. Please stop using this to advance your political aspirations."

"Oh, Detective." Her cackling laughter grated on his ears. "Don't you know that serial killers want to be caught? The interviews, the book and movie deals…they live for that notoriety."

"Some do, but not this guy, not in the way you think. Sure, notoriety contributes to the adrenaline rush and the feeling of having power, but it's got to be on his, or her, terms. The killer wants to be in control, and a big part of it is to control every minute of the narrative, and every minute of my existence…and he, or she, is not done with me."

"Oh?"

"I've got a few theories. One being that in his, or her, warped mind, this lunatic is punishing me, and when he, or she, feels they've tortured me enough, I'll become the final victim. At that point, the killer will either be caught, killed in a blaze of glory, or disappear, never to be found."

"He or she?"

"I don't wanna underestimate the evil that some

women could be capable of. That would be sexist, yes?" His deliberate tone was obvious.

"Interesting theory." She offered up a small bowl filled with peanuts and white raisins. Henry declined.

"It's only one of several that I've been working on."

"Yes, about that. Now that you've been suspended, tell me, who's taking the lead on this case?"

"I can't tell you."

"…you can't or you won't?"

"I'm suspended. I'm out of the loop. I've turned over all my files, and I'm no longer privy to any official information about this case. That includes the name of the detective or detectives now heading it up."

"Do you really expect me to believe that? Do you expect me to believe they're not going to contact you to pick your brain?"

"They haven't yet, so I don't know who's been assigned. Even if I wasn't on suspension, I couldn't and wouldn't give you any information about this case that hadn't been approved for release by the brass. Besides, you know that asking me to do so is an ethics violation."

"As I said, you know very little about politics. Frankly, I was surprised that you were assigned to this case in the first place. After all, with your wife being the first victim…being brutally and sadistically murdered the way she was. I saw some of the photos. How anybody can do that to another human being is beyond me." She briefly waited for his reaction. "You don't seem surprised that I know about that."

"Would you be surprised if I told you I don't care if you know it or not?"

"No."

"It was a detail that the department decided to keep quiet for obvious reasons. But obviously you have your contacts at HPD, and I suspect you already know what you wanna know."

"You were mentioning ethics violations?"

"That was a decision made by headquarters, not by me."

"So why and how did you get this assignment?"

"...since we're being frank, it's because I'm the most aggressive detective on the job. I've got a record of accomplishment. I'm not afraid to speak my mind, knock down doors, and I get answers. I get results. I get criminals locked up."

"And you've had many complaints filed against you...a testament to your style?"

"Like I said, I get results. The kind of results that anger the people who go to jail. They file complaints. And it's because of politicians that those complaints are given the time of day. It plays well in the press, doesn't it?"

"And yet you've been unable to get results with this case."

"Don't kid yourself. In spite of the politics, the prejudices, the budget constraints placed on the department by the city council, and what selected information I've revealed to superiors, I *was* making significant progress."

"So, you *have* been keeping secrets?"

"As you undoubtedly know, the department has a number of people who talk too much...to the media and to elected officials who also love to talk to the media. And you know how quickly facts get twisted and false information spreads. Your little cub reporter friend is a perfect example. In spite of many challenges over the past several months, I've been able to make progress because I'm selective with what I disclose. I've questioned and ruled out a whole bunch of possible suspects over the previous eight months, and regardless of many avenues of resistance, I've been narrowing that list."

"Sounds like you're still on this case."

"Let's just say I'm able to continue an investigation of my own, on my own terms, independent of those with a personal agenda...departmental or political. There's a good number of people on this island looking to cash in if you know what I mean. They're just not gonna get any nuggets from me." Henry's laser-like stare made Ramos-Brown uncomfortable.

"You're a very interesting individual, Detective."

"That's what I hear." He looked at his watch.

"And I see I'm boring you."

"I've got a lot on my plate, and there's only so many hours in a day."

"...okay then, enough of this banter."

"Yes. So, if you don't mind, what was so important that you insisted on seeing me this early?"

"Believe it or not, I wanted to talk to you because we're a lot alike."

"On the surface to the untrained eye maybe. But we're nothing alike, Councilwoman."

"Oh, but we are. We just have different styles is all. I tend to be more refined and diplomatic in my approach, but we both see things for what and how they are, and we go after what we want."

"You're right; I'm no diplomat. My motivation or my approach is not for personal gain. It's more honest, and I have no respect or time for people who pass the buck, lie about their intentions, or exaggerate their accomplishments, because we both know that's all about personal gain. Now, if you could please get to the point."

"You're right; you are no diplomat. So be it. Rumor has it that the mayor and the police chief want you out permanently. In spite of your accomplishments, people on this island don't appreciate your aggressive style. And given the disrespectful way you talk to me, you could understand why I'd want to help them. But I'll be straight with you. Even though you've yet to catch the guy who took Malia's life, and the lives of those other poor girls, I actually like you. Hard to believe, I know. But I appreciate your work ethic and your no-bullshit attitude. I actually wish we had more people like you at HPD and in city government. No doubt you have seen the early polling that shows I'm the odds-on favorite to be the next mayor."

"Sorry, I don't pay attention to that sort of stuff."

"I doubt that." She laughed. "Regardless, I'll be announcing my candidacy very soon, and I'm looking for somebody exactly like you who tells it like it is. Of course, we'd have to make sure you weren't in the public eye."

"No, we couldn't have that, could we?"

"Yes-men are a dime a dozen, and I'm looking for that special person to be a personal advisor and the head of my security team."

"I can come up with a few recommendations for you."

"I already found the man that I want." Her smile was cold and sinister.

"No, you didn't. I'm not that guy. Sure, if in some altered reality I did work for you, I'd tell you things that would take you out of your comfort zone. I'd tell you things you'd need to hear, but you're not gonna want to hear them...ever. We'll clash from day one, and it won't be pretty. And that's when you'll come up with some phony controversy to justify my termination."

"Just to be clear, there are plenty of qualified individuals who've expressed an interest in working for me...and if I didn't know any better"—she snickered—"it seems to me you're just trying to negotiate a big paycheck to come on board my team. I need to remind you that salaries for my administration's top appointees will have to be approved by the full council. But there's always cash to be found for special situations. I may have some wiggle room."

"I don't think you're hearing me. I'm not your guy. I'm not looking to be a part of your team, and I'm not interested, Councilwoman. Now, if there's nothing else..."

"I don't think *you're hearing me*. As mayor, I'll have the power to reinstate you, get you whatever back pay is owed to you, have you promoted in rank, and as head of my security team, you'll only have to answer to me."

"Oh, I heard you loud and clear. The answer is still no." Henry stood to leave.

"I'm offering you an opportunity to have input that can affect the future of this island."

"Are you serious? You must live in a bubble. First of all, do you really think you're gonna be the next mayor? Don't answer that."

"You are dangerously close to crossing over a line you won't be able to walk back."

"People in and out of this building know how you wheel and deal. They've seen how you go back on your word, how you always pass the buck, throw your friends under the bus, and the way you always play the woman card. Did I cross it yet? You're always the victim, aren't you? Hell, your constituents even—"

"My constituents love me!" she shouted and slammed her desk, startling Henry as she jumped up from her chair.

"Actually, they hate you. You forget, I used to be assigned to the West Oahu precinct, *your* council district. I was there for many years. I was the HPD rep who attended those monthly community meetings…the meetings you refused to go to because *those people* were beneath you. The meetings that poor Malia had to put up with listening to a barrage of complaints from the people you've ignored. Every month I'd hear those complaints about all the promises you made and never kept and about all the phone calls you never returned. Even I'd have people come up to me, asking if I knew what their council rep looked like because they've never met you."

"You lie! I've been to my district plenty of times!"

"Yeah, for photo ops to take credit for someone else's hard work. Trust me, Councilwoman, your reputation on the Westside is far worse than mine. When you talk stink about *those people,* as you refer to them, you're doing it from a place of contempt. To quote what Malia had said about you, *'those people* are uneducated! *Those people* don't vote! I have better things to do with my time.' Those were your responses when she asked you to attend meetings in the district. You want me to work for you? Based on everything I had heard from that poor girl and other former staff members, even if you did have a chance of getting elected mayor, there's no way in hell I'd compromise my principles to work for you! Is that straightforward enough for you? Did I cross that line yet?"

Henry couldn't help notice that Ramos-Brown trembled with anger. A line had definitely been crossed, and he half expected her to throw the oil diffuser she now grasped—he didn't care.

"I can see that I misjudged you, Detective. Apparently, you're not as astute as I was led to believe. The fact that you believe the lies told to you by a few disloyal staffers who were all about to be fired for incompetence shows me you're not a smart man. Malia was lucky she was murdered. Now she's forever an innocent angel in the people's eyes instead of going through life branded as just another ignorant malcontent from Waianae! You have no idea the bridge you just burned. But that's okay, because now I know not to waste any more of my time trying to save your petulant ass."

"Your attitude is disgusting and pathetic on so many levels. You not only spit on the memory of that sweet girl. You disparage an entire community, as well as the culture you know nothing about. My wife's mother and her ancestors were Hawaiian. They lived, farmed, and fished the Waianae Coast for generations. All of these folks busted their collective asses to make a life, a good life, an honest life, and they're a proud people who've continuously had the rug pulled out from under them by self-anointed deities like you."

"That's enough!"

"You all look down your noses and toss scraps from your table and then wonder why they're angry? From where I stand, they've got just cause to be."

"Cry me a river." She lifted the diffuser. "We're finished here, and I can guarantee you that your career is also finished. You will never be reinstated as long as I have any say in the matter. Now show yourself the hell out before I call security."

"It was nice seeing you again, Princess," he mocked. "Yeah, I know about that warped fantasy too. Please know that I'll be burning some sage tonight to smudge your dark energy off my petulant ass."

****

Nicky Costa purposely drove over every sizeable pothole, rock, and tree branch that littered the narrow rural road leading to a remote area in the Makaha Valley—laughing every time he heard the dull thud from the trunk of Judy Coleman's bright-yellow Oldsmobile. It was a classic 1970 Cutlass 442 that her husband came across at an estate sale and had painstakingly restored to mint condition. And for many years since his passing, and except for the rare occasions that she used it, the car sat undisturbed in her garage until that morning.

"There's another one for you, bitch," he yelled when the right front fender sideswiped the trunk of a Koa tree that had long ago been victimized by poachers.

By the time he pulled up to the entrance of the barbed-wired chain-link fence surrounding Keahi's wrecking yard, he was sure that he had heard the last from her.

"Why the fuck you have to be this far away from everything?" Costa cursed the old man.

"Ya ask me dat every time ya come out here. To have da best 'disposal' business on da island, location is everytin', mon!" He winked and brushed away the dreadlocks coming out of his rastacap. "And city property inspectors too afraid to ever come out dis way, yeah?"

"What's with the fucking rasta talk, huh? You gotta be smoking that shit again, 'cause you ain't no Jamaican. Now look, damn it, I had to come alone, so you're gonna have to drive me back."

"No can, brah. I can't leave wit no one here to watch da place."

"Who's gonna come up here to steal anything? Besides, you got dogs. Stop feeding them so much, and they'll take care of any trespassers. Now open the gate and let me in."

Keahi directed Costa over toward a large hydraulic machine away from the entrance—waving as if guiding a jetliner into a docking gate. When he crossed his arms and the car came to a stop, he gave a quick walk around, skimming his hand over the mirror-like reflection of the hood.

"Wow, except for dat gash in da fender, she's a beauty. Look almost new, like it never been driven. How many miles she got?"

"I didn't look." Costa handed him an envelope. "It's all there like we agreed."

"I bet some *kupuna* lady drove to church on Sundays, yeah? Ya sure ya wanna put dis ting in da crusher? It's so clean."

"I promised the owner I'd get rid of it no questions

asked, understood?"

"Yeah, sure, but damn, it's a shame, brah. Dis a classic 'cause they don't make Oldsmobile no more, ya know what I'm sayin'?"

"Yeah, a real fucking shame."

"This could fetch a couple tousand, don't ya tink?"

"Yeah, maybe."

"I go find a buyer. You and me, we split the cash fifty-fifty."

"The car goes in the crusher."

"Okay, okay, sixty-fifty. C'mon, Nicky, who gonna know?"

"Look, I don't gotta lot of time to screw around. You got your money, right?"

"No need get upset, brah. I'm just tinkin' we can make some extra, you and me, and someone get a nice ride. Dats all I'm sayin'."

"Look, if the owner wants this thing crushed, he's probably got something to hide. And if this thing is seen on the street, HPD gonna find out you had something to do with it. You want that, you little shit?"

"Hell no, Nicky, I don't want dat, don't want dat at all."

"And if the owner starts feeling the heat, he never trusts me again, and then no one ever see you again, understand, mon?" he mocked.

"Yeah, sure, Nicky, sure!" Keahi said, taking one more walk around before firing up the diesel on the junkyard crane he called jaws. "Is my brain playin' tricks on me, or did I just hear sometin' move in da trunk?"

"You been smoking and drinking, haven't you?" Costa's ice-cold stare startled the old man.

"...you right, da alcohol be playin' tricks on me, yeah? Okay, okay, hang loose, bruddah, and in a few minutes we have one more cube ready for da landfill."

****

Detective Fred Becerra greeted Henry as he passed through the oversized black and green-stained copper-clad doors of city hall and emerged to bask in the warmth of the sun.

"Go toward the light, the voices counsel." He raised his hands to the sky and inhaled as deeply as he could. "There's nothing like solar radiation to burn off the impurities."

"That bad?"

"I shouldn't have to remind you, Freddie. You got any sage?"

"What?"

"Never mind. You got that information I asked for?"

"Yeah, right here." Becerra held out a small envelope. "He's definitely Kanakina's uncle. You gonna confront her about it?"

"I have no choice. If she can't or won't get a search warrant to go through his place, I'll end up asking Iona to do it for me and, to be honest, I'm more than a little concerned about him. I can't figure him out."

"Sorry, I wish I could help you with that one. What about your meeting with the dragon lady? Was I right?"

"Pretty much, Freddie, pretty much. She went as far as to offer me a position in her fantasy administration, which, right out of the starting gate, we know is bullshit. If that woman didn't hate me before today, I know she hates me now. And if she practices voodoo, I'm definitely gonna be experiencing some

161

pretty intense acupuncture, if you get my drift. This woman has contacts at headquarters, so I know she didn't need any information about the case from me."

"Then why'd she ask you to drive all the way into town for a one-on-one?"

"That's what I can't figure out. Why would she want to see me first thing in the morning if not to keep me tied up, and from what? Think about it—morning rush hour's a bitch. It took me just over an hour to get down here. Then she kept me waiting another forty-five minutes, and the drive back at this hour will be at least another forty. It doesn't make sense unless…unless you have some clue that I'm not seeing."

"Maybe that's got something to do with it." Becerra pointed to Ramos-Brown walking out of city hall to a limo waiting at the far entrance of the semicircular driveway. A well-dressed woman exited the car and greeted the councilwoman with a handshake and a smile. They spoke, seemingly unaware both detectives watched from a short distance away.

"You recognize her, Hank?"

"Very attractive, but no, I don't recognize her at all. Who is she?"

"Noelani Mendoza. Peter Mendoza's mother."

Chapter 11

Fear not the ocean.
She is neither enemy nor friend.
Watch the duality of her waves,
one moment caressing the sands,
softly molding, reshaping, concealing,
or uncovering with patience and resolve.
The next she is a woman scorned.
Pounding with relentless anger
against the jagged rock and coral.
What was once laid bare for all to see will,
with time, be buried again.
What was once buried will be revealed just the same.
So it is with all things in life.
Set aside your ambivalence,
but fear not the ocean.
She is neither enemy nor friend.
She simply is.

Billy Iona tried to concentrate on the dozen or so messages filling his voicemail box with the same energy he used to ignore the stares his lieutenant threw from the other side of the bullpen. Neither effort was successful nor was it convincing. Iona had become distracted by Mendoza's sudden obsession of him as much as he was preoccupied about his former partner. For the past several days, the negative energy directed toward Billy was palpable, and it began to weigh heavily on him without reprieve.

Of the many things he disliked about the young lieutenant—country clubs, private school education, access to the best of the island's offerings throughout his life—it was his political connections and fast-tracked advancement in the police department that was the hardest for him to ignore. He never realized it was the one thing he and Henry had in common. For a number of years, Billy had been looking to cast blame on anyone or anything for his station in life. Although Henry and Hokulani had been favorite targets of his frustrations, when he did think about all the times he'd been passed over for promotion compared to Mendoza's meteoric rise, he'd find himself fantasizing about situations where he'd have sole dominion over his superior officer's life:

****

"I don't wanna actually kill him," he once told a department therapist, "but like I said, sometimes I become so resentful and angry with this man, with this boy, because I'm the one that ends up on the side of the road, and this guy flies by in the fast lane. I get so angry that, if he were lying injured in the street, and I mean life-threatening kind of injured, and I was the only one who could help him, well, I wouldn't lift a finger. Not one! I'd sit there and watch him suffer. I'd sit there and make sure he knew I was watching him as he pleaded for help…pleaded for his life."

"And you would actually do this if you had the chance?"

"I don't know, I don't think so, but I think about it…sometimes a lot. I've asked myself what I would actually do if the situation ever actually happened."

"And what conclusion do you come to?"

"Well, I...I mean, while I think about him lying there, I don't ask that question too often. I guess I don't wanna know the answer. But if it means anything, I do feel a little guilty afterward."

"Is that because you're afraid to admit that given the chance you couldn't fulfill this fantasy? Or maybe the resentment and anger that you harbor for this man is actually a substitute for the real issue."

"The real issue? I don't know what you're talking about."

"Do you see how this could be a metaphor for your issues with intimacy, with an inability to perform sexually?"

"What? I never said I have problems with sex."

"Didn't you? Let's be honest, William. Isn't that the core issue here?"

"Are you saying that I have problems with my manhood? Anger issues with women? Are you suggesting that I wanna hurt them in some way?"

"You said it, not me."

"But I don't have those issues, do I? I...I never thought about that."

"In that case, it's a good thing this is finally coming to the surface, isn't it?"

"I...I guess."

"So, now that you are thinking about it, how does it make you feel?"

"Confused, unsatisfied...completely confused. But, Doc, I've never hurt a woman before."

"No, not physically, but there are other ways. Think deeper, Detective. Have you ever heard about micro-aggressions?"

****

If there had been a silver lining from his recent interactions with Henry, it was the reminder that he needed to expect the unexpected. That was why, from the minute he stepped off the elevator, he had been formulating a host of responses to the questions he knew would be coming. But preparation would only take him just so far. He had a reputation for being a terrible poker player, and under the right circumstances his body language gave away more than just the power of the cards he held in his hand. Mendoza knew this, and he exploited the weakness every chance he got.

The robotic way Billy moved about his desk irritated the lieutenant to the point he gave up trying to shoot telepathic messages to the other side of the room. With comparable levels of anxiety, he put forth a predictable attempt to appear nonchalant as he made his way toward Billy.

"Detective Iona." He sat on the corner of the desk. "Nice reading glasses. I've never seen a cop wearing purple frames before. Don't get me wrong—they look good on you."

"Thanks, Lieutenant," Billy responded without taking his eyes off the computer. "You should try hanging out in Kaimuki once in a while. Better still, cruise down Monsarrat in Diamond Head if you really wanna improve your fashion style."

"I'm surprised you know about that sort of stuff."

"You don't think I get outta Waianae that much, do ya?"

"I'm not saying that, but somehow I can't see you anywhere near Kaimuki."

"You're right. I got them as a present from an old girlfriend. She liked purple, and she wanted me to get more in touch with my feminine side."

"You've been staring at the same screen for the past fifteen minutes. What's so interesting?"

"You can tell that from the other side of the room?"

"Not that I've been watching you, but I happened to notice you haven't touched your keyboard or mouse in all that time. So, what has you so consumed?"

"I'm not consumed, not distracted, not preoccupied at all. I'm just focused and thinking about what I'm reading here. You know, analyzing, that sort of thing."

"Like I said, consumed. Put it aside for a minute. We need to have a little talk."

"Can't it wait? I've got a backlog of voicemails, emails, and reports that I gotta get to. Captain called me at home this morning asking about reports and stuff, and I don't need him coming over here to bust my balls."

"Funny, unless I missed it, I haven't seen Tanaka come out of his office all morning. And I'm sitting right here in front of you now," he whispered.

"You make a good point. How can I help you?"

"The offer I made a couple nights ago...I'm still waiting to hear your answer. Are you with us or not?"

"I'm really sorry. You know I've been busy, and I just haven't had the time to consider everything."

"Busy? With police work? Billy, I'm your lieutenant. You're no busier than any other detective in the squad. You got a side job going that I don't know about?"

"With all due respect, we're all busy because we're

understaffed. So no, I don't have time for a side job."

"Then what?"

"...well, if you must know, it's my uncle. He's been ill lately," he lied.

"I see how that can keep you distracted from other important things."

"I appreciate that, I think. I promise I'll give you an answer tomorrow. Don't worry, I'm sure you'll be pleased with my response."

"Then I'll take that as a yes, and I'll let the group know. You see how easy that was?"

"Easy, yes, of course."

"Is there anything I can do to help you with your uncle?"

"My uncle? Oh, my uncle. No, of course not. Thanks for asking."

"No problem. We Kanaka gotta stick together, yeah?"

Mendoza patted Billy on the back and began to walk away—stopping abruptly, he looked back.

"Oh, and by the way...I haven't heard about that errand I asked you to take care of. Did I mention that it's time sensitive?"

"I'm working on it. Do we really need to discuss this within earshot of Tanaka's office?"

"No, we certainly don't." Mendoza glanced at the captain's door. "It's been two days, and I'm concerned that nothing's been done. Other than your uncle, are there any other problems that I should know about? I hate being surprised."

"I told you, I'm working...no, no other problems. I'm making arrangements."

"Arrangements? What kind of...no, don't answer

that. I don't wanna know."

"Don't worry, I'm gonna get it done soon."

"Get it done tonight, Billy. Take care of it tonight."

"But—"

"No buts, understand?" Mendoza waited for acknowledgment, and Billy nodded without comment. "Good. I'm glad you appreciate how important this is. Now, I have to head out to Aina Haina. I doubt I'll be back by the time you leave for the day, but you never know."

"Sure thing, Lieutenant. Give my regards to your mother."

"What makes you so sure I'm on my way to see my mother?"

"She has a big beautiful beachfront house over there, yeah? If she were my mom, that's where I'd be if I was going to the east side on a Friday afternoon. I just assumed you were…"

"Don't be so quick to…" He stopped himself. "You're right. That's where I'm going…for an early dinner with my mother. Since my father passed away, I make it a point to have dinner with her a couple times a month. She's lonely, and it makes her happy to have my company."

"You're a good son, Lieutenant."

"I trust you'll have a good report for me tomorrow?"

"…yes, tomorrow."

Watching from the breakroom, Iona waited to see Mendoza's car exit the parking garage, then returned to his desk. Again, he stared into his monitor, his mind drifting off:

****

"Help me, Billy. I've been shot."

"Yes, you're right, Peter. You've been shot, and you're bleeding too. Tell me, you sonofabitch, does it hurt?"

"Please, Billy, please. It hurts, it hurts really bad. Help me, call for an ambulance, call my mother, do something. I think I'm dying."

"Yes, you're right again. You're dying. I should do something. But what should I do? I am kind of hungry. Are you hungry? I can get us a snack. Hey, I know, let's have a talk. You always like to interrupt me for your talks, right? So, we can talk about my reading glasses, or you can tell me why you think you deserve to be saved?"

"Billy, for the love of God, please!"

"Come on now, Peter, man up! It can't be that bad, can it? I'll tell you what. We'll have the ambulances take care of all the deserving people first. Then I'll have one come for you. That seems fair, doesn't it?"

****

When Billy realized he was laughing out loud, he scanned the room to see he had become the center of attention for a dozen pair of eyes. He wondered how long they had been watching or if the imagined conversation left his lips. One by one, his colleagues returned to their tasks without saying a word. He swallowed hard and picked up his phone.

"It's me. You got a minute? Did you get any of that conversation? No, not that one. The one I had with the lieutenant." He reached for the micro recorder mounted underneath the middle drawer of his desk. "So do you believe me now?" He half smiled. "I've got, we've got a big problem...yes, he's pushing me to get it done tonight...no, I don't know where he is right now, but most likely he's up to no good...agreed...yes, I'm heading out to track him down. I was thinking of driving by his place, but Hank lives a couple houses down from him, so I gotta wait until dark, otherwise, there's a good chance he'll see me...no, I haven't started following him yet, not since Kaelani...yes, I was going to, but things got crazy...you're right, Hank will be quick to spot it. I should use a different car. I'll call the motor pool and pick one up tomorrow. I'm sure they have something other than black...who, Mendoza? You heard him, he just left. I believe he's really gone for the day...yes, that's true, if she summoned him, he's not gonna ignore her, not while she's still subsidizing his lifestyle...no, I haven't updated Kaelani yet...I'll try and meet up with her later to fill her in. Captain, about Costa...yes, okay, I'm gonna pick him up...yes, put him on ice, I understand...I was actually thinking of bringing him downtown to HQ so Mendoza thinks I took care of that detail, but there's something else. I told you about his connection to Kaelani, but I still haven't told you...well, it's just that they're not the only two who are related."

The door to the captain's office opened with the same slowness Billy placed the phone receiver back in its cradle. He glanced over to find Tanaka standing there with hands on hips.

"I..."

"Billy, don't! Don't say anything just yet."

"Cap, look, please don't get mad."

"That good, huh?"

Billy nodded.

"Great! Just what I need. Are there any other little

secrets I should know about?"

"Not that I can think of."

Except for a few ringing telephones calling out for attention, Tanaka took notice of a sudden absence of office noise—the chatter, the tapping of fingers on keyboards, the opening and closing of file cabinets—until a stern fatherly look, known to precede a scolding, redirected everyone's focus.

"Perhaps you and I better step inside my office."

Chapter 12

It is always calm before the storm,
yet people wait to seek shelter.
It is always darkest before the dawn,
yet they wait for the light to live.
The sun will always rise before it sets,
but it does always rise,
so why fear the night?
Storm clouds are gathering,
but they do not always portend a heavy rain.
Should we be any less prepared?
There was a time
a true medicine man of my people
could stand alone on a hillside,
brave the lightning,
feel and smell the winds whipping up on the prairie,
and spy the flight of a Northern Harrier Hawk.
And from that he knew the heavens were about to open,
deliver our karma, fulfill our destiny.
Be it good or be it bad, it was what we deserved.
No more, no less.
Be it the spring rains to grow our crops,
provide the rainbow trout from Black Hills streams,
or the buffalo sent to provide us with our nourishment
and their hides to keep us warm.
And sometimes, those winds brought warnings
of the white man coming to steal our land.

Let us listen to the wind and observe the sky.
You have always carried that medicine with you,
and it is strengthened by the virtue of our union.
This is our karma.
Do you feel it?

In spite of Kaelani's explanation, when Henry pulled up to Hokulani's house he scanned the block for any car or anything out of place—especially a standard issue unmarked police cruiser. With all the aerodynamic advancements made in automotive design over the years, to the trained eye the plain-brown-wrapper cars used by Honolulu police detectives were the most easily recognizable cars with their telltale blue strobe lights mounted behind the front grille and their all black or brown paint schemes layered with the dark-red volcanic dust carried everywhere by the trade winds.

Even while parked, he waited for something, anything to appear in his rearview mirror or from the cross street a hundred yards ahead. He knew the likelihood of that happening before sunset was rare, unless it was Billy, who was known to have an occasional lapse in judgment. Still, his cautious nature was on high alert as the hairs on the back of his neck had been up all day trying to figure out the real purpose of his meeting with Councilwoman Ramos-Brown, or why Noelani Mendoza had paid her a visit.

He was about to light another cigarette when he heard the unmistakable sound of a straining engine working its way up the winding two-mile incline of the seldom traveled street. His eyes shifted back and forth between the mirrors, and he relaxed when he recognized Kaelani behind the wheel. He watched her make the standard call to dispatch that she could be reached by portable radio or cellular, then waited for her to approach.

"I see the motor pool gave you a new car." Henry was jealous.

"It's not new. I just like to keep it clean."

"You do it yourself, or do you have a favorite car wash place?"

"I bring malasadas to the boys in the motor pool, and they do it for me. When you come off suspension, you should try it sometime."

"Given the way you look, and you do look good, I'll bet they'd do it for you even if you brought them a box of dirt."

She surprised him with a rare smile.

"So, you're finally gonna fill me in on our Jane Doe in the morgue?"

"As I promised. But there are some things we need to discuss before we go inside."

"Such as?"

"First, before coming up here, I went to look into something that turned out to be nothing."

"And you're telling me this because…"

"I'm bringing this up because I thought I'd dust off my old shield, the one I was issued as a patrolman." He caught a wide-eyed stare from her. "Come on, don't look at me like that. I wanted to have it with me in case I needed it. You know as well as I do that I don't exactly look like a local and, if people see me as a cop, there's a better chance they'll answer my questions, and a much better chance they won't mess with me."

"Okay, first off, keep in mind that you don't need a

shield, or a uniform for that matter, for people to see that you're a cop. You stick out like a sore thumb. But if you do use a badge, if something bad happened and you got caught, you could find yourself out of a job permanently."

"Something tells me that's gonna happen anyway, but that's beside the point. I couldn't find it."

"Maybe you misplaced it. How many years since you got your gold shield?"

"Long enough, but I know I didn't misplace it. I kept it in my nightstand drawer."

"What, exactly, are saying? You think I took it?"

"No, of course not. I know your fetish is women's underwear."

"Now what are you trying to say?"

"Relax, Lani…can I call you Lani?"

"No."

"Fine. It was just a bad attempt at a joke."

"You got that right…you're thinking it was stolen?"

"I don't know. I don't think so. But if it was, the house was never broken into as far as I can remember, and I have no idea how long it's been gone. The only person who has access to my place is my landlady. I know she's been going into the house to snoop around when I'm not there, but I can't imagine she'd steal my badge."

"I hate to say it, but I think I might know who. But then the question remains how."

And with that, Henry recalled the conversation he had with Judy Coleman about paint:

****

"I've got the best painters, Hank. They'll be in and

out of the cottage before you know it."

"That's okay, Mrs. Coleman. I don't mind taking care of it."

"It's Judy! And I'd be here the whole time to supervise."

"Judy, yes, of course."

"I'm not trying to be pushy, but the guys I use are professionals. Everything will be done quickly, efficiently, and most of all, neatly."

"Are these the same guys who painted the cottage before I moved in?"

"Yes of course they were. I always use them."

"And these professionals, they're the ones who left chip marks on the back door and paint that bled from the window moldings onto the glass?"

"Chip marks on the back door? I didn't see any chip marks?"

"Around the door latch. They're real small. It's no big deal. However, you can't miss the over-paint on the windows."

****

"Chip marks on the back door, of course. Chip marks on the back door by the lock, like it was jimmied. But they're so small."

"Chip marks?"

"Yeah, on the back door to my place. I assumed it had been done by painters who removed the lock when they painted the back door. But those guys weren't that meticulous. They wouldn't have removed the lock. They would have painted around it. Now that you've brought it up, I think we both know that brings us to the other thing needed to be discussed."

"No!"

"Look, we gotta talk about this. I had Becerra look into it for me, and we know—"

"What the fuck, you were spying on me?"

"Hell no! Well, not intentionally. I had him doing more digging on Costa. The guy has an axe to grind with me—of course he's a suspect."

"I can name a dozen or more people who have an axe to grind with you, and I'm becoming one of them."

"You gotta admit it, with his rap sheet as long as it is, and the creepy shit he's been involved with over the years, how can he not be a suspect? The link to you came up during Freddie's investigation."

"I'll handle him."

"I know about your auntie Tesha."

"You what?"

"I know she was married to him. I know she went missing without a trace."

"You don't know what you're talking about."

"And I already told you that I know about Nicky Junior."

"Don't go there."

"We need to talk about this, partner."

"You can't call me Lani, and we're not fucking partners."

"Back off, girl! You're starting to piss me off. I don't know what your issue is or what you have against me, but let's get one thing straight. We *need* to talk about this, or we're not going inside Hoku's house. Damn it! Here I am willing to trust you with something that means everything in the world to me, and you're gonna have to have the same level of trust and transparency, or I swear, as God is my witness, you'll get nothing further from me if you can't bring it to the table."

"…God, I wanna punch you so bad right now! I wanna bash your face! I hate you!" She growled and walked a few yards away from him, only stopping when he countered.

"You wanna hit me? Okay, come do it. Go for it, get it outta your system, but I'll fucking hit you back."

Her fists tightened, and she began to rock forward and back on the balls of her feet. Henry waited for the attack.

"You'd really hit a girl? Is that the kind of man you are?"

"No, but I'd hit you."

"Fuck you, okay?" she shouted.

"Yeah, okay, fine. Okay? Now back it down a few notches and take a breath."

"Yeah, fine." She allowed her hands to relax, turned, and walked toward her car.

"What, you leaving?"

"I need a minute."

"So, we're gonna talk about it, right? We're gonna talk about Costa?"

"As long as you promise you don't ever refer to him as my uncle, we'll talk about that bastard, but not right now."

"What? What do you mean not right now?"

"I need a day…give me that, will ya? But first things first, agreed?"

"I'll give you a day. I just hope you're not trying to avoid this. You pull an end around on me, and I'll—"

"You'll what?" She clinched her fists and walked back toward him.

"…fine, we'll talk about it afterward, but I gotta

get inside his house. I need you to get a warrant so we can search his place."

"I don't know about that."

"The way I see it, you can put in for a warrant, Captain Tanaka can get one for us, or I can just bust into his house."

"Bust into his house while on suspension or without a warrant, and you'll be giving his lawyers exactly what they'll need to keep him from facing any charges. And, on top of that, you'll be the one who ends up in jail, or dead if he doesn't shoot you."

"I know that! So, work with me on this. Let's do it the right way and get in there before there's another victim."

"Don't worry, Hank, I've got unfinished business with that sonofabitch, so I'm not letting him off the hook, okay?"

"Unfinished business? Like *you're* gonna kill him kind of unfinished business?"

"Only if he forces the issue, only if he pulls a weapon. Then I'll have no choice."

"…okay, I'm good with that."

"Do you want me to file a report for you…about your missing shield?"

"Yeah, I guess I should do that, shouldn't I?"

"What was your number?"

"Seventy-five eleven. Now let's go inside. It's time you met Maya."

Chapter 13

Not a day goes by
that I do not think of you.
Not a night goes by
that I am not dreaming of your arms around me—
holding, squeezing, caressing, teasing.
Not a moment goes by
that I am not grateful
for how much I've been blessed.
For each time we return, we reunite.
No matter the forest, the desert,
the mountain, or the valley,
no matter the river
or the ocean that comes between us.
No matter the span of time that separates each
incarnation
will my love for you be any farther from my heart, my
soul,
and every fiber of my being.
Your breath fills my lungs,
Your heart beats in my chest,
Your strength fuels my existence.

Along the eastern shore of Oahu, multimillion-dollar waterfront homes from mansions to modest beach cottages graced the palm tree-ladened shoreline from Diamond Head to Hawaii Kai. From the wealthy neighborhoods of Kahala to Aina Haina, where Hollywood screenwriters based their fictional heroes and police cars and private security patrolled regularly, strategically placed home surveillance systems went far beyond the common doorbell camera. Noelani Mendoza, widow of Ernesto Mendoza, the former boss of the island's largest labor union, took her afternoon massage by the heated saltwater pool at her gated estate. Her private secretary dutifully took messages from the many callers who desired a few minutes of her time, and a member of her kitchen staff diligently refreshed her iced tea. From politicians seeking reelection, to environmental groups seeking financial assistance for their latest lobbying effort, no cause was more important to her than preserving her deceased husband's legacy—and by extension, her standing among the island's social royalty. But even a tarnished reputation among the elite, though a temporary inconvenience afforded the most-wealthy, still dominated the gossip at the country clubs and, in her view, had to be avoided at all cost.

Ernesto Mendoza had been a strong and powerful figure throughout the Central Pacific while he was alive, and more so as his legendary exploits were embellished after his death. A force to be reckoned with, a single word or the nod of his head could put a stranglehold on national and international commerce to and from the islands in an instant—with a domino effect stretching as far as Southeast Asia. When he spoke, politicians not only listened. They obeyed. With his endorsement, the rank and file voted in lockstep. Family members of longtime friends had him to thank for civil service careers that ranged from clerical positions to supervisory roles. He turned community leaders into local and state legislators, and legislators into mayors, governors, and even representatives to the United States Congress. One time, when a congressional representative overstepped his authority and dared mention a repeal of the Jones Act which would have helped lower the cost of goods for the state's residents, a Mendoza-led wildcat strike stopped the loading and unloading of ships for ten days that caused local panic and a political firestorm with a message that still carried weight in the halls of Congress.

When he met Noelani, she was a stunningly beautiful but physically battered single mother of a five-year-old with learning difficulties. She was also thirty years his junior. Regardless, she was a goddess in his eyes, and her beauty, as well as her quick wit and strong will, captured his imagination and fueled his fantasies from the bedroom to being the talk of the island's power-players when his entrances were all the more spectacular with this native beauty on his arm. It was no secret his interest in her was mostly physical as was his interest in many of the young women of the Waianae Coast—too young and too financially compromised to resist his advances. His victories in and out of the bedroom were no secret, and he loved being the envy of the local people with whom he provided jobs and philanthropy. Noelani, too, was well aware of his insatiable need to bed every young girl that caught his eye. But their relationship, however, was symbiotic. She was lifted from poverty and well taken care of— never again suffering from want. Her young son, Peter, would take his stepfather's name, attend the finest private schools on the island, and while he seemed to have inherited the lower intellect of his biological father, a successful and admirable career path was planned for him nonetheless.

When he died from a massive cerebral hemorrhage during one of his sexual conquests, he was one day shy of his eightieth birthday. His young partner received compensation to ease the trauma of having had the old man's bowel and bladder empty while on top of her during his collapse, and a handsome bonus with a warning was issued to ensure her silence. What was to be a grand eightieth birthday celebration turned into a statewide remembrance attended by dignitaries and celebrities alike who paid their respects to the grieving and soon-to-be most-eligible widow who had played her part to perfection.

And while Noelani Mendoza had continued to relish in her good fortune and the power that came with it, she was convinced that her son, more than her devotion to the tropical sun, was the reason for her regular sessions with the island's best cosmetic surgeon.

"You're late, Peter," she said without lifting her head from the massage table.

"It's nice to see you too, Mother. Am I interrupting?"

"We're almost done. I thought I asked you to arrive here by four. Why so late?"

"I had business at the station that couldn't be ignored, and rush hour traffic was heavy and slow as usual."

"Once this issue is finally put to bed, you'll transfer back to headquarters where the right people will always be able to see you. Traffic won't be a problem then, will it?"

"No, it won't. But if I'd come at four, you wouldn't have been able to get your afternoon massage, and you know how you love Matthew's...it is Matthew, isn't it?" He watched the muscular therapist's hands slowly glide up his mother's thighs. "You know how you love Matthew's *lomi lomi* work."

"Don't be disrespectful, Peter. I don't like it."

"That wasn't my intention, Mother."

"Be a dear and go tell Angel it will be just the two of us for dinner." She waved off the therapist and sat up to face her son. "Why don't you have her make you a cocktail, and I'll go shower and dress."

****

Mother and son shared a meal and the sunset but little conversation on the lanai that overlooked Maunalua Bay. It wasn't until the table was cleared and the staff dismissed for the evening did they begin to truly engage. Peter, knowing he was there to be scolded, attempted to redirect.

"I've noticed you have new servants—I mean domestics."

"Filipino girls, yes. They're cute, aren't they?"

"Very much so. I think I'll go introduce myself."

"Don't be silly."

"Silly? Don't you think others deserve a rags-to-riches fantasy?" Although rhetorical, his comment was ignored. "Anyway, what happened to the previous girls?"

"The Mexicans from Los Angeles? I didn't care for them." She shrugged. "Your father had always said Filipino girls make the best workers, and I tend to agree."

"And yet you always hired Mexicans in the past."

"I couldn't use the Filipinas when your father was alive because of his appetite for his own people. They would never be able to get any work done unless he was in a meeting somewhere or out on the golf course. For some reason, the Mexican girls didn't appeal to him."

"Is that what he told you? Sorry to disappoint you, Mother, but he was interested. He was very interested, and he took full advantage every time you were off to some charity event."

"And how do you know this?" Her tone was dismissive.

"There was this one girl he was particularly fond of. If I remember correctly, her name was Rosie. I had a friend over to play. It was one of the few times Ernesto allowed me to have anyone over while you were out. He was insistent we didn't make noise or wander around the house, but we snooped around anyway. You want to talk about noise? We heard thumping and grunting coming from the game room, and, well, there was good ol' Ernesto, pants down around his ankles, and he had Rosie bent over the billiard table. He was grinding away, and she was moaning like there was no tomorrow. To top it off, it didn't faze him when he realized we were watching. He wasn't even embarrassed. And without missing a stroke, he turned and yelled at us to leave the room and to make sure we didn't slam the door."

"…I'm not surprised. He was such a pig."

"And you let him touch you too. So what does that say about you?"

"How dare you talk to me that way!" she said with restrained indignation.

"The staff is gone, Mother. You can drop the high-brow act with me."

"And what makes you think this is an act?"

"You always told me that you can take the *tita* out of Waianae, but you can't take the Waianae, or the *tita*, out of the girl. I've been on the receiving end of many of your lectures of how I was a disappointment to your husband. It's funny that I had to live up to his expectations, his standards, when he was as corrupt, perverted, and unfaithful as they come. So, can we just acknowledge who he really was and allow ourselves the honesty of who we are…at least when no one else is around?"

"My, you've become so articulate and emboldened…oh wait, emboldened isn't the correct word for a *tita* to use, is it. Okay, you little *fakkah*. So what helped you grow a fucking pair of balls?" she said with a straight face before he could no longer hold the laughter.

"There she is. I knew she was in there somewhere." He sighed. "I guess my hanging around cops and criminals helps the testosterone flow."

"Well, you better watch that. Ernesto may be dead and buried, but the goal and the plan for you to be chief of police is still looking good…very good. In a few weeks, Carmen Ramos-Brown will be announcing her candidacy for mayor, and when she wins, you'll make captain during her first year in office, then major, and by the beginning of her second term, you'll be an assistant chief. And shortly after that, you'll become Oahu's next native Hawaiian chief of police. Though not the first one of our people to hold that position, you'll be the youngest chief in the department's history. And it doesn't end there. She's got plans for the governor's office. Do you know what that means for you? For us?"

"I can only imagine. Mother...Mom, why do you need her? Why are you so involved with her? Don't you have enough money, enough power?"

"What are you talking about? She's the one who's attracted to power and money just like Ernesto was. She allowed herself to get involved with your father."

"What are you saying?"

"For one thing, he was doing her too. She came to him when she was fresh out of school and wanted his blessing and support when she started her political career. She needed him because she needed the unions. Because of him, money flowed to her campaign from practically every dock worker, every truck driver, every operating engineer, and so on. He's literally financed her past campaigns, formed PACs, and used his media connections to destroy her opponents, and dictated legislation that benefitted every union worker on this island...in this state. He paid for her house, her cars, and her cosmetic surgeries. Why do you think every investigation or audit into the mismanagement of the rail project never got off the ground? Because Ernesto ordered her, and the others he owned, to make sure they never did."

"Are you saying good ol' Ernie was responsible for billions of cost overruns on that project? Are you telling me she helped provide cover?"

"If it wasn't for him, all those workers would've been out of a job years ago. He got that project extended with payoffs to inspectors, well-timed lawsuits, shortages in materials, worker slowdowns…that's what pushed the project long past the original timeline. He saw to it that federal and state money kept flowing. Sure, she helped, but she wasn't the only one in the government who was in his pocket. Ernesto had people at the state legislature as well as in Congress. But Ramos-Brown…she was into him for a ton of money. Because she was so greedy, she kept coming back for more. He owned her, Peter, and now, I'm the one who owns her ass. She is indebted to me and this family. She takes her marching orders from me, understand?"

He nodded, then walked over to the bar and poured himself an iced tea.

"Refill?"

"I'm good. But enough of this. It's time to talk business. This situation with this Costa guy it's *pilau*. It stinks. It's out of control, Peter, and I want you to clean this dog shit off my freaking lawn. I'm mad that you didn't investigate this guy more thoroughly. He had one job to take care of, one! And he's gone off the deep end. My God, those poor girls. They didn't deserve it. It makes me sick to my stomach. And apparently, he's not going to stop until he gets caught or gets killed. He's got to be killed, because you know what happens with guys like him who get caught? He's going to squeal like a wild pig. It's your name that will roll off his tongue. It's time you put an end to it. Do you understand me?"

"I've already arranged to have it taken care of."

"With somebody a little more professional?"

"I admit Costa's *lolo*, he's crazy, but how was I supposed to know he's a psycho? But my God, Mom, look what *we* asked him to do. Look what you wanted him to do, and for what, to protect Ernesto's name?"

"Well, how was I to know the girl would actually come back to Oahu after all these years?"

"Look, I know it's been eight months, and it's way too late to ask this now that she's dead. But how were you even sure it was her? Let's face it, what Ernesto did was almost thirty years ago."

"I'm sure it was her! I recognized the face. I recognized the look in her eyes. A mother doesn't forget these things. And I know what I know."

"That's not good enough! The deeper we get into this, the greater the risk that everything is going to come tumbling down. And Carmen Ramos-Brown is going to run from us faster than a wildfire races through the Makaha Valley in mid-August!"

"Well, this thing wouldn't have gotten out of control if you had picked the right person."

"There is no right person when you're hiring somebody to commit murder. And in this case the woman who was killed was the wife of a cop! A cop who is not going to stop investigating until he uncovers every rock and hiding place. Tell me, Mother, how could you be sure she was *that* little girl!"

"Because I was there, damn you, I was there!" She jumped to her feet. "I saw that little girl's face. I saw the look in her eyes. I saw the way she looked at Ernesto, and I saw the way she looked at me! I thought about that face for almost thirty years, worrying that she would return to get revenge. And when I saw her that day volunteering at our Christmas food drive in Maili, I knew instantly by the way she looked at me she knew who I was. I knew instantly that no matter how many years had passed, details of that day would come flooding back for her, and I couldn't take the chance of that happening to us!"

"Happening to us, or happening to you?"

"What fucking difference does it make?"

"It makes all the fucking difference in the world, Mother."

Chapter 14

The other night I had a dream,
a vision actually.
One of many, each unique unto itself.
You were there as my spirit animal.
I always knew you were.
Together we are one and we are safe.
There were others, interlopers all.
They lurk in the shadows,
the shadows camouflage their weakness.
Their faces hidden by the darkness,
the darkness a reflection of their earthly spirit,
a telltale of their intent.
You are my spirit animal,
and you remind me that we walk in the light,
the light of which they fear.
We walk the path, we stay the course,
we are invincible,
and we are almost free.

When she opened her front door to find Henry and Kaelani, Hokulani ushered them in as if she were hiding fugitives on the run. She stepped out onto the front entryway to see if they had been followed.

"Is it all clear? Are we safe?" Henry laughed.

"You're still quick with the wisecracks." She slapped him on the shoulder. "I heard you guys arguing outside, and, you know, I was just checking."

"You're becoming quite the detective, but don't worry, there's no blood in the street, no fresh bruises on either of us, and we promised not to kill each other. We weren't even followed. Besides, we're the good guys, right?" he reassured her.

Kaelani nodded and exchanged a polite smile with Hoku who directed them to her kitchen.

"Have a seat, make yourself at home. There's plenty of coffee already made, and there's more than plenty of last night's special from the café in the fridge. It's Mary's...I mean it's Maya's recipe, and it really is quite good," she said and felt an awkwardness as if being an unwanted chaperone. "I'd stay to referee, but I've gotta get back down to the café."

"It's all right if you wanna stay. You should, you know? We're not gonna talk about anything you don't already know."

"That's okay, Hank. I should get back. You guys take your time."

"I could use a drink. Mind if I help myself?"

She hesitated, looked over at Maya's bedroom door, then said, "I'm all out."

"Since when?" He looked at her suspiciously.

"From this day forward. The bar in my house and at the café is closed for you. Maya will be out in a minute."

"...thanks. Any other changes I should know about? Everything else is good? We're good? Nothing out of the ordinary?"

"It's all good. The coffee is strong. Help yourself," she said, then grabbed her handbag and was off to work.

Henry apologized to Kaelani, excused himself, and ran to catch Hokulani before she drove off.

"Hey, wait up a sec. What did you mean from now on the bar is closed?"

"I had a long talk with Maya about some changes we're seeing in you, and let's just say we're both concerned. What you do to address the issue is your business…and Maya's. I'm not gonna be the person you come running to for a fix. We're worried about you, Hank, so don't be mad at me, and don't look so surprised."

"…I don't know how…"

"You don't need to say anything else. Just don't ignore this. I gotta go."

"Wait…I need to ask you something. I got something in my car I want you to look at."

"Sure."

"I've got this picture and was hoping you could confirm something for me. I already know the answer, but I thought, well, here, take a look." He showed her a small black-and-white photo he had received from the California State Department of Corrections. "Is this him? Is this the uncle you were telling me about the other day?"

She took all of two seconds before nodding her head.

"Oh my God, yes, that's the crazy bastard. I thought I'd forgotten what he looked like, but that's her uncle. Wait a sec, is he the same guy you busted, what was it, six, seven years ago?"

"Ten. Yeah, he's the same guy. This whack job is Nicky Costa, and he not only did time here, but as you can see…"

"In California too. What for?"

"The list is long. From petty theft and attempted rape to assault with a deadly weapon. He was even a member of a neo-Nazi biker group."

"What? He's a racist?"

"A racist, an anti-Semite, he's a total nutcase. Prison psych records describe him as bipolar, manic, paranoid, you name it, a full fruit salad. How or why he ever got out of prison is a testament to our broken justice system."

"I'm not surprised. We got lots of these guys walking around, yeah?"

"Yeah. Believe it or not he lives a few doors down from me, moved there several months ago, shortly after I did. If you ever see him at your café, you call me right away. If you ever see him anywhere near your house, you call me, and if he ever tries to get into your house, even if he's knocking on the front door, you shoot the bastard. You shoot him dead, then call me, and I'll take care of the rest. You got it?"

She nodded. "Do you think he's the guy? Do you think he's been killing those girls?"

"At this point, I couldn't swear to it in court, but my gut says he is. He's at the top of my list, and I'd have no problem punching his ticket."

She stared at the photograph, and he could tell she was shaken.

"I don't know why, but I feel a little more worried now that I know this."

"It'll be okay…trust me. Kaelani's got a score to settle with him, and we have a couple others who've got our backs. It'll be okay. Now go ahead and get back to work."

****

Kaelani sat opposite Henry and Maya, not knowing what, if anything, to say. For many months she had only known Maya as Mary from Hokulani's Oceanside Café, and Mary the waitress had served her many breakfasts, sometimes lunch, occasional dinners, and had become the focus of her fantasies. They'd had coffee together on her days off, talked about their favorite things to do on the island, favorite movies, and especially their relationships. Kaelani had shared personal experiences that she never did with anyone before. And although she would never admit it, she was now experiencing a crushing ache about the waitress who was the motivation for her increased patronage at the café. She now assumed that the special guy "Mary" had often lamented over was actually Henry, and until that moment, she never considered him to be a romantic, let alone someone who had honestly cared about the Hawaiian people. Now she wondered how much of everything else Maya spoke of was true or part of a made-up persona to maintain her cover. She felt betrayed and hurt by the deception while admiring her ability to maintain it for so long.

"I have a lot of questions. I honestly don't know where to start," she said while studying the contours of Maya's face—a face she had caressed and kissed so many times in her dreams.

"Then I'll simply start, and you can ask any questions that come to you," Maya replied in a calm, collected voice.

"Before she starts, Hank, please tell me who's the girl in the morgue wearing Maya's toe tag?"

"Henry, Leilani deserves to have her full story

told," Maya softly instructed to his nod.

"Wait a minute," Kaelani said. "You call him Henry?"

"Yes, I've always called him Henry." She smiled at her husband.

"She's the only one who does. I actually like that she's the only one. It keeps the cop part of me separate from my personal life," he said. "When we're together and she says my given name, it reminds me that I'm human. The poor girl in the morgue was our tenant, and she was also a friend. Please understand that in her death, if it means anything, she has continued to honor that friendship by providing cover for Maya because at the time, I believed, based on the note that was left with her body...I believed the killer thought he was murdering my wife, or he wanted us to believe that was what he thought."

"What are you saying, Hank?"

"It has been, and it still is, our belief that Maya was the original target. She wasn't picked at random by a serial killer. When this guy got into our house and found Leilani, he killed her thinking she was Maya. Now, keep in mind that there's a chance he knew it wasn't her, and Leilani, having seen his face, paid the price for being in the wrong place at the wrong time."

"Wait, stop, let me get this straight. If Maya had been targeted, you're saying this was a contract hit, yet it's possible the killer had no idea what she looked like. But if it's true he was hired, how would he not know his target?"

"Except for the few years' difference in their ages, Leilani and Maya do look similar to the untrained eye. Same height, weight, hair, and skin color."

"But it was ritualistic. A contract killer wouldn't take the time to do what was done."

"True, but maybe it didn't start out that way. Maybe the whole thing flipped a switch inside this guy's brain."

"And the other four killings?"

"Well, you see, that's the curveball that's thrown me for a loop. I've also been thinking that this guy has something against me. We discussed this, remember? Every one of those girls were tied to me in some small way. And that's why I want us to discuss Costa. So, before we get any further on that detour, let me add, if whoever wanted Maya dead had found out the hitman missed his mark, she would've still been in danger. It was my decision to let people think that Leilani was Maya. Are you with me so far?"

"Go on, Hank."

"I enlisted Hoku to help us. We gave Maya a new identity. New name, changed the way she wore her hair, she started wearing glasses instead of her contacts, and Hoku agreed to let her live with her and work as a waitress at the café…just until I was able to find the killer and the person who ordered it," Henry said, then stood to get a cup of coffee.

"Okay, but how did you get away with using this Leilani person as Maya's corpse? Who is she? Didn't people know she lived with you guys? Weren't you concerned she would be missed?" Her eyes darted back and forth between the two.

"Maya, I'll let you explain how Leilani Kalua came to live with us."

Maya thought for minute, turned to Henry, and asked for a glass of water.

"I was a teacher at the Prince Kuhio Academy in Manoa. There was this girl, a young woman actually, and she was homeless. That was Leilani. She said she was twenty-eight and had been living on the streets since she was twenty-one. I'd see her every morning when I arrived at the school. How and why she chose that location I can't tell you; she never said. She'd be in the parking lot, and some of the academy staff would bring her breakfast each day. Sometimes they'd bring her a new blouse, some old tee shirts, a pair of slippas, stuff like that. Day after day, month after month, she was there in the parking lot waiting for breakfast. She never spoke to any of the staff, and they never really made any attempt. They would just leave the stuff for her and go about their business. One day during lunch break, I noticed she was still out there, so I brought her a lunch from the cafeteria and asked if she'd mind some company. She really appreciated the contact, the human connection. It became a regular thing. She looked forward to it…and so did I.

"She was nice, I liked her and, to be honest, I felt bad for her. She was all alone in the world…no family, no friends, no partner, nothing. She wasn't even born in the islands. Her parents were, they were Kanaka, but had moved to Vegas because they couldn't afford to live here anymore."

"That's a familiar story," Kaelani said. "That's happening more and more these days. Go on, I didn't mean to interrupt."

"She told me both her parents were addicts and had died within weeks of each other from overdosing. She ended up on the streets, started hanging around the casinos, and started selling her body just so she could buy food. After having been beaten a few times, she figured if she was going to die, she didn't want to do it in a seedy motel room on the strip. She wanted to do it here, her ancestral home."

"One day Maya comes home from work and starts telling me all about Leilani and how she wanted to help her," Henry said, returning to the table with coffees for all of them. "I ran a background check with the information I had. Las Vegas PD confirmed the girl's story. She had a record for petty theft…food from a convenience store, stuff like that. We did a search to try and find family of any kind. She had a grandmother who lived windward side, but she died years ago."

"I began bringing her sack lunches and sometimes took her out for dinner…even brought her home one night so she could have a hot bath and get a good night's sleep. That's when I asked her if she would like to live with us. Henry looked at me like I was nuts, but we had an extra bedroom, and I figured if she had a safe place to stay, healthy food to eat, and people who cared about her, she could find work, find purpose in life, and get back on her feet…ironic now that I think about it."

"Ironic? In what way?" Kaelani asked.

"I thought I was giving her a safe place to live. If I had left her on the street, she'd still be alive." She looked at Henry.

"Oh, Maya, that's not on you at all," Kaelani offered. "So, she had no family, no friends, just you two."

"That's right," Henry continued. "Leilani lived with us for about a year, right, Maya?"

"Yes, that's right. She was the perfect tenant. Quiet, clean, respectful, and she became a friend. Henry and I would go off to work, and she took it upon herself to clean for us, do laundry, and she even cooked. She was a fantastic cook. She would have been great at the Oceanside Café. She said it was the least she could do to repay our hospitality and friendship."

"The night she was killed, Maya and I had gone out for dinner and a movie. When we got back, we found her bound, gagged, partially naked, and sliced up…just like the girls who followed. Maya went into shock. I think I did too. I read the note several times, and something came over me. All I could think about was protecting my wife. I realized the killer had no idea what she looked like and thought he had the right target. I called Hoku since she lived a couple blocks away, told her what happened, and asked her to let Maya come over. Then I called HPD. I'm sorry, Kaelani, I'm sorry I deceived people, I'm sorry I deceived you, but I didn't know what else to do."

"So you're telling me Hokulani is an accomplice in this coverup?" she asked and waited for a response. Henry and Maya were momentarily silenced. She continued. "Don't worry, I'm not telling anyone. That story stays in this room for now, until we find this guy, and then the truth will have to come out…you both know that, right? So why do you think you were targeted, Maya? Who would want you dead?"

"I believe this began when I was a little girl…I was nine years old. My mother brought me to Oahu to meet family. Uncles, aunties, cousins. They lived here on the Waianae Coast. One day the whole family went to this big harvest party at one of the farms in the valley. All the adults and most of the children who were there were sent out into the fields to gather a wide variety of fruits and vegetables to be sold at the farmer's market. And everybody got to take home a basket of produce for free. At sunset, we gathered under the stars for a big luau in celebration of a successful harvest."

"I'm sorry, but what does this have to do with anything?"

"The man who sponsored the event was famous among the people. They honored him with leis and tributes. He walked around as if he were King Kamehameha himself. People lined up to talk to him, little children sat on his lap as if he were Santa Claus, and we each got a dollar from him. And his wife was so young and so beautiful. She too held court among the women who were there. They all knew her and were so proud of her. I remember the women would want to have their picture taken with her, and they kept saying she was *'O kā mākou pono 'ī*. Am I saying that right?"

"One of our own. Yes, you said that correctly." Kaelani smiled.

"Between the food and the music and the fireworks, it was like Christmas, New Year's, and the Fourth of July all rolled up into one big party. Anyway, this man who walked around as if he were the king took a fancy to my mother, but I could tell she was uncomfortable around him, so she kept trying to avoid him. The more she did, the more he pursued her and showered her with compliments. I kept trying to follow, but there were too many people, and it was getting dark. I lost sight of the two of them, and it seemed as if they were gone for hours, but it couldn't have been more than twenty minutes. Eventually I saw him coming out from a heavily wooded path. He had scratches on his face and a bloodstain on his shirt. People came running to help him. He said he had gone for a walk and tripped in the darkness, falling into a culvert of some sort. I ran down the path to look for my mother…and I found her. Her clothing had been torn off, her face was beaten and bloody, and my relatives learned later on that the doctors said she had been raped. At the time I didn't know what that meant. She was beaten so badly that she was in a coma for several weeks. My father flew out here so he could bring her home to the rez, the reservation where we lived. She never fully recovered and had many health problems during that next year…eventually she died. I knew that man was responsible for what had happened to her, and he and his wife had known I was aware of what he had done. They acted so surprised and sad that she was so badly injured, and they insisted that she too must have taken a walk in the dark and fell into the culvert."

"What did the police say?"

"No one called the police. There was no ambulance, nothing. The old man ordered somebody to put her into the back of a pickup truck like she was cattle, and she was driven to the hospital in Honolulu. The wife volunteered to pay the hospital bills and pay for us to fly back home to South Dakota. I was told that the local news ran a story of her bad accident and the generosity of this man and woman. They were celebrated by everybody. Later on, after my mother passed, my father tried to talk to the doctors or get records from the hospital, but he was told there were no records of her ever being there."

"Maya, who was the man that did that to your mother?" Kaelani asked.

"Isn't it obvious? Ernesto Mendoza. He was the

one who raped and beat my mother. He killed my mother, but I have no proof, and who is going to believe my suspicions all these years later? Henry, water…please, I need some water. For many years I suppressed the memory, and for many years I had nightmares and dreams of my spirit guides coming to counsel me. I kept a journal of those dreams."

"That's the leatherbound book I saw on Hank's nightstand, the one next to your picture."

"When Henry and I moved here after college, I wanted to live in Nanakuli, close to those cousins of mine. But it wasn't until last year when I volunteered at a food bank that I ran into Noelani Mendoza. I didn't recognize her at first, but when I watched the way she talked to little children, handed them dollar bills saying that it was her deceased husband's tradition, the memories flooded back. I must've said something, I don't remember, but she suddenly turned in my direction. That's when I saw the recognition in her face. She looked horrified and angry all at the same time. A cold chill ran through me. I didn't know what to do. The next thing I know, she's rushing to her limo, and she was gone."

"Are you saying that she's the one who wanted you dead?"

"Help me with this, Henry…I'm a little light-headed."

"Hank, this is crazy. A woman of her wealth and position?"

"Think about it. A woman whose deceased husband's name and reputation still opens doors for her. A man whose existence, corrupt or not, lifted up impoverished people better and more consistently than any politician ever did and as such has buildings, high school athletic fields, and streets named after him. Maya's story can take it all away. This woman has wealth and social standing that she wants to desperately protect, and she's not gonna let someone from the past destroy that life."

"Did you ever question her?"

"Several months ago, I was going to. I set up an appointment to meet with her, and the next thing I knew, I was transferred to Waikiki, got purposely bogged down with more crap than you can imagine. Anytime I tried to pursue her as a lead, I was conveniently derailed. I had to work this case when I was off the clock, and of course, her secretary could never find an opening on her calendar. Doesn't it make sense that her son was the one who got me transferred?"

"So you let it slide?"

"No, not exactly. I got Freddie Becerra to do it for me. He dropped in on her unannounced. And while she was polite to him, by the time he got back to the station, he got called in on the carpet and took one hell of a rip for doing that."

"And what did he find out, anything?"

"Are you kidding? She had to have known that a day would eventually come where she would be questioned. She was well rehearsed, and without having the actual killer to say 'yes, she's the one who hired me,' with her legal team and connections to police brass, politicians, and judges, I'd be the laughing stock of the island. I need the killer. Without him, that woman will never see the inside of a jail cell. I know Nicky Costa is your uncle, and I'll bet anything he's the guy."

"We're not blood."

"Exactly!"

"Why do you think he had anything to do with this?"

"Why are you protecting him? You know as well as I do he's responsible for the disappearance of your auntie. You know his history. You've seen his rap sheet. How long are you going to let him get away with it?"

"That's my issue and my issue alone."

"No, not anymore. If I didn't know any better, you're waiting for an opportunity to take him out. Believe me, I understand that, and I don't wanna take that away from you, but I want…I need that waste of a human life alive. I need him to give up Noelani Mendoza. You're calling the DA, and I'm driving you in to town so we can get that search warrant. Please, you know we gotta do this."

Chapter 15

There are times when I wake,
it is the middle of the night,
and I feel lost.
I panic, and then like magic
I feel my mother with me.
Her perfume fills the air
like it did in my childhood.
I hear her calling from the porch,
her apron flowing in the heat of the summer breeze,
she brushes errant strands of hair from her face.
My name echoes off her lips,
I feel comforted knowing she is here.
And while I cannot embrace her,
her presence has never been more real.
Her love is unmistakable,
her message has never been so clear.

Nicky Costa cruised up and down the Farrington Highway along the Waianae Coast, trying to burn off steam. In fact, just the opposite was occurring as his rage continued to build while preoccupied with the events of the past couple days. Not only did his meeting with Peter Mendoza release a flood of digestive acids that stole the brief pleasure from his linguica and mac salad plate lunch—*I can't believe that worthless piece of shit has the balls to threaten me.* He belched. He also began to think Keahi, too, could be a possible threat and considered making an unscheduled visit to the wrecking yard to rectify that situation. What bothered him most, however, was the thought that Henry Benjamin seemed no closer to figuring out that it was he who butchered his wife.

After eating too many meals off of cold tin trays, and spending many sleepless nights on an institutional mattress fantasizing about his revenge, Mendoza's offer had not only provided a financial windfall that had eluded him throughout his life. It allowed him to link the suffering he wanted to inflict on Henry with his long-desired quest for the purification of a people who rejected his warped obsession with, and his need for acceptance from the Hawaiians. *What do I gotta do for this guy to figure out that I killed his little bitch? Write him a note with my name and picture? Do I gotta go knock on his door and hand it to him?* He heard her pleas and cries dance around in his head. He watched her in his mind's eye, and it aroused him just as the other killings did—an arousal that he was never able to bring to a satisfying conclusion. He blamed Henry for that too. As physically big as he was, in prison there was always someone a little bigger, a little stronger, and a little more mentally disturbed. Costa had learned that painful lesson when he tried to claim another man's bitchmeat. After he was beaten within an inch of his life, he spent weeks in traction and many months in physical therapy to regain his ability to walk. He had been taunted by his attacker that the resultant sexual dysfunction was well deserved. It was his karma, because of his appetite for underaged girls. And although the brutal beating had earned him an early end to his incarceration, his injury-related inability to now pleasure himself, coupled with the humiliation he suffered from the jeers and laughter that had vibrated off the walls throughout the cell block, caused his resentment to escalate even more.

That shithead Mendoza doesn't know the gift he handed me to get back at that motherfucker transplant. But his slut deserved it anyway. She was unclean, not pure. No matter how many others of his little dirty whores I lay at his feet, that dumb transplant still can't figure out it's me. Is he that stupid, or am I that much smarter than he is? Should I even have to ask that question? It goes without saying that I'm smarter. I'm smarter than all of them! I'm smarter than these mokes who mock me. Can't they see I'm more Hawaiian than all of them put together? I'm the one trying to keep the bloodline pure. I'm the one trying to wake them up to be something greater. Maybe it's not enough for them? Yeah, that's it. I gotta demonstrate how serious I am about saving these islands from these fucking outsiders. They sit in their cave up in the mountain, and all they do is beat their chests. They're only big and strong among themselves, but they're nothing but losers! All of them losers! They need a real leader. They need someone who's not afraid to show them what a real warrior looks like. That's it, that's the key. I'll lead them, and they'll have no choice but to accept me as one of them.

Lost in his indignation, he didn't realize the traffic light had changed until a car horn jolted him. It made him think of how Mendoza had snuck up on him a few nights before. Refusing to proceed through the intersection, he held his ground. Once more, the horn blasted him, and he cursed into his rearview mirror while flipping his middle finger at the young Asian driver behind him. The driver, accompanied by several friends, quickly changed lanes, pulled up alongside the black Mercedes, and launched into a verbal tirade that included threats and comments referring to a myriad of sexual acts between farm animals and his mother. Before he could respond, they raced off. Costa felt another wave of spasms in his abdomen as the taste of Portuguese sausage and bile burned the back of his throat.

"Fuck you too, you...you goddamn foreigners!" he screamed while pointing his fingers as if his hand were a gun. "Take that, you motherfuckers!" They were already too far down the street to hear or see his reply, and he surely knew that.

At that moment, however, a giddiness came over him as if he were a child on Christmas morning eyeing the splendor of a tree covered in tinsel and flashing colored lights. *They're just as bad as those rich white people from the mainland. I'll do an Asian this time. Hell, they deserve it. They've been buying up the entire island for years. First it was the Japanese, and now it's those damn Chinese. I'll show them all. I'll show those morons up on the mountain how to take back the kingdom. They'll see how great I am, and they'll be begging me to join them and to lead them. Even that fucking transplant cop will see. I'm gonna do another one, but an Asian this time. I gotta see his face when he sees how powerful I am. I wanna see his face when he sees that he paid the price for jamming me up, for arresting me, for publicly embarrassing me, for hurting my reputation in front of my people, for spoiling our women, for everything! I wanna see the look in his eyes just before I put a bullet in his head, and I say to him 'I killed your whore, you goddamn transplant! I violated her! I carved your name into her belly. I burned a hole in her face. I did it, you fuck.' And then bam, I'll splatter his brains all over the front door!*

Costa reached over to his glove box, removed a hand-held police radio scanner, a gun, a handful of zip-ties, and a police shield.

The longer he drove up and down the coast highway, the more clouded his scenarios had become for the next abduction. From where the initial stop would take place, to the language he would use, to where he would perform the ritual, his impatience and the daylight hours created confusion for him as the sketchy details of one plan bled into the next. And while his frustration grew, the one constant was that at midnight he was going to leave number six on the doorstep of Henry's cottage, bang on that door until he woke, and then pull the trigger at the moment recognition filled his eyes.

****

The late afternoon sun began to cast palm tree shadows on Henry and Kaelani as they strolled the Royal Palace grounds in downtown Honolulu, waiting to be notified by the district attorney's office that their request for a search warrant had been approved. They smoked, drank coffee, and watched the tourists take selfies and group photos at the King Kamehameha statue across the street. But mostly, they talked about the black sheep of her family—Uncle Nicky.

"Every fiber of my being says he's the guy. Everything points to him, and I can kick myself for not looking at him in more depth until now."

"Don't take offense, Hank, but given your typical way of doing things, I'm glad you're willing to do this by the book...not that you don't do it by the book, but in cases like this, you've got a take-no-prisoners reputation, and we can't afford any mistakes right now."

"I'm not gonna argue with you about the pros and cons of my style. The results speak for themselves. But consider the options if the D.A. isn't on board. What if we don't get a warrant, what then? What if the D.A. says she doesn't have enough to prosecute? What if she, like so many others on this island, is in Noelani Mendoza's back pocket?"

"Hopefully she's not. Hopefully...knowing the fear these murders are creating, she'll give us a little leeway. Earlier this morning the lab's preliminary findings were still inconclusive for Nicky's DNA on the cigarette butt as well as in the blood found on the Kiawe branches that came from Auntie Lily's. Apparently, the samples were contaminated. The D.A. knows or should know we need to get into his house."

"And when we do find what we need, will she, the police commission, or Kelly Cho"—he pointed to the reporter headed their way—"be convinced it's enough to justify one of us killing him? Assuming of course if it comes to that."

"It all depends on what kind of spin we put on it. We'll have to discuss that further."

Kaelani turned to the approaching news crew. Henry walked far enough away to avoid the distraction and thought about the lab results. Recalling a past encounter with Costa, he tried to connect the pieces:

****

"Hey, cop! Yeah, you, come here a minute. I wanna talk to you."

"What's the matter, Costa, this holding cell giving you flashbacks of being somebody's bitch?"

"Very funny. I'm thirsty."

"What am I, your personal wait staff?"

"What the hell, I'm not asking for a cocktail."

"I'll see what I can do."

"In the meantime, can you at least give a guy a smoke?"

"...sure, why not."

"Now that's a pretty package. I don't see too many men smoke those girlie brands. Well, not real men anyways."

"You're a real piece of work, aren't you? If you're too much of man and don't want it..."

"No, no, I'll take it."

"Yeah, you'll take it any way you can get it. Especially from little kids, right?"

"You think your charges are gonna stick? You targeted me. You harassed me and publicly embarrassed me. I think you even planted that coke on me. My lawyers will have me out of this place in no time. And that's when I'm gonna file a complaint against you for false arrest, defamation, slander, all that stuff. Yessir, bruddah, I'm gonna sue the city for millions."

"Defamation and slander? Let me get you a dictionary, genius. And as far as being embarrassed...possession with intent to distribute and getting a blow job from a sixteen-year-old? Good luck with that. Oh, and by the way, she already signed an affidavit that you gave her the coke in exchange for sex. She already told us that it wasn't the first time you picked her up or other girls at the high school. So have at it, you lowlife piece of shit. Do what you gotta do. The pathetic thing about slobs like you, Costa, is that you're more concerned about people seeing you dragged out of your car with your pants down than you are about selling that poison on the street or your desire for little girls. When you get convicted, I'm gonna make sure the inmate population knows all about you. And one more thing: all those bystanders who watched you get dragged out of the car, they're still talking about the big fat guy with the shit-stained boxers pleading and crying like a little kid. I think I'll take a ride back out that way to make sure they know your name."

"Fuck you and go to hell. Just know this: karma has a long memory."

****

Henry heard those words as clear as if the conversation had happened the other day. Thinking about the look in Costa's eyes during that discussion gave him a chill and made him question why he had forgotten so much about that encounter until now. *What else am I missing here?* He had no answer other than the fact that Costa was one of several similar arrests he had made over the course of his career. There was nothing in particular that stood out for him. He now thought about the evidence bags that Captain Tanaka had found on Mendoza's desk. *I owe Kaelani an apology.*

Henry noticed that Cho directed a perfectly timed stink eye in his direction when she finished her interview with Kaelani.

"That was fast. Did you shut her down?"

"Yes and no. I'm sure she really didn't come over here for an interview, though. She mentioned she got word that we were down here getting a warrant but didn't know who for. I told her I couldn't comment. She wasn't happy, but she didn't even press the issue. I don't think she even had her mic on now that I think about it. My guess? She really came here to deliver a message…a message for you."

"I could probably guess, but please, go right ahead."

"She wanted you to know that Councilwoman Ramos-Brown is on the warpath. She filed complaints against you with the ethics commission, the police commission, and the civilian review board. She's also going to meet with the mayor and the chief to demand your termination."

"What, no complaints from Ms. Cho?"

"She's filing a harassment complaint too."

"Go figure." He smirked.

"I can see you're all broken up about it," she replied. "Based on what she told me you said and did, I understand now how you got the nickname Dirty Henry."

"No, you don't, and I'm not even gonna comment."

"Just the same, she's got the means to influence public opinion."

"Look, she hasn't been on island long enough to have a serious following, and she certainly doesn't know anything about me. If she's getting any of her info from Ramos-Brown, then she's as gullible as she seems, and she's gonna end up destroying what little

215

credibility she thinks she has."

"Then why don't you fill me in? How'd this nickname stuff start?"

Henry figured he had nothing to lose at this point. "Do you remember Tommy Kekoa?"

"I've heard of him. I heard the story of what happened to his wife and daughter. Everybody heard that story."

"You and everybody else only heard part of it. Tommy was assigned as my training officer when I got out of the academy."

"I didn't know that. I thought Billy trained you."

"Billy came way after that, when I got my gold shield. I got assigned to Tommy right outta the gate. He was a decent guy. Had a lot of years on the job, he knew his stuff, and I learned a hell of a lot of things about the Waianae Coast that came in handy over the years. Knowing all that trivial stuff even saved my life a time or two. But he was just another one of those guys on the job who seemed to be related to everybody else up there. And because of that, he looked the other way on a lot of things. Not my style, but I didn't say anything, ever, to anyone. I kept my mouth shut, kept my head down, and while I was under his wing, he was the ultimate authority. One day we were on patrol, and this car came flying out of the Waianae boat harbor…almost took out a minivan. So Tommy lights him up, and we pull him over. No license, no insurance, expired inspection sticker, car's unregistered, and on top of all that, the guy was drunk. Really drunk. I smelled it before we even walked up to the car. He and Tommy get into this long conversation, they start laughing about a bunch of stuff, and then he cuts the guy loose."

"He let him drive away?"

"Yup. That was the first and last time I opened my mouth to him. We got into an argument. It was the first time he saw me lose my temper, and it was the first time he threatened to write me up because I dared question his judgment. And then he begins to dress me down right there in the middle of the street. 'Are you a specialist in field sobriety? Are you a doctor? Are you a toxicologist? Can you give expert testimony in court that the guy was impaired?' "

For a moment Henry felt transported back in time, then grew silent.

"Hank?"

"He yelled and screamed at me. I'd almost shit myself I was so scared. I'd never seen him so angry. Turned out the guy he let go was a brother-in-law of one of his cousins. I should've guessed they were related before I opened my mouth. About twenty minutes later all's forgotten, and he's laughing and wants to buy me a plate lunch...and then we get this call from dispatch to respond to a three-car accident with fatalities over at the elementary school. The guy he let go had been flying down Haleakala Avenue. He hit a speed bump that launched his car into the air like a missile and came down head-on into a parked car, then bounced off and smashed into one coming out of the school driveway. The occupants of that second car were killed instantly. We were the first to arrive on the scene. Tommy's wife and daughter were in that second car. We already knew the subsequent investigation by internal affairs was gonna be brutal, but Tommy had already charged, tried, and convicted himself for the accident and the deaths. The night before he was to be questioned, he ate his gun. Left a note explaining his guilt and exonerating me. I decided that I wasn't gonna be the kind of cop that looked the other way. And I decided that I was gonna do whatever I needed to do to get answers and get bad guys off the street. So maybe I've bent the rules and been a hard-ass at times. If that earned me the nickname Dirty Henry, fine, I really don't care."

"I'm sorry. I never knew. That's a sad story. It's a sobering story."

"Do me favor…keep it to yourself."

Kaelani nodded, checked her cell phone, and worried if the district attorney's office would call.

"Wanna cheer me up while we wait for this warrant? Tell me about your auntie, Costa's wife."

"I don't know if this will cheer you up, but here it goes. Auntie Tesha was always known as someone who pushed the envelope. She liked to walk on the wild side, as they say. When she was young, she ran with the wrong crowd and did things that bent the rules."

"Like you did?"

"Like I did," she admitted. "But I was lucky. I got nailed and faced a judge who showed me a path to redemption before I became a lost cause, not that she did anything *that* bad. She just made bad choices, but she was a good lady…very loving and caring. Of all my aunties, she was my favorite because in spite of her faults, she was very protective of us kids. She fed us…good stuff from all the fast-food places"—she laughed—"and watched us after school. She even took the time to teach us to surf. That was her true passion, and I loved to watch her shoot a curl. She could've been a competitor had she run with the right crowd. She was great with a net...fishing. She loved all us kids equally. Every weekend, the whole family—the aunties, uncles, and cousins—would get together at Nanakuli Beach Park. The men would set up the tents and the barbecue grills. Some would then walk down to the water and cast their nets and fishing lines...Auntie T always joined them." She smiled at the memory. "The women brought all the food. We had salads of every kind, huli-huli chicken, and lau lau. We'd be there all weekend long. You ever sleep out on the beach?"

"No, haven't had the opportunity, but I'd like to. Maybe when this is all over."

"It was a way for the adults to blow off steam from a hard week, yeah? They didn't have the kind of jobs that paid a whole lot, and we all didn't have much, but we had family, food from our gardens, meat from the wild game that roams the mountains. We had the beach and the ocean...that's life for us here, ya know?"

"Yeah, I know. Maya once told me about it. I still see that going on all the time. It's nice."

"One weekend, Auntie T shows up with this loser...Nicky. Right away nobody liked him. He had this bad energy about him. We all felt it. We could see it in his eyes, especially the way he leered at the women. He was this big know-it-all thinking he was gonna teach us everything about anything. And he'd be telling these stories about how he was in the military and how he had PTSD from Desert Storm and stuff like that. Two of my uncles were in that conflict. They'd never talk about it like this guy did. Hell, years later I was over there with the guard. I saw too many of my sisters and brothers in uniform lose their lives, so if there's one thing that really pisses me off, it's stolen valor. Anyway, he'd force himself into conversations and claim to be an expert on everything. He'd even try to tell one auntie how to improve her mac salad. Bruddah, when you're an outsider, you don't do that shit. But the thing that got people mad was how he tried to convince all of us that he was one of us. In private he had a short, violent temper. When the men of the family mocked him or the aunties told him to mind his own business, or even when the kids started to laugh at him, he'd go home and take it out on Auntie T, that fucking coward."

"I don't get it. Why'd she put up with that? Why'd she stay with him?"

"Why does any woman stay with a man who beats her? Many reasons, yeah? Anyway, he got her pregnant, and she didn't wanna be a single mom. We got too much of that up on the coast. Too many girls getting pregnant in high school. Too many sixteen- and seventeen-year-old babies raising babies." She shook her head. "Anyway, when some of the uncles found out about the baby, they had a long talk with him. It kind of settled him down for a while, but he couldn't help himself. He needed the attention and started up with his shit again. Kept getting into fights at work and fired from his jobs. HPD would show up in the middle of the night, wanting to question him about a break-in somewhere or a stolen car. The family told Auntie T that he was not family and to not bring him to our gatherings anymore. That's when he started running scams on the people in the homestead. He'd spend whatever money he got on drugs or in the illegal gambling rooms. He'd steal things, then use that stuff to pay off the bookies. Got caught with young girls. And the more he got mocked for trying to tell people he was one of us, the more he'd take it out on Auntie T. One day when I came home from school, she was at my house. Her face looked like she was in a boxing match. She couldn't open one eye, and her lips were so swollen she could hardly speak."

Her eyes glazing over, Kaelani grew quiet as she remembered seeing a cigarette burn mark on her Auntie Tesha's cheek. It surprised her that she had forgotten about that.

"What? What's that look? You okay?"

"...everyone in the family tried to get her to leave him. She was always a bit pigheaded. About a week later we all stopped hearing from her. She disappeared. Nicky said she ran off, but I know my auntie. She wouldn't do that and leave the baby with that bastard. But he's the one who ended up running off to California because he knew if he stayed, he was gonna get his. He was gonna get it the Waianae way. You know what I'm saying?"

Henry nodded.

"Any idea what happened to your auntie?"

"Oh, I've got an idea all right. He had rented a boat for a 'nighttime fishing trip' the same time she went missing. We all think he beat her to death, chopped her up, and dumped her into the ocean."

"And no one called HPD?"

"The police were called. Unis came out, looked around, and took a report. They said they'd turn it over to the detectives, but we should be patient because they were backlogged. About a week later a detective showed up to investigate. A fucking week later! Not surprised he found nothing if you can believe it. The guy who rented the boat to him claimed he saw nothing. The harbor master saw nothing. And except for fish blood, scales, and that kind of stuff from later rentals, the boat was clean. His car was clean."

"The house?"

"No evidence of a murder found anywhere."

"Maybe she did run off?"

"Do you really believe that? Do you really think he didn't kill her, chop her up, and feed her to the sharks?"

"No, of course not. So what do you think? Sloppy investigating or just a lack of the technology we have today?"

"Both. But now you know why I got pissed off when you called my investigation sloppy. It's a sensitive subject with me, and I was already pissed that the lieutenant kept getting in my way."

"I see that now. I'm sorry…really, I owe you an apology for that…so, what happened to the baby?"

"Nicky Junior? Thank God that prick wanted nothing to do with his son, so he was raised by the other aunties. I hear he turned out good. He lives on the mainland now…has no contact with his father, but then again, he has no real contact with the rest of us."

"I can see why you've got a score to settle with him."

"And I'm going to. You can count on it."

When Kaelani's phone buzzed with a text from the D.A.'s office, she smiled at Henry.

"We got our warrant!"

****

Amy Nguyen jumped when she noticed the flashing blue lights in her rearview mirror. She pulled her car over to the shoulder and readied her license, registration, proof of insurance, and a notepad with pen while cursing her luck.

"Fuck me, not again! I can't afford another ticket," she vented before lowering her window and took notice of the officer's badge number. When she got stopped for running a red light a few weeks prior, that officer had propositioned her in exchange for ignoring the infraction. She said no, a traffic ticket was written, and she filed a sexual harassment complaint with the city against the wishes of her family.

Having escaped the communist government in Vietnam many years before, her parents were still afraid to confront the authorities on any level or for any reason. Among the other lessons to help their children navigate life in America, Amy's parents often warned her and her siblings about the many pitfalls of questioning those with any power. Amy, however, was American born, grew up in an environment that also taught her to stand up and speak out against injustice, and was no different than many of her generation. She couldn't help but wonder if, because of her actions, she was now being targeted.

"License, reg—"

"Registration, proof of insurance, yeah, yeah, I know the drill," she said while handing over her documents. "Do you mind telling me what I did wrong, Officer?"

"A few things, actually. You ran the stop sign after you pulled out of the convenience store, and you made an unsafe lane change. I've been following you for a couple miles, hoping you'd see me and begin driving a little more responsibly. But I guess you were too focused on your cell phone."

"You gotta be kidding me, I wasn't on my…" She quickly checked herself, took a breath, and began again. "I can explain, Officer. I wasn't on my cell phone, and I honestly didn't see the stop sign. It must have been covered over by tree branches or something. And I swerved to avoid that pothole. Did you see how big that was?"

"Uh-huh, I see. Shut off your engine and sit tight. I'll be back in a bit."

"*Shit, I'm screwed*!" she said under her breath. "*My mom's gonna freak all over me!*"

Because of her previous experience with HPD, she was quick to write down the officer's shield number after he had walked back to his car to run her information and check for any outstanding warrants. In the meantime, she phoned a friend from her acting class who counseled her to livestream the event and "make sure you show a little cleavage, but not too much. A little more thigh is good too, but don't be too obvious about it. You don't wanna come off as a slut. Oh, and don't spare the tears, baby girl. Let 'em flow, just like when we do a scene in Scott's acting classes. That's your strength, so use it." When the officer finally returned with citation in hand, her performance, while convincing, failed to play on his emotions.

"The stop sign is clearly visible, young lady. If you want to contest that in court, you have that option. And since you're recording all this on your phone, I recommend you drive back there, use it to take some pictures of the intersection and that stop sign. Bring it with you when you fight your ticket. If the judge feels the sign is obscured, the picture will help get the ticket dismissed. I also suggest that you dress a little more conservatively and try to hold off on the tears, and maybe that too will be taken into consideration. As far as swerving to avoid a pothole, I recommend that you drive the speed limit or a little slower and stay in your lane so you don't risk causing an accident." He then looked directly at the cell phone camera. "My name is Officer Tadesco, shield number eight-three-two-two. Please drive safe and have a nice day."

Amy remained parked on the shoulder and continued to livestream about the experience, adding salty commentary about her previous encounter with the police when a black sedan pulled up behind her.

"What now?" she remarked to her video audience. "I hope this isn't another cop!"

She spied the plainclothes officer's badge and gun holstered on his hip, lowered her window one more time, and set the phone on the dash to allow the livestream to continue.

"Excuse me, miss. Inspector Benjamin, Hank Benjamin from HPD's special investigations unit," he said, failing to notice her phone.

"Yes, sir, is something wrong?" she politely inquired while noting shield number 7511.

"Yes, I was parked a little ways back and was watching the officer who pulled you over. I noticed you got a ticket. I'd like to see it."

"Sure, here you go. What's this about?"

"One second, Ms...Newjen, Nig...guy..."

"Wen, it's pronounced Wen."

"Right." He resented being corrected. "Officer Tadesco, just as I thought." Nicky Costa lifted the police scanner to his mouth as if it were a two-way radio. "Inspector eight-one to dispatch. Have Officer Tadesco meet me at the station, over." The scanner crackled, naturally with an unrelated call. "Yeah, copy that, dispatch. Will do."

"Inspector, do you mind if I ask what's going on?"

"We've been watching this guy for several weeks now. We got several complaints he's been pulling over young girls like you just to get their addresses. Then he shows up where they live saying he feels bad about giving them the ticket, and, well, you can figure out the rest. I'm gonna bet he said you ran a red light."

"A stop sign. He said I ran a stop sign. But it shows that on the ticket."

"Yeah, I know, his handwriting is bad, but that's him all right. I'm gonna have to ask you to come with me to the station."

"Why, what for?"

"It looks like we're gonna have to suspend him, but you'll have to give us a statement for the record."

"I'm not so sure about that. I already have one complaint against a cop, and I don't want…"

"Look, come help us out, and I can get this ticket canceled for you."

"If you know it's not a legit ticket, you should have it canceled anyway, and you don't need me to—"

"Hey, if you don't wanna help us, I understand," he interrupted, his patience growing thin, "but look, the department needs your help to get these creeps away from the public. If you don't help, he's gonna just keep doing this to Asian women just like you. Do you want that? Do you want that to be your fault?"

"No, I don't…okay, but I'll drive over and meet you at the police station."

"No!" he shouted which startled her. "I mean, if you're worried about your car, don't be. It'll be safe here. I, uh, I also need to ask you some important questions on the way. So, come on, we're wasting time!" His tone made her more uncomfortable.

She heard her phone vibrate against the dashboard and glanced over to see a text:

—I don't think that guy's a real cop. Don't go with him! Lock your doors! I'll call 911!—

"On second thought, I don't wanna go with you. I wanna see some I.D."

"Here's my badge"—he pointed—"go ahead and write down my number. Now enough of this, I'm trying to do you a favor." At the sound of the lock engaging, he pulled hard on the door handle.

"I want you to get your supervisor here."

"Okay, that's it. I'm gonna have to ask you to step out of your car."

"Wait, what? What's going on here?"

"The computer shows that you have a suspended license, and the car is unregistered. Step out from the car right now!"

"That's ridiculous! The other cop didn't say anything about that, and I know you didn't check any computer!"

"I...I got the report on the radio when I pulled up behind you. Now for the last time, get out of your car"—his voice loud and serious—"and slowly, with nothing in your hands."

"You're not a cop! I'm not getting out!" she yelled and tried to turn the ignition key.

Costa felt the surge of power when he saw panic on the girl's face. In an attempt to maintain the façade, he turned up the volume knob on his scanner for added realism, then held it to his mouth while grabbing for the ignition key.

"Inspector eight-one to central. Let Lieutenant Mendoza know that the driver of the vehicle matches the description of that Chinese drug dealer we've been looking for, and she's resisting."

"You're crazy! I'm no drug dealer, and I'm not even Chinese, you racist fu—"

Before she could say another word, he grabbed her by the throat, pulled her through the open window, and used his large frame and meaty hands to slam her head into the windshield. He landed another blow to the side of her face. Her body went limp and couldn't fight back as he tie-wrapped her wrists and dragged her off to his car—tossing her into the back seat as if she were a stuffed toy. Costa glared at the few homeless bystanders. And while most swiftly walked away, to make the charade complete for the couple onlookers who remained, he went back to her car, pulled a small bag of white powder from his pocket, grabbed her phone, and brought both items back to finish the scene.

"So, you're not a drug dealer? You wanna tell me about this?"

"You're c-crazy," she slurred, too woozy to sit upright. "That's not m-mine, and you're not a c-cop."

"Tell me another one, liar." He held up the bag in full view of the livestream. "I found this in your glove box."

"Not t-true. I don't do…"

"Look at you, you're all doped up on your own merchandise. I'm taking you downtown. You're going to jail."

"It's not mine, I t-tell you. I'm n-no drug d-dealer. I'm an h-honor s-student at the u-university."

As they drove off, she helplessly watched Costa bashing her phone before tossing the shattered pieces onto the roadway.

****

Going through his planned dialogue before heading out to confront Costa, Billy decided to check with Captain Tanaka how Mendoza's arrest would go down. Channeling what Henry would do to a cop who had ordered an assassination—even if it was on someone like Costa—Billy had strongly lobbied for a public display that would send a strong message to the rank and file at the West Oahu precinct. Tanaka, however, explained one more time why it needed to be done with discretion, cautioning against personal retribution or any advocacy for a public thrashing which would have repercussions as word traveled throughout the entire department.

"You gotta keep in mind, Billy, there are others in this building who are part of that group. They'll condemn you as a rat, a traitor. And if that happens, who's ever gonna work with you? Who'll watch your six? Do you think you'd be safe going on a call into the back country not knowing what or who could be waiting for you in the bush? Do you wanna spend the rest of your life looking over your shoulder? Look at me. I've got this thing handled. I'm sending Mendoza down to headquarters on an errand. He'll think he's there to pick up some important documents. Federal agents will be waiting to take him into custody, and no one will know we had anything to do with it."

"But he will definitely think I had something to do

with it. He'll still spread the word to everyone he can think of."

"Or, once he's detained and being questioned, an agent could let it slip that they've had a man on the inside of his separatist group for quite some time."

"And he'll think I was helping in some way. He'll think I was wearing a wire."

"You're overthinking this. I don't think he's that smart, and I think you're a little paranoid. Anyway, it'll definitely stir up a lot of distrust among their ranks while trying to figure out who the inside man is or what, if anything else, is going on." Tanaka smiled.

Back at his desk, Iona checked the ammo clip in his gun, holstered his weapon, and stood to leave when his phone buzzed. It was Mendoza.

"Now's not a good time, Lieutenant." He looked across the room to Peter's desk.

"It's never a good time, is it? Look, about our boy—"

"No worries, I'm on my way to take care of it now."

"I hope so. You promised me you were gonna do this last night."

"There were too many people around. I would've been seen. Trust me, there's nothing to worry about. In a little while he'll be the last thing on your mind. I guarantee it."

"Good, very good. Check in with me when you get back."

"Will do," he said and ended the call when he noticed a sudden flurry of activity. "Hey, Kalima, what's going on?"

"Front desk got a call from someone saying her

girlfriend was being abducted by a cop."

"A cop? In uniform? In broad daylight?"

"Plainclothes. She sent a recorded copy of the livestream. We got a shield number, and we're running it now."

Detectives gathered around Billy's desk to watch the video. Although they could only see his waist and the HPD badge, he and Mendoza immediately recognized Costa's voice.

"That looks like Farrington Highway, town-bound side just after the power plant," said one officer.

"I got a hit on the shield. It's Hank Benjamin!" called out another.

"That's not Hank," said a third. "This guy's language, his voice, that's somebody else. And look how fat that fakkah is!"

Tanaka came rushing out of his office.

"Calm down, ladies! Is anybody working this yet, or are you all just going to stand there? Yes? No? Let's go! Is there a patrol unit on the scene? If not, is there one on the way? Do we have any other information on the girl that just got grabbed? What about the kidnapper's car? Do we have a description? If so, did anybody put out a BOLO? What direction was this guy heading when he took off? I want some answers, and I want them now! This girl's life is in danger, so let's get to work!"

****

With search warrant in hand, a cautious Kaelani allowed herself another bonding moment over the shared victory—she thinking, albeit briefly, that he'd be an acceptable partner.

He was beginning to perspire in anticipation of his

eight-month-long nightmare finally coming to an end.

"Hey, Hank, wake up! Didn't you hear anything I just said?"

"Sorry, my mind is getting ahead of me. Tell me again?"

"Never mind, it was just a silly thought."

"Something about when I come off suspension? I heard that much. Go on."

"I was just saying that eventually the whole incident with that tourist will blow over, and you'll be reinstated. I was just thinking that if you could, you know, with Tanaka's help, get reassigned back to West Oahu, we could—"

"No, I don't think so. At this point, I think I'm gonna get the deep six."

"Are you kidding? Call the union rep and fight this thing."

"I don't know if I even want to. But if I did, I'm not coming back to work the Westside, no way. Not now, not ever!"

"Like I said, it was a silly thought."

"Wait, were you suggesting that we, you and I, partner up?"

"Oh, hell no, are you kidding? You think because we shared a personal moment back there, or because we got this warrant and it looks like things are breaking our way, that I wanna team up with you? Is that what you want?"

"Shit no, are you kidding me? But you gotta admit that's what it sounded like you were suggesting."

"Not. On. Your. Life. No! We are oil and water, baby. We got two different styles that would not work well together. You and me partners? Ha!"

"Exactly! Now if you don't mind concentrating on the road, I wanna get up to Costa's house before nightfall."

"Keep your shirt on, wiseass. At least I'm fucking sober." She tried to swallow that last word. After an awkward moment of silence, she said, "I'm sorry. I didn't mean…"

Henry didn't say a word. However, it finally hit home his drinking had become that obvious.

"We'll be there in thirty minutes, Han—" She was interrupted by the explosion of chatter coming over the radio as Henry's cell phone buzzed simultaneously.

"Yeah, Billy, what's up?"

"It's Costa! He's definitely the guy. He's the killer!" Iona's voice was frantic. "I'm certain of it!"

"Calm down! What's going on?"

"Will you keep your voice down!?" Kaelani scolded. "I'm trying to listen to this BOLO!"

"Billy, radio traffic's going crazy. What's going on? Where are you?"

"I'm heading over to Costa's house. He just abducted a girl. He's using your old shield. Seven five one one, that's you, right? He's got it. I think he's been using it to get his victims."

"Are you sure he's headed back to his house?"

"It's the middle of the day. Where's he gonna go?"

"Holy shit, Costa just nabbed a girl right off Farrington, not too far from Electric Beach," Kaelani said to Henry.

"I know. I'm talking to Billy. He's heading over to his house," he said, and Kaelani ripped the phone from his hands.

"Don't go into the house without backup, Uncle

Billy!" she shouted. "Not until we get there, you understand? You wait for backup."

"Uncle Billy!?" He grabbed for the phone.

"Not now, Hank. Not now!"

"Give me the goddamn phone and hit the after-burners on this beast." His face was bright red and eyes bulged from the adrenaline dump.

With lights and siren helping to carve out a path through the lunchtime traffic, they raced for the closest freeway on-ramp.

"I think he's heading back to his house," Billy repeated.

"We're fighting our way through this fucking Nimitz traffic but—"

"Hold on, Hank!" Kaelani's arm shot out across his chest as she slammed on the brakes.

****

Billy Iona parked a few houses from Costa's, again checking the ammo clip in his gun, the spare clip secured to his trouser belt, the telescoping baton that he shoved into his back pocket, and then sidled up behind the black Mercedes parked in front of the garage. He crouched and duck-walked to the passenger side and steadied himself against the door. It felt wet and sticky against his hand, which was now stained a dark red. Feeling the arteries pulsating in his neck, he swallowed hard, then continued his advance to the overgrown hedgerow separating the gravel driveway from the front yard. As best as he could determine from his position, there was no movement visible in either of the two front windows of the house. He held his place and listened for what seemed like eternity. Convinced that all was quiet on the inside, he proceeded to inch his way across the weeds, crabgrass, and piles of dog excrement. Billy nearly lost bladder control when a gust of wind liberated a dying palm frond that landed by his feet. With that, he froze to consider Kaelani's insistence he wait for backup, then thought he heard a faint whimpering coming from the house. Bent at the waist, he now tiptoed to the front door, which, to his surprise, hadn't been closed all the way. *Could it be that easy? No, not with this guy. Okay, Billy boy, relax...relax...relax. It's not a trap if you're ready for it.* Crouching on the front step, he took note of the fresh blood on the entryway floor and eased back the slide of his nine-millimeter to advance a round into the chamber. He tried to get a better grip on his weapon, but the tackiness from the blood on his hand made it feel clumsy. He reflexively wiped it against his shirt, then cursed, having stained the newly purchased hundred-dollar designer print.

With the least pressure possible, he inched the opening wider—momentarily stopping when the rust-covered hinges cried out to reveal his presence. *Damn it!* He waited for a response. There was none. Neither was there any counsel from the heavens as his eyes looked skyward. "If ever there was a time, Jesus, be with me now," he muttered and hoped unused training from his academy days hadn't escaped him. *Easy now, one step at a time.* He pushed the door as far as it would swing and took aim, somehow expecting to see piles of junk sitting on top of cheap mismatched living room furniture. *What the...it's completely empty!* With his gun firmly secured in a two-handed grip to point the way, Billy swept his aim back and forth across the width of the room, waiting for a closet door to blast open. Baby steps guided his advance, stopping again at the muffled sobbing coming from the hallway. Hearing no other noise save for the creaking floorboards beneath his feet, he crept toward the bedrooms in back.

****

"Kaelani, you okay?"

Noticing a dazed look and a small bump forming on her forehead, Henry grasped her shoulder.

"Yeah...I think. What the hell just happened?"

"Seriously? You drove into a light pole to avoid hitting that woman."

"What woman? What pole?" She leaned back into the seat and looked over at Henry. "My head, it feels like it split in two."

"Holy crap, are you serious? Okay, um, look at me. Look at me and follow my finger."

"Do you know what you're doing?"

"I saw this on one of those TV cop shows."

"You're kidding, right?" Kaelani's eyes tracked the movements to his satisfaction.

"Good, now what day is it?"

"...Tuesday, right?"

"Right. Any neck pain?" His hands felt and pushed on her spine.

"...what are you, a chiropractor or something?"

"Just answer the question."

"You touch anything below my shoulders and I'm gonna shoot you."

"You'll be fine. Now slide over. I'm driving." He jumped out of the car, surveyed the damage, then scanned the street to make sure nobody besides the two of them were banged up. Except for a few items from a dropped bag of groceries, there was no sign of the pedestrian who had stepped out into the oncoming traffic.

"The car...I fucked up the car," she worried.

"I'm fine, thanks for asking."

"How bad? The damage, how bad is it?"

"You crunched the front fender. Light pole is scarred but still standing." He shifted into reverse, rammed his foot into the gas pedal, and smoked the back tires while backing off the raised median strip. "And, as you can see, the car still works. I say it was a tie match."

"Where the hell did you learn to drive?"

With equal intention he banged the shift handle into drive, then almost caused another accident on their way to the freeway entrance. Feeling for blood, she rubbed the bruise on her forehead.

"You're not bleeding, but that's gonna hurt you for a few days. By the way, your arm saved me. You got good parental instincts."

"The car...I fucked up the car."

"Yeah, so what? At least you didn't kill anybody, so stop worrying about the damn car. At least now you'll get to see if all those donuts to the motor pool guys was a good investment."

****

Without the benefit of any electricity, Billy inspected the walls of the first bedroom with a penlight he had swiped from his doctor's office. He was almost too scared to venture any farther past the doorway. His intuition screamed for him to leave the house and wait for assistance. His refusal to obey his gut instinct to retreat would have surprised any one of his colleagues. It certainly surprised him. Even if he tried to leave, a physiological response that he couldn't comprehend had kicked in, affecting his legs, making each step extremely difficult to take. In all his years on the job, he had never personally witnessed, outside of crime scene photos reviewed in the safety of the bullpen, what he was now seeing with his own eyes. Had he not been awake, he wouldn't have believed what lay before him. *Please tell me this is a bad dream.*

Several dozen photos, some with comments, others with circles and punctuation marks written in red, were the most graphic he'd ever encountered. And that was just the tip of the iceberg. Forgetting the dried blood on his hands, he reflexively brought one to his nose to block the intolerable stench. Ignoring the shaking in his knees and coming close to letting the weight of the gun slip through his weakened grip, he remained fixated on the images until the shadow of a door moved across his field of vision, and the muffled distress call could be heard once more.

Costa's presence was so palpable it made him spin into a defensive posture—permitting himself to continue breathing when he was convinced no one was behind him. His left knee gave way, and he found himself toppling over, only to be saved by roach-infested garbage bags filled with the remnants of practically every fast-food restaurant known to mankind. Repulsed, Billy scurried to his feet, frantically swiping at his head and shoulders. He forced a swallow to the objections of a sandpaper tongue. No matter how hard he tried to produce saliva, none would come, and his throat protested with every attempt. *Where the hell are Hank and Kaelani?*

The door to the second bedroom had to be forced

open over a thick layer of plastic painter's tarp that had bunched at the base of the door. It ran the length and width of the room, and a double layer of soundproofing insulation covered the walls as well as the windows. Billy patted his pockets, looking for the penlight, and concluded he had dropped it when he fell. Rationalizing he'd get a new one at his next doctor visit, he decided not to retrieve it. When his eyes adjusted to the darkened room, they fell upon Amy Nguyen—naked and tied to a floor-to-ceiling wooden cross that was bolted to the far wall. She was gagged with the same style bandana that had been used on Makani Palahia. And through the glistening red lines snaking down her chest, abdomen, and legs, dripping onto the plastic, he could almost make out Henry's initials etched into her torso.

Already shaken to the core, Billy had a hard time maintaining focus. The room spun, and the walls appeared to be closing in, his heartbeat deafening to the point he couldn't hear himself think, and with each labored step forward, he felt as if his legs had abandoned him altogether. In his determination to free the girl, he could no longer process the threat to his personal safety and momentarily forgot about Costa. *Never in all my years...*

Unlike the other victims, Amy was the first one Nicky had brought back to his house. He didn't want to risk having the neighbors hear her cries for help, so he sedated her with a suppository, which compounded the effects of the concussion suffered during the abduction.

She attempted to lift her head when Billy came into the room, thinking through the fog that her ordeal was about to become worse.

"C-can you hear me? A-are you okay?" he asked.

Her tear-filled eyes struggled to stay open, her words unintelligible while mumbling through the bandana.

"Calm down," he whispered more for himself than for her and began to remove her gag. "It'll be okay. I'm with HPD, and I'm here to help you. Where's the man who brought you here? Where's the man who did this to you?"

"I'm right behind you," Costa said, stepping out from the closet.

Before Billy could turn, the crack of a powerful blow to the back of his head echoed like a Louisville Slugger sending a homerun ball deep into centerfield. A lightning-strike sensation bolted from head to toe while a simultaneous flash of light, a few seconds of blackness, and a loss of muscle control overwhelmed him, and he folded like a punch-drunk boxer who hit the canvas for a final ten-count. He rolled over in an attempt to stop the room from spinning and quell the intensity of his nausea. Costa towered above, waving a two-by-four and motioning as if daring him to get up to finish the bout that had already been won. Billy tried focusing on the drooling face above him while his hands searched the floor.

Costa laughed and taunted him, "Looking for this?" He displayed Billy's gun just as the detective's eyes rolled back into his head.

****

When Henry whipped onto Palehua Street, he knocked over several garbage totes set out for the weekly pickup and came close to taking out a neighbor's fence.

"Sorry, Lani," he said and pulled the car to a stop. "It almost got away from me."

"Never mind that. What are you doing?" She was startled. "Why you stopping this far from the house? Something wrong?"

"Just wanna check that you're okay before we proceed. Your head clear? Can you engage?"

"Killer headache, my ears are ringing, but I'm good. Now let's go."

He rolled his window down and motioned for her to do the same. Placing the transmission in neutral and shutting off the engine, he eased his foot off the brake and allowed the car to coast down the street.

"You hear that?" His voice was barely audible.

"It's quiet. I don't hear a thing." She copied him.

"Do you notice anything else?"

"Yeah, no sign of Billy's car for one thing...and I told you don't call me Lani. That fat bastard called me Lani when I was a kid. Teased me all the time with 'little lolo Lani' this and 'chubby lolo Lani' that."

"Chubby crazy Lani? Really?"

"Don't you dare repeat that to anyone."

"I won't, and I promise I'll never call you Lani again. Billy's car isn't here, but check it out. That's Costa's." He pointed to the Mercedes.

"I thought he would've been here by now, unless...you didn't see him pass us, did you?"

"No, but that doesn't mean he hadn't been here. There's a number of other streets he could've used to get out of this neighborhood." He rolled up his window. She followed suit. "Call his radio. I'll try his cell."

"Do you think he already arrested Nicky?" She keyed the radio mic. "Detective nine-nine to seven-oh, over."

"Maybe, but I doubt it. I've never known him to go it alone. Besides, Costa could easily overpower him...unless Billy shot him first. At least that's what I'd do. When he called before, he said he was on his way here, so I'm thinking something happened."

"Like what?"

"I don't know, but if he did get here, wouldn't he have called it in? Assuming Costa brought the girl here, wouldn't he have called for an ambulance to take her to the hospital? Standard procedure, right? We heard nothing come over the radio."

"He could've used his cell."

"Still, I didn't hear or see any sirens or lights, did you?"

"No."

He let the car roll to a stop in front of his house. Kaelani called Billy several times—getting no response. Likewise for Henry when he tried by phone.

"Something's not right," he said, studying the street.

"Right? He's not answering either of us."

"And that's not the only thing. It's quiet, but it's way too quiet."

"Like how?"

"I don't like what I'm seeing at Judy Coleman's house."

"Your nosy landlady? Where is she?"

"Exactly, where is she? Usually, when I come pulling up, she'd be out here waiting to fill me in on every little thing. I know she's mad as hell at me, but at the very least she'd be peering through the windows and..." He noticed the torn curtain. "Call for backup.

Get Tanaka on the phone. Get everybody you can. I'm gonna check out Judy's. Make the call, then meet me over there."

As he made his way down the side of her house, Henry noticed the busted lock on the garage door along with several plastic pieces from a broken taillight. *She shivered over that car.* He drew his weapon, chambered a round, then continued on to the back of the house.

"Judy, you in there?" he shouted through the shattered door, then stepped over splintered wood and blood splatter. Fragmented glass crunched under each step. A smashed chair, a porcelain cup in pieces, grocery coupons soaking on a coffee-covered table, the kitchen looked as if an explosion ripped through it. "Judy!"

Kaelani met him at the front of the cottage. "Tanaka's on the way with a crew. What's going on in here? Anything?"

"Looks like he got to her too. Kitchen, living room, all torn up, blood everywhere. Thing is, her car's gone."

"Maybe she drove herself to the hospital?"

"Let's hope. Call the E.R., but my money says no. She would've called...holy shit...she did try to call me! The other morning when I was meeting Ramos-Brown. We better get over to Costa's house."

****

When Billy came to, the pounding in his head was made worse by the sun setting in a cloudless sky. It took him a few minutes to realize he was up in the mountains looking out over the dense forest of the Waianae Range. If his hands hadn't been bound behind his back, he'd have rubbed the dried blood from his eyes to get a better look. However, he could still make out the valley and beyond that, the diamond-like sparkles dancing across the Pacific Ocean.

"Recognize it?" Costa asked from behind him.

It was at that very instant Billy knew he was never leaving the mountain.

"Yeah, I recognize it. I've hiked the Kolekole Pass many times when I was a kid, and with better company. I know these trails like the back of my hand, and I know why you brought me up here. By the way, how'd you get me up here?"

Costa tossed a shovel at Billy, then knelt beside him holding a gun to his head.

"Car, you idiot. How else was I gonna drag your sorry ass almost seventeen-hundred feet up this mountain, huh?"

"You drove a car up this road? You are crazy! That dirt road is so unstable it could give way under the weight. That's why they've had it closed for years."

"Do you really believe that story? Unstable roads? Nah. Government's got the roads up here closed to keep this sacred land away from her people, our people."

"You're crazy and stupid if you believe that nonsense."

"Crazy and stupid, huh? Who's the prisoner? Now, listen up so there's no mistakes. I'm gonna free your hands, and you're gonna start digging me a hole. You try anything funny"—he smacked his face with the gun—"you're gonna be begging me to pull this trigger. Now get a move on it. Unstable roads my ass. I've been driving up here for years. If this road were unsafe, I'd know it. Where do you think I dump my shit, huh? And why the fuck you worried about a dangerous road? You should be worried about me. Right now, I'm more dangerous than any fucking road, you dumb moron. You're gonna die here today anyway, yeah?"

"Is this where you dumped my sister?"

"Tesha?" He laughed. "Everybody thinks I fed that bitch to the sharks. Don't you?"

"I don't know. You tell me."

"It was a good cover, yeah? Rent a boat out so everybody sees me go, then bring it back after an hour, and everybody's convinced that's what I did. Because that's what I wanted them to think. Not so stupid, huh? So, they go through that boat as best they could and found nothing, not even a strand of hair. That's 'cause I took her up Makaha, to the heiau at Kaneaki. I cut that bitch up and left her for the wild pigs. I still laugh thinking somebody bagged one of them suckers and a whole bunch of people ate some kalua Tesha at their next luau."

"And that's what you're gonna do to me, yeah? In that case, why should I dig? Why should I do your dirty work?"

"Because of hope. Hope that somehow a miracle will happen at the last minute and you'll be saved. Hope that when the sun goes down, it'll be dark enough for you to make a break for it. Hope that I'll let you live. Just like those filthy, unclean bitches who betrayed their culture and betrayed the kingdom. You should have seen the hope in their eyes, thinking that I'd let them go. But I didn't." He laughed. "And nobody came busting in at the last minute to save them like on those stupid television cop shows. But maybe things will be different for you, Billy. Maybe your fucking transplant friend will come riding in at the last minute to save you from the gates of Hell. So, you'll dig. You'll dig his grave because we're running outta daylight and you're wasting my time. Dig, and maybe I'll let you live long enough to see him die first. You know something? I'm surprised you even woke up after I hit you. That is some nasty swelling on the back of your head. I must be losing my touch."

"You think you're gonna get away with this? Hank's on to you. He knows you killed those five women, and he'll find you, and it don't have to be up here. He'll hunt you down like the sick animal you are. The whole department knows you butchered five innocent women. Do you think you're getting off this island? Off this mountain?"

Enraged, Costa pistol-whipped Billy—knocking him over and distorting his already broken nose into a three-dimensional Picasso.

"Hank Benjamin knows I'm the killer? First, he couldn't figure it out, and now he's blaming me for all five? What a fucking asshole! I didn't sacrifice five sinners, only four! Four, damn it, four! Give credit where credit is due!" he screamed.

"What the hell do you mean you only killed four?"

"You think I'm the only one who's been called by the ancients to rise up against the injustice to our people?"

"*Our* people? You have nothing to do with *our* people, you psycho sonofabitch!"

Costa pushed Billy onto his stomach and cut the plastic restraints binding his hands—making sure to push his face into the dirt, making sure Billy's pain was amplified.

"Now get the hell up, you weak little man, and dig his hole. And if you don't, when he gets up here, he gets to see you die just before I send him off to hell to meet his maker."

****

In addition to the mixture of colored flashing lights from police cars, a fire department HAZMAT unit, and a tow truck waiting for the forensics team to finish a preliminary once-over of Nicky Costa's Mercedes, the dozens of onlookers gathered around the yellow crime scene tape at both the Coleman and Costa cottages gave Palehua Street a carnival-like atmosphere typically reserved for Christmas and New Year's Eve celebrations. The only thing missing was the countless amount of illegal firework displays so common throughout the island. Adding to the combination of excitement and tension was the rush of media crews to go live with a "Breaking News: The Hunt for a Serial Killer" exclusive. Neighborhood men and women gathered together over beers and speculation, while kids engaged in "high-speed chases" on their bicycles— most preferring to be gangsters instead of cops.

Henry and Kaelani elbowed and shouldered their way past Kelly Cho and other reporters to update Captain Tanaka while walking him through the team of CSU investigators and other first responders now swarming throughout Costa's front yard and cottage. Peter Mendoza tagged along in silence, taking it all in from a few yards away.

"Any word from Billy?" Henry asked.

"No, nothing yet." Tanaka turned to Mendoza who confirmed. "What's the latest on the girl?"

"She was barely conscious by the time paramedics arrived," Kaelani said, "but still able to talk."

"Drugged?"

"Head trauma for sure. They don't know about drugs, gotta run a tox screen at the hospital."

"As you can see, Cap, she lost a good deal of blood, but when she was awake, she was able to confirm that Costa was using an HPD badge. That bastard was using my old patrolman's shield."

"Did she say anything at all about Billy being here?" Tanaka asked as he studied the torture room, then looked at Mendoza. "You wanna get in here and get briefed on this, or what?"

The lieutenant, unable to speak while trying to comprehend the magnitude of it all, hesitantly stepped closer.

"No, Cap, not a word. But she didn't have to." Henry held up Billy's purple-framed reading glasses. "They were on the floor near the wooden cross."

"Hey, Cap, come this way. You gotta see this other room." Kaelani led the way. "You can see from the placement of these cushions this is where he slept."

Lost for words, the three of them stepped over bags of trash, boxes of stolen merchandise, fake I.D.s, adult and child pornography, and a variety of handguns, to bear witness to four walls that Tanaka could only describe as sheer madness. One wall, with pictures of the royal monarchs, old Hawaii, members of the separatist group he hungered to belong to, and reprinted news articles of the illegal overthrow of the Hawaiian Kingdom appeared to be a shrine to the former independent nation. Plastered over another wall were what appeared to be computer-generated certificates lauding his achievements ranging from "Top Thoracic Surgeon of 2009" and "U.S. Air Force Ace Fighter Pilot" to "2015 Placer County Deputy Sheriff of the

Year" which sat alongside computer-manipulated pictures of Costa dressed in a number of different uniforms from all branches of the military—each adorned with a chest full of medals and ribbons. And then there were the other two walls with dozens of photos of his victims pictured with Henry before and individually after they'd been tortured to death. He noticed, however, there were no photos of him with Maya, and no pre-death photos of Leilani or Malia Opunui. He didn't comment. There were plenty of photos of Henry too—going in and out of his home, at work, and coming in and out of Hokulani's Oceanside Café. On a corner desk, Kaelani skimmed through a stack of photos of Henry with a number of other young Native Hawaiian women—women who were next in line as the writing in red marker on each picture stated, "Still to be purified."

"I hate to say it." Henry broke the silence without taking his eyes off the walls. "But at this point, I gotta believe both Billy and Judy Coleman are dead."

"Do either of you three have any idea where this lunatic would be hiding?" Tanaka turned to his detectives.

Mendoza thought of the mountain bunkers but remained silent. He knew Costa wouldn't go up there and risk being caught by members of the loyalist group. At a loss to come up with anything else, he defaulted to the other two.

"...I do," Kaelani said as long-buried childhood memories began to resurface. "I have a pretty good idea where he is."

****

Costa had fashioned a couple of torches, providing

just enough light for him to monitor his captive's progress. He was impressed with himself and bragged about his craftsmanship.

"Did you get a good look at these torches? I gotta admit, of all the ones I made before, I think these are my best ones yet. Did you know these are great for setting fires? It's true, Billy. Listen up, and you'll learn something. Do you remember that big brush fire down by the landfill a few years ago? That was one of mine. Yeah, I did it, but I didn't expect for it to get so outta hand. I felt bad about that. But whaddya gonna do? I had some special 'stuff' that had to be dumped, and I needed to be sure I wouldn't get interrupted. So I made one of these torches. You listening to me? I made one of these torches, set it up near a big pile of dead overgrowth, and took off to wait for the sirens. You see, I made the bamboo pole real short so it was closer to the ground than these ones right here. Then I placed it in the ground so it was really loose because I knew when the wind kicked up, it would knock it over and then boom, brush fire. By the time that happened and HPD and the fire department were on their way, I was on the other side of the valley, dumping a couple drums of used motor oil. Can you believe it?"

Having enough light to keep an eye on Billy wasn't his only motivation for making them, however. Sitting on the hood of the unmarked police car was, in addition to the torches, an added measure of protection for him from the myriad of ravenous bugs that took advantage of the darkness. He watched and produced a gleeful laugh each time Iona swatted a mosquito, slapped an ankle, or stomped at the ground as if he were performing an Irish river dance. Still, the thought of being bitten to death by a large centipede or swarmed by an army of tropical fire ants competed for his attention as he too alternately brushed at his head, neck, and shoulders.

"You know they're gonna see the light," Billy commented, then threw another shovelful of dirt onto the growing mound by the side of the deepening hole.

"I don't understand. What's your problem?"

"I said they're gonna see the torches…down there in the valley. It's so dark up here, they'll be able to see the light, and they'll come investigate."

"Good, that's what we want, isn't it? We want Detective Benjamin to work his way up here over the weak and unstable road you're so concerned about. By the time he gets here, if he doesn't take a wrong turn and fall to the rocks below, he'll be so worked up, won't he? The only thing is, it'll be so satisfying to kill him, your death will be, I don't know, routine maybe? Whaddya think?"

Billy continued to dig, tossed another shovelful of dirt, then stopped to wipe the sweat from his forehead.

"I think I need a break. That's what I think."

"Come on, you weak, lazy man, dig that hole!"

"Can I get something to drink?"

"Thirsty already?"

"It's hot. It's humid. I'm sweating like a pig."

"Poor baby! What can I get you? Oh, I know, how 'bout a nice cold beer, or maybe an iced tea?" Costa mocked. "Maybe you'd like to see a menu?"

"Do you want me to get this hole dug or not? I'm soaking wet with sweat. I'm dehydrating. I'm still feeling off-balance from being hit in the head. I need water so that I can keep going."

"Whaddya want me to do, take a drive down to the convenience store? Are you hungry too? Should I get you a musubi?"

"You know something, Nicky? It's this shit right here is why everyone thinks you're the biggest fucking shithead in the world. You've always been fucking crazy and full of shit. We all knew that from the first time Tesha brought you to a family gathering. Your condescending negative attitude was always the black cloud that robbed the joy out of everything."

"Watch your fucking mouth, or I'll pop you right here and now." He hopped off the car and waved his gun.

"You're gonna do it anyway, so go ahead. Then you'll have to climb down in this hole with all these bugs and dig this shit yourself." His dare stopped Costa in his tracks.

"…you almost had me there, Billy. You almost had me." He nodded and smiled. "You almost got me to do it. You know something, maybe you're not as dumb as everybody says. Yeah, I remember how the family used to talk about you behind your back and they—"

"The family? What family you talking about, because it ain't my family. You were never part of my family."

"You better be careful, or I *will* pop you right now. I don't need no fucking hole. I can dump you off this ridge, and no one will ever find you. I've gotten away with it before." Again, he waved the gun toward Billy—stopping when he realized he kept taking the bait. "I know what you're doing. My, my, you're good. It's not gonna work. You can dare me all you want, but I know you. I know you're holding out hope for the cavalry to come riding up this hill and save your ass at the last minute. You know what? That'll be my big favor to you because, of all the other family members, you were the only one who never made fun of me...not to my face anyway. So I'll do you a favor. I'll allow you to hope and pray to be saved at the very last minute. It makes for a good story. Spoiler alert!" He laughed. "I know the ending!"

"Water...please." Billy stuck the shovel into the dirt and sat down. "Not one more scoop of dirt until I get some water. I keep a few bottles in my trunk. Please, all I want is one."

"Well, why the hell didn't you say so, you dumb shit. I'm really thirsty," he said, opened the trunk, and returned to stand over Iona with two bottles of water and a shotgun. "And look what little toy I just found. I'd forgotten you guys carry these with you. You know what they say, finders keepers!"

"Do you mind?" He held out his hand.

"Oh yeah, I almost forgot." Costa opened one bottle, drank half, then poured out the rest. "Can water taste stale? Because this tasted stale. I wouldn't want you to have stale water. Let's try this other one."

He drank a little, held the bottle out, then jerked it away before Billy could grasp it.

"Stop fucking around," he scolded before getting hit in the chest with it.

"There's your water, you little pussy. Drink it before I change my mind."

Billy took some in his mouth, poured a little over his head, then tossed it back, making sure it landed on the ground between the two of them. When Costa bent over to retrieve it, a handful of dirt was tossed at his face. Billy grabbed the shovel and swung it with every ounce of energy he could muster and caught his captor on the side of the head. Falling to his knees, Nicky dropped both guns to rub the dirt from his eyes and protect his face from further assault—his scream echoing down the mountainside. A less powerful second strike nailed him in the shoulder, and with even less force, a third struck him on the back of his head. Although drained of his strength, Billy still cursed himself for missing an opportunity to strike a fatal blow.

"Doesn't feel so good, does it?" Billy asked, then stumbled backward from his own light-headedness. Weak and in pain, he did his best to crawl his way out of the hole. Dazed, Costa now held on to the back of his bleeding head, growling like a wounded grizzly.

"Billy, you motherfucker, you're dead! You're dead!"

Iona had the presence of mind to know the shotgun was unloaded and dove for the pistol lying on the ground between the two of them. In the midst of the scrum, they fought for control, neither getting the upper hand. The much bigger and awkward Costa tried to bull his opponent out of the way, but equally unsteady, his legs betrayed him, and he rolled onto the smaller man instead.

"Get the hell off me, you fat pig!"

Billy's free hand started hitting and pushing in an attempt to get out from under the crushing weight. Undeterred by the blows landing onto his face, Costa leaned forward to bury his teeth into Iona's cheek and thrashed his head back and forth as a shark would attack its defenseless prey. This time it was a high-pitched scream that put the wildlife on notice as it reverberated across the expanse of the Waianae Kai Forest Reserve.

As Costa shifted his weight, trying to gain further advantage, Billy managed to roll free and stumbled back into the freshly excavated earth in his failed effort to get to the trees.

For a moment all was quiet save for the heavy breathing coming from both men. One lay motionless at the bottom of a hole, head spinning, face throbbing with blood oozing out of the torn flesh. The other just as exhausted, experiencing his own physical hell, now fighting to catch his breath and struggling to stand. There was no way he was going to let Billy Iona get the best of him. There was no way he was going to let him escape into the darkness. He drew the hunting knife used to commit his murders and had been using on Amy Nguyen when his work was interrupted by the detective.

"Look at you lying there," he wheezed. "What's the matter, Billy, no more fight left in you? Of all the men in your family, you were the one who always stepped out of the way to let the others do the heavy lifting. Why do you suppose that is? They even had to fight your battles for you. I gotta admit I'm impressed that you tried to take me on. Big mistake, yeah? You would have never survived in prison."

He jumped on top of Iona, grabbed a handful of his hair, ripped his head backward, and placed the edge of the serrated blade against his neck.

"You thought you could beat me? You thought you could get away? You thought you had hope? Well, you thought wrong. You're gonna be here to greet Detective

Hank Benjamin. You will be the welcoming committee." He laughed, then pressed the blade with more force. "It's just too bad you're so spent and have no more fight in you. It almost takes the fun out it…almost."

Chapter 16

When I doubt myself,
I tend to think of the plains.
The winters cold, dark, and barren,
harsh and unforgiving.
I've often wondered why
were we forced to live there.
What did my people do to deserve this?
Was it not a lesson, a test, a challenge?
But then the spring rains brought change.
The trees, the mountains, the rivers and valleys
reborn, exploding with life.
The summer and autumn yielded our bounty.
Spirits and faith renewed
with abundance for all,
and all was good again.
Was it not a lesson, a test, a challenge?
I think of these islands
and in many ways see similar obstacles,
similar struggles, and in many the same despair.
In many ways I see the same blessings.
But it is the passing of seasons that make us see,
that give us hope.
I know you've had your challenges,
but I know you have the faith deep within your soul.
There is no obstacle, no challenge too great to
overcome.

There is an abundance of all that is good.
I know you see it.
Let it give you hope, bring you peace, renew your spirit.
Let it bring you back to who you once were.
I will be waiting.

Serving as the main command post for HPD's uniformed officers, detectives, and SWAT team, Hokulani's Oceanside Café was teeming with so much activity the regular morning customers were happy she set up an outdoor station for those managing to get into the parking lot for takeout orders. Still, she had a full complement of kitchen and wait staff serving up more coffee and breakfast sandwiches than she ever had before.

"These guys are packing it away!" Hokulani said to her crew. "Keep that food coming and make sure you guys write down everything that leaves this kitchen—sandwiches, coffee, muffins, everything. I gotta give them an accurate bill, or I won't get paid, you got it? After all, I'm not running a charity."

Officers in and out of uniform, some from other precincts, some still half asleep, gathered around hastily constructed wall charts, maps, and handouts of the Makaha and Waianae Valleys, and the infamous Kolekole Pass. Not since local boxer Kid Kimo captured the heavyweight title thirty years prior had the Waianae Coast experienced such a large police presence. But the commotion this morning wasn't about a parade for a local boy who made it big. This was about a manhunt for a local serial killer, a missing cop, and an elderly woman who was already feared dead.

Even though onlookers couldn't get near the café,

Farrington Highway, as well as the side streets, was clogged with residents capturing cell phone video and buzzing with misinformation ranging from the number of killers taking refuge in the hills to the inflated number of female victims. One blurred image of a "body" washed up at a beach park during a large birthday celebration was posted to social media and quickly debunked when a local marine biologist identified it as a sleeping monk seal. Television news reporters were eager to put any number of storytellers on the air as long as the tale being told was more sensational than what the competition was broadcasting. When word got around that HPD was looking for Nicky Costa, about a dozen men who had fallen victim to one or more of his scams had already taken up arms and headed into the mountains. There was no doubt among police brass and reporters alike that there would be a number of casualties before nightfall.

Captain Tanaka, Henry, and Kaelani huddled with several assistant chiefs and the SWAT commander to discuss the latest intel and how available resources would be allocated. Once brought up to speed, the captain began banging on the table to get everyone's attention. Slowly, the chattering of coffee cups, plates, and utensils ceased, and a myriad of conversations faded to a barely noticeable hum.

"Listen up, people. Everybody settle down." Tanaka started the briefing. "You all have handouts with a photo and a description of Nicky Costa. He is armed, dangerous, and mentally unstable. Do not, I repeat, do not take any chances with this guy. He will kill you in the blink of an eye. You sergeants make sure the men in your respective search groups understand that. But he's not your only threat. It is my understanding there are roughly ten to twelve vigilantes already on the hunt. Their being up there is not sanctioned by this department. We are in the process of trying to identify these individuals and then have friends and family members try to reach out to them to get them to stand down. Unfortunately, cell service up in those mountains is sketchy. Be advised they are trigger happy and, to complicate matters, I'm told two people offered up a bounty on Costa's head, and a third is willing to pay for a boar or a goat. Be careful, and make no mistake that any encounter with these motivated individuals can also be deadly. With that said, if you run into one of these guys and you think your life is in danger…well, let your training take over and do what you gotta do to protect yourself and your team. I'm going to turn this over to Detective Kanakina, but first, you all know Hank Benjamin." Tanaka pointed to Henry who was cheered with a well-meaning chorus of *"Dirty Henry!"*

Maya, who was one of the wait staff serving coffee to the officers, looked at her husband who could only shrug in his embarrassment.

"In spite of his current status," the captain continued, "Hank has been working this case with Detective Kanakina, and he will be joining in on the search."

While caught watching Maya work the room refreshing empty coffee cups, Kaelani was greeted with a few whistles and catcalls when she stepped forward to speak.

"Nice, very nice! A very professional response,

you guys. I think you should keep in mind that those vigilantes may not be the only ones up on that mountain today who could be trigger happy." She focused on a few of those vocal officers. "I know some of you are familiar with Costa. You've either had minor run-ins with him over the years, or if you grew up here on the coast like I did, you know him pretty well, and you know what he's capable of. I'm sorry to say that I know him too well. At least I thought I did. But what I do know of him is that he is a creature of habit. Up here on the wall is a map of the three main areas where he has been known to do most of his illegal activities over the years, and on top of that, they're places he's been known to disappear when people or various law enforcement agencies had been looking for him. Anyone who knows these areas also knows how to avoid being found and/or set a successful ambush. One area that he loves is over here in the Waianae Valley"— she pointed to the map—"way up on the Ka'ala Hiking Trail, especially as it runs along the Hiu Stream. To the teams that are assigned to that area, keep in mind that the backwoods all along Plantation Road going up the mountain are areas that he's also been known to do his dirty work. So, what I'm saying is, stay completely focused as no stone should remain unturned."

"You sergeants just arriving, especially you guys in the K-9 units, you'll each get assigned grids where you and your teams will focus. Each time you complete a grid, make sure you call in," added Tanaka.

"Another area that needs to be covered is in the Makaha Valley up near the Kaneaki Heiau. As you know, this is an ancient and very sacred site. The cultural significance cannot be overstated. A number of times over the years, my relatives told me that he would sometimes go up there, but for whatever reason that area seems to spook him, or at least it used to. I guess it has something to do with the legend that the original temple was a site for human sacrifice. You all know Detective Iona is missing. He might be a hostage. There's also a picture in your packet of an older woman, one of Costa's neighbors. It's possible that she too can be a hostage or that both of them could already be dead. But either way, if he did go up there, in his current state of mind, he could very well have taken either one there to perform a sacrifice. Regardless, any teams heading up that way please be respectful of the site."

"Costa's other favorite place is over here along this closed section of road that goes to the top of Kolekole Pass," Henry continued. "As you know, this property up here is under control of the U.S. Army. They've gotten word that we're conducting a manhunt, and we have permission to search this area. For now, all training exercises out of Schofield Barracks have been suspended in this region until they hear from us. But their patience and cooperation has its limits. If you should encounter anybody wearing the current ACU or any other form of army combat uniform, you can be confident they are not military personnel. And while we don't know what Costa is presently wearing, he does have a history of dressing up in military-style clothing. But if he is, trust me, nobody that fat is gonna be an active-duty soldier," he said to a round of laughter. "Just like with the other areas we're searching this morning, anywhere along these roads, trails, and backwoods areas leading up to the pass are fair game, and they need to be carefully canvassed."

"One more thing to keep in mind, people...given the extent of this search, and knowing the rumors that we've all heard over the years, don't be surprised if you come across the remains of a hiker, a runaway, or even one of our *kupuna* with Alzheimer's who wandered off and disappeared. Lord knows we have a ton of cold cases. So, it's already hot, it's gonna get hotter, and if you're not used to this kind of physical activity, there'll be a tendency to get sloppy and miss things. Take breaks and stay hydrated as much as you have to, but please, let's not get cavalier out there. Guard your six. If there are no questions, come get your grid assignments, assemble your men and supplies, and let's get to work," Tanaka said, then turned to Henry. "You're gonna stick with Kaelani, correct?"

"Yes, we're gonna head up to the Kolekole Pass."

"Oh? You got a strong feeling about that location?"

"Kaelani does. She remembers Costa always threatening her Auntie Tesha with a 'one-way trip to the pass.' She feels that's where he's gonna be. I'm going with her to make sure she doesn't do anything she'll regret."

"Uh-huh." Tanaka was skeptical. "Who else is going with you?"

"Just the two of us. If she's right, the more people we have with us, the less chance of surprising him."

"And what about you? Is she gonna keep you from doing something you'll regret?" Henry didn't answer. "I want you guys to take someone else with you...just to be safe."

"To be safe, or to babysit us?"

"Hank, you're in enough hot water. I want another

person with you two, understood?"

Reluctantly, Henry agreed that one more person would be beneficial. While he looked around the dining room for an acceptable addition, Maya had come over with a to-go bag packed with sandwiches. They hugged, kissed, and he noticed Mendoza watching him from the other side of the café. When their eyes met, the lieutenant tossed his food into a wastebasket, nodded, then left through a side door.

"Don't even think about it," Tanaka said. "I've got other plans for him."

"I was actually thinking about Taberejo, the rookie who blew chunks all over the place at Auntie Lily's a few days ago."

Chapter 17

Sometimes I pace the floor,
unable to quiet the messages
that come in the night when all is still.
They come at all hours,
at times without warning.
Some with reverence for what was,
some with caution for what is to come.
What is to come is yet unknown,
but still I am guided.
I have wondered if I am truly an oracle.
While I dare not claim to be a prophet,
many of these prophecies have manifested.
Nonetheless, there are times I worry
that I might have misled you.
Please heed this message that comes back to me.
As it is always most quiet before the daybreak,
the birds still sing with the sunrise,
and it always rains before the rainbow,
or so it seems.
Sometimes I pace the floor
because I know this is our destiny.
I see you ready to storm the gates.
You do not fear this final conflict.
I am told what was could be again
if we believe it is within us to make it so,
but should we?

*I believe what happened in the past
happened for a reason.
Caution is the key.*

Even with the borrowed four-wheel drive they used
to negotiate the large potholes and downed tree
branches on the partially paved road leading up to the
Kolekole Pass, the heavy downpour that rolled over the
island in the pre-dawn hours caused a rock and
mudslide. Considered minor by some, it nonetheless
presented an insurmountable challenge for the aging
truck and forced Henry, Kaelani, and Officer Taberejo
to abandon their attempts and continue the journey on
foot.

Already feeling inconvenienced having the rookie
officer with them, Kaelani began to complain to Henry
while simultaneously chiding the young man—now
cramping and growing nauseous from a hangover and
impeding their progress up the mountain.

"Of all the people you had to pick to come with us,
Hank, you had to pick this kid? He's one of the reasons
I got blamed for a sloppy crime scene."

Still embarrassed from his performance at Luau
Cove a few days prior, Taberejo worked hard to keep
his breakfast down as he tried to keep pace with the
veteran detectives.

"How long you been on the job, Officer?" Kaelani
asked without having to look back to know he was
struggling.

"I graduated the academy a few months ago, top
half of my class," he replied with bravado.

"Seriously? A kid as young as you shouldn't have
to be working this hard to keep up with us. How'd you

266

get so outta shape already?" she pressed.

"If I wasn't out late last night…" he began, then leaned against a tree to vomit.

"Boozing it up and then stuffing yourself at an all-night buffet? How many greasy bacon sandwiches you pack away this morning?"

"Ease up on the kid, will ya?" Henry interceded.

"What's the matter, Hank? Am I stealing your thunder?"

"Just the same, there'll be plenty of time to make him feel inadequate. Right now, I think it best for all of us to focus on the task at hand."

"And how do you think that's gonna work out for us if the end result of this guy's lack of self-control's gonna alert Costa we're up here?"

"I'll bet he already knows we're on the way," Henry offered although he knew she was right and empathized with her internal struggle over what was going to happen. The noise Taberejo was making as he surrendered his breakfast would surely announce their presence. He walked back to counsel the officer.

"Taberejo…it's John, isn't it?" He placed a hand on his back to comfort him as another eruption came to the surface. "Steady, son, watch the shoes!"

"Richie, my name is Richie."

"Wipe your mouth, Richie, and take some advice about something I learned early on. If you know you're gonna be working the next day, you can't be out the night before acting like you're a frat boy. It doesn't work well with this kind of job. Understand?"

"Copy that, Detective." Again, he heaved.

"Okay, you wanna be a big help to us and this mission? You go on back to the truck. There's a cooler full of water back there that we'll need to keep us hydrated, and you obviously need some now. But there's also a small shovel in the utility bin. Start moving the debris to create enough clearance so you'll be able to get that truck up here. Otherwise, we'll have to hike the whole way. And if you think Detective Kanakina is in a bad mood now, you just wait and see how nasty she can get, got it?"

"By myself? It'll take forever," Taberejo protested.

"Then you better get on it right away."

A dejected Richie Taberejo headed back down the path, and Kaelani nodded her approval as the two of them continued their trek.

"Hank, you've never really seen me get nasty, let alone real nasty."

"I'll bet that's one helluva sight to see."

"Pray you never do. I can't believe the decisions he's making, but I gotta say, though, you handled the kid pretty well. You and Maya gotta have kids, am I right?"

"C'mon, are you telling me you weren't like that when you were his age?"

"What, you think I look that much older than him?"

Henry nodded.

"Hell, I'm not *that* much older than he is, and when I was his age, I just finished the roughest youth boot camp designed to keep me from doing stupid shit like that. What about you?"

"I'm a guy. We make mistakes."

"So you're saying you were just as stupid," she stated as a forgone conclusion.

"More like educated through experience," he

countered.

"So I interpret that to mean you were just as stupid, and you survived a few close calls."

"More than a few, but that about sums it up," he surrendered.

"And yet you became a cop."

"You proved your point. Are you happy now?"

After another mile of switchbacks, their pace slowed considerably from the combination of increasing thirst, heat, and altitude. They agreed to catch a breath at the next vista point where Henry reflexively dug through his pockets for a cigarette, then realized the irony.

"I think it's time I gave these things up."

"I was just thinking the same thing. I'm glad the kid isn't up here to see us gasping for air."

"He'd be justified to criticize."

"And then some. Our secret?"

"Our secret! I wonder how much longer it'll take him to get up here with that water?"

"Don't know, I'll bet he's working on a good case of dry heaves by now. If he does manage to get the truck through, he'll quickly catch up to us, so I think we should wait for him."

"Just another minute or two. I wanna keep moving."

"Not for nothing, but since you brought up smoking, that Japanese brand that you smoke…even with the large number of Japanese tourists we get every year, it's still an uncommon brand. It's the same brand of cigarette found in the bushes at Auntie Lily's." Her remark more probing than curious.

"And with the other vics…except Leilani. There

was a different one left with her body. Still, it's pretty freaky, if you're not looking at the specifics of the case."

"And that doesn't bother you in some way? You know, because of how it looks to those who don't know all the details?"

"I know perfectly well how it looks, but I think we both know that it was just one tool Costa was using to taunt me, just like with the notes. He got into my place and stole my shield, right? I figure he saw the butts in the ashtray and..." Henry stopped mid-sentence, squinting to get a better look through the trees. "Hey, come here and take a look. You see that down there?"

"What, where are you looking?"

"Way down there." He pointed to the bottom of a cliff. "Look through the breaks in the trees. You see that thing?"

"That black thing next to the pile of white things, yeah?"

"Yeah, that looks like, what, a hundred-fifty, maybe a two-hundred-foot drop? Does that look like a car to you? Like maybe Billy's car?"

"Hard to tell from the shape or from the way the light is hitting it. But he had a dark-blue unit, didn't he?"

"It could be dark blue, but I thought his car was black. You're right, though, I can't tell."

"It could be a big pile of garbage bags, no? I mean people come up here all the time to dump their old refrigerators, bathtubs, stuff like that. See that white pile?" She studied the length of the drop.

"But does it make sense they'd drive that far up to throw the stuff back down? That's nuts."

"Unless there's no trail down there to drive their loads in. Check it out." She pointed to the rock face. "I don't see any fresh gashes in the rock or in the pine and eucalyptus trees along the way down."

"Like a heavy object made of metal would do. I see your point. But there are some gash marks on those trees. See them?"

"Those look pretty weathered if you ask me. But if it is Billy's car, and if he's in there, and assuming he wasn't already dead, I doubt he would've survived the impact," she theorized.

"Either way, we should call it in to Tanaka so he can get a team in there to investigate."

"Okay, agreed. But I'm not getting any signal, are you?"

"Hell no, not a thing. Try anyway, just in case."

After three attempts and no reply, she motioned to Henry it was useless.

"So much for that idea. We can try again when we get closer to the top. Want me to try checking in with Taberejo?"

"Let him work," he said. "I don't want him to think we don't trust him."

"I'm beginning to think you like this kid."

"He's all right. I just feel sorry for him is all."

"That's on you. Let's take a look at the map. If I'm not mistaken, the trail forks after this next bend. Split up or stay together? It's your call."

****

Cursing with each shovelful of dirt, mud, and softball sized rocks that weighed about five pounds each, Richie Taberejo worked as hard as he was physically able. He desperately wanted to be a viable asset to the team, and he was determined to demonstrate he wasn't an irresponsible screw-up—not that anyone had accused him as much, but in his mind, he surely gave that impression to the people he wanted to impress the most. When he heard Kaelani's voice crackle over the portable radio, he attempted to fight off another wave of dry heaves while continuing to clear a path through the debris field. "I'm almost there. I can do this. I can get it done," he chanted over and over to himself before he retched again.

"Damn it! I'm almost there. I can do this. I can get it done. Just a few more shovels full, and I'll be able to move that damn rock…that big, damn rock that's in the middle of the path."

He tried to rally until exhaustion got the better of him. In frustration, he tossed the shovel to the ground, grabbed a bottle of water from the cooler, and made himself comfortable on the front seat of the truck. He leaned back, closed his eyes, and told himself it would only be for a minute—just until his strength returned. Then he'd make the final push necessary to get moving up the mountain. "I can do this. They'll be proud of me that I came through."

The bottle felt good over his forehead and cheeks. He eased it over the back of his neck, the coolness sending a shiver down his spine. He let out a long sigh. "Drink it already, and let's get back to work." He sucked down half of the sixteen-ounce container when his empty stomach rebelled with cramps from the sudden shock of the cold. Taberejo doubled over, then forced himself into a fetal position when he fell across the bench-style seat. Holding onto himself and rocking back and forth, he remained that way for several minutes as the intensity gradually faded—pushing himself to an upright posture when he heard footsteps squishing in the mud and heavy breathing coming up from behind him.

****

It had been twenty minutes since Henry and Kaelani split up at the fork. The path he won by coin toss began to narrow to the point that no vehicle would be able to navigate. "She practically busted a gut when it came up tails. I'll bet she knew all along I was making the wrong choice," he complained through standing puddles of muddy water as the mosquitos feasted. Regardless, he was grateful for the machete she insisted he bring—finding it useful to help clear the overgrowth that increasingly blocked his way. That overgrowth, however, was the least of his worries as the crack of distant gunshots shattered the silence and reminded him of the civilian posse who were also on the hunt for a crazed killer. When he imagined one of them crossing paths with some wild game, he remembered the importance of staying vigilant, as the slightest rustling could signal an angry goat or boar ready to charge out of a thicket. To him, that was more of a threat than a few trigger-happy warriors whose lack of stealth would provide plenty of warning that they were nearby. *At least there's no snakes on this island,* he thought while swinging his blade through a few more of the tenacious vines.

After several more minutes of fighting nature and stumbling over the occasional remnants of a teenage rendezvous, Henry decided to double back and rejoin Kaelani. Using the pre-selected channel on his portable radio, his attempt to check in with her, or Taberejo, was unsuccessful. Both the radio and his cellular were useless, and he cursed the lack of reception as well as the absence of a cell tower. *Hopefully, the kid got up here with that water.*

****

Richie Taberejo held onto his stomach and prayed to God and his guardian angels with all his might. As he crawled on his belly, images of flowing magma came to mind in a scenario that had him describing his pain should a team of paramedics miraculously happen by. He knew the chances of that occurring were next to impossible and once again felt embarrassed. But this time it was for his recent lapse in faith, and he now found himself wishing his social life hadn't been such a betrayal to his Catholic upbringing. He rolled over onto his back and used his legs to prop himself against a rock while watching the truck creep up the mountain road until it was out of sight.

"Father Dominick, Lord Jesus, I need you," he cried, then lifted a muddy hand, now covered in blood from his wounds, and raised it toward the sky.

"All things are possible through Christ our Lord, Richie." He heard his priest's voice.

"Yes, Father Dominick, I know."

"Even in our darkest hour, he stands with us."

"Yes, Father Dominick, I know."

"Your faith and belief in him, accepting him as your lord and savior, is all that he asks of us to be granted eternal life."

"Yes, Father Dominick, I have, I have."

"Then confess your sins and pray with me, my son, and all will be forgiven."

Tears and beads of sweat coalesced into larger

drops that streamed down over his boyish face. His lips quivering, he crossed himself and began:

"Forgive me, Father, for I have sinned..."

****

From her crouched position behind a tree, Kaelani was flooded with emotions she had not experienced since she was a little girl—when family members gathered to discuss the different ways Nicky Costa could have killed and disposed of her Auntie Tesha. With each theory more graphic than the one before, it was almost as if the relatives were intentionally trying to outdo one another. She had carried those stories to bed each night for many months, only to wake up screaming from the horrific images that filled her dreams and soaked her sheets.

For years she had also dreamed of revenge—her temper boiling over each time she was inadvertently reminded of how Tesha must have suffered. She also dreamed of carrying out any one of those tortuous theories on Costa. She was angry and carried that anger within her for all these years. And she blamed that anger for her behavior as a wild teen as well as for the severe beating she had inflicted on a girlfriend who had cheated on her. Just the thought of being betrayed by anyone with whom she confided her most inner feelings and secrets triggered an internal rage—the same rage that necessitated a late-night emergency session with her therapist after she had learned Mary was actually Maya.

With the realization Nicky Costa's judgment day had arrived and that she would finally be able to get payback, she was unexpectedly blindsided by the sight of his latest act of brutality. She was almost breathless, and now it was Kaelani's turn to force down a wave of nausea.

"Oh, Uncle Billy." She fought back tears. "You poor, sweet man. You didn't deserve this. You didn't deserve this at all."

Gun drawn, she stepped away from her cover for a better visual of the dense tree line that bordered the open field before her. And although her scrutiny proved fruitless, she knew Nicky was still there: hiding, watching, waiting to pounce. She felt his presence—a dark, unholy energy that weighed as heavy on her now as it did when the fear of haunting dreams and night terrors dominated her youth.

"Nicky, you sonofabitch," she yelled loud enough for her voice to carry throughout the forest and give cause for birds to protest as they took flight from the trees. "I know you're still here. I know you're watching me. Come on out from under your rock, you sick pervert, and face me like the man you desperately wanna be. We settle our business today, do you hear me? It all gets settled today! It's time for you to go back to hell!"

His mix of laughter and coughing also breached the stillness.

"Well, if it isn't little lolo Lani! What makes you think you're so innocent?" His voice not as threatening as it once was, he remained unseen and attempted to provoke her.

"What in God's name is wrong with you?" She ignored the bait. "Did you have to do this to Billy? Did you have to kill him this way? What did this gentle soul ever do to you to make you wanna cut off his head and put it on the end of a stake?"

"Don't you like it? It's my way of showing you what I'm gonna do to you and your partner. That's right; you've got a lot to answer for too, yeah? You don't think I know what you've done?"

"Ha! Typical paranoid narcissist Nicky, always trying to turn it around on people. Well, I'm not falling for the mind games you've played on the people you've scammed all these years."

"You think you're better than me? You think that goddamn transplant is better than me? Where is he by the way? I always knew he was a pussy. At least *you* have the guts to come up here to take me on. I wanted to ask him how he's doing without the comfort of his beautiful wife." He coughed a little blood. "I guess he was just too scared to come face me. It's pretty funny when you think about it."

"I'm right here, Costa," Henry answered, "and my wife's doing great! Gave her a big hug and kiss this morning."

Kaelani turned to find Henry standing by Billy's car.

"She doing great? Bullshit! Wanna know something? I fucked her that night. That's right, I did her like she'd never been done before, and she loved it. She told me she wished her man could do her like I did her. And you know what the best part was? It was when all her moaning of pleasure turned to squeals of pain. She squealed just like the wife of a pig would squeal. She squealed like the pig she was when I stuck her and carved her up. I did it nice and slow. So I don't think she's doing so great because I killed your little bitch! And you know what? Today I'm gonna make you squeal like a pig too!"

The intensity of Costa's diatribe increased the volume of blood now flowing freely from his mouth. What he couldn't wipe away with his shirt, he forcibly spit to keep from swallowing.

"You've been reading too many of those porn magazines, Costa. We all know you're blowing smoke outta your ass, because everybody knows you're unable to screw anything anymore, not even those little girls you used to do before your prison days. Yup, we all had a good laugh about that down at the station when I dug out those photos of you being dragged off to county lockup in your shit-stained underwear."

Aided by the tree that shielded him, Costa pulled himself up to his feet, steadied himself, and tried to take aim at Henry.

"Keep on talking, boy. I'm gonna enjoy putting a bullet in your head and cutting you up. I'm gonna enjoy neutering you."

"Hank, please," Kaelani pleaded through clenched teeth, "this guy's mine, so take a backseat, okay? I'm gonna take him out."

Although he acknowledged her, Henry still cautioned he needed Costa alive.

"I forgot to tell you, Costa," he continued, "you killed the wrong girl that night. You screwed it up. Like everything else you've done in your worthless life, you messed up. You can't get a damn thing right because you're so incompetent. You're a loser, Costa, a major league failure."

"Come outta the woods, you coward," Kaelani said and made her way up to the six-foot bamboo pole that supported Billy's head. She toppled it with one push and watched it fall into the open grave where the rest of his body lay. "You've got a lot to answer for. Those girls, Judy Coleman, Uncle Billy, Auntie Tesha!"

"You think I'm stupid? You think I'm gonna show myself and let you shoot me? Not a chance. I'm not the one who's gonna die today."

"You wanna know something, Kaelani?" Henry yelled. "When Nicky was in prison, he was somebody's bitch. Isn't that right, Costa? I heard you enjoyed being on the receiving end."

Costa fired off a round from Billy's gun—the ricochet missing Henry's ear by inches.

Taking cover where they stood, both detectives continued to study the gaps in the trees—looking for any sign of movement. There was none. But they both knew he was still there as any attempt to run off into the woods would have yielded the telltale sounds of Costa's heavy feet pounding over layers of dead needles and cones from the rocket-shaped pine trees.

"Would you please back down and let me handle this, damn it!" she chastised Henry.

Henry debated having her provide him covering fire so he could make a break for the trees, until he heard the grinding of transmission gears coming up the path. *I can't believe this kid doesn't know how to drive a stick. At least he finally got here.* Without turning to see Mendoza behind the wheel, he called out to Taberejo. "Careful, Richie, we got him, we got Costa up ahead, and he just took a shot at us. Stay down and get over here behind me, okay, kid?"

"Sure, I'll stay behind you," Mendoza responded.

He didn't have to turn around to see that it wasn't Taberejo, but he did anyway. With Mendoza bleeding profusely from a gunshot wound to the shoulder, Henry suspected the bullet hit a main artery that ran from the neck to the upper arm. The ashen-looking lieutenant supported himself against the front fender. Noticing Taberejo wasn't in the truck, he recalled hearing the two gunshots and now suspected the rookie officer was dead.

"Look at you." A weakened Mendoza smirked. "Caught between a rock and a hard place, aren't you?"

"You're hurt, Lieutenant. Let me help you," Henry said, trying to get the advantage.

"You wanna help me? Now that's funny. You've never wanted to help me with anything."

"Where's Richie? Where's the kid?"

"All he had to do was listen to me. All he had to do was get out of the truck, give me his gun, and put on the cuffs. Would he listen? Nah. Somehow, he knew…and he tried to stop me, stupid kid. He should've listened." Mendoza's knees buckled, and he went down.

Henry saw the opportunity to disarm him and charged. Off balance and panicked, Mendoza fired without taking aim—the hollow-point bullet ripping into Kaelani's hip—fragmenting the bone as if it were papier-mâché.

Costa came stumbling out from the trees before Henry could shift his focus away from Mendoza to his wounded partner. He came up from behind her, got her into a crude version of a chokehold, then rested the barrel of Billy's gun onto the side of her head.

"I told you, I'm not the one who's gonna die today." He slobbered into her ear while tightening his grip.

Trying in vain to break free, she clawed at his arm but got nowhere.

Mendoza lay bleeding out from the wound he sustained during his struggle with Taberejo—the pain more than he could tolerate. Henry, now held hostage at gunpoint, remained standing over the stricken man.

"It looks like I've got the upper hand." He struggled to keep his head up.

"I don't know exactly why or how you're involved in all this, or if you're just looking at this as an opportunity to kill me, but I'm looking at your wound, and one thing's for certain…" He dove for cover as several bullets fired by Costa shattered the truck's windshield. He scrambled to knock the gun from Mendoza's hand—the resistance all but absent.

"I got your partner, Detective Benjamin. I got little lolo Lani right here." Costa jerked her up, then slammed her down, her shattered hip hitting against the ground. "You gonna come and rescue her?"

Henry took the gun from Mendoza's lifeless hand, zeroed in on Costa, and proceeded to walk back up the path.

"I'm right here, Nicky. Put her down, and me and you will settle our business, because that's what this is all about, isn't it?"

"Hank," Kaelani called, "take the shot, take him out."

"Too dangerous. I might hit you."

"You're a great shot. I saw all your trophies," she lied. "You can hit anything from fifty yards. You can do this. I trust you."

"Yes, Hank," Costa mocked, then turned Kaelani into a moving target, "go ahead and take the shot."

"Don't mind him, Hank. Take the shot, take ten shots, just kill this bastard already."

Distracted by Henry taking aim while he walked briskly toward them, Costa had loosened his grip enough for Kaelani to ram an elbow into his groin. He doubled over, lost control of his prisoner, and Henry fired a round that took off three fingers on Costa's gun hand. He had been aiming for his chest. Continuing to advance for the final kill shot, he raised his gun, squeezed the trigger, but nothing happened. He squeezed again. Still nothing. Eyes bulging with sheer terror, Costa began to backpedal past Kaelani while Henry ejected a jammed round, then slammed in a new clip. He raised the weapon again and sighted his target. With Costa's eyes locked onto him, Kaelani grabbed the length of bamboo that had been used to mount Billy's severed head. She shoved it between Costa's legs, causing him to fall onto his back, barely escaping death as the second shot grazed his forehead. Grunting and still coughing blood, Costa now peed himself. Henry drew closer, pulled back on the hammer, and watched Nicky inch backward, crying and pleading the same way he did when Henry busted him ten years earlier.

"Say goodbye, you worthless waste of human life," Henry said without emotion.

Their eyes locked one final time, with one man taking a deep breath, and the other now too frightened to breathe at all. Henry took aim, then lowered the weapon to watch Costa back himself over the cliff— falling two hundred feet into the piles of garbage he had helped to create.

Chapter 18

Once the war is over,
the healing can begin.
At least that is what we tell ourselves
time and again.
But no warrior, I am told,
be they victor or vanquished,
emerges without scars.
Deep or shallow, real or imagined,
earthbound in anguish,
or freed from our chains,
the residuals hurt just the same.
And regardless of their claim,
there are no innocent bystanders
who willingly send their loved ones off to the fray.
I am guilty as charged.
An act of indiscretion?
A feeling of remorse?
Perhaps.
But had we not acted,
would we even be here to lament the cost?
While I suffer this paradox
I beg your forgiveness.

Richie Taberejo brightened up when Henry stopped in to visit. Although it had only been a week since his surgery, he greeted each new day with a positive attitude and amazing progress that impressed his doctors. And while they were quick to accept praise from the media, Taberejo credited his progress to all the single nurses at the Kamehameha Medical Center who made it a point to visit the handsome young police officer as often as they could. Henry marveled at the display of flowers, chocolates, and a variety of stuffed animals deposited by his growing band of admirers—some going as far as to offer personal services as soon as he was discharged.

"Looks like you've got it made, kid."

"It can be embarrassing at times."

"Yeah, sure! Tell me you're not in heaven with all this attention." Henry picked up a small panda to read the note—his eyes widened at the suggestive nature. "The bullet didn't kill you, but what this girl wants to do to you just might."

"My dad is bragging to all his buddies and, when my mom was here yesterday, she kept asking the nurses if they were married. She even invited a few to come by for dinner when I get released—of course, not at the same time."

"No, of course not. This is your fifteen minutes, kid. Enjoy the attention while you can."

"I'm glad you stopped by because I have questions, and nobody'll give me any answers about what really went on that day…like with Lieutenant Mendoza…I just don't understand."

"Don't worry about any of that. After we debriefed, I heard the department is not even close to thinking about charging you with anything. They know he attacked you, and you shot in self-defense. Case closed."

"To be honest, I wasn't worried about that. I just don't understand what that whole thing was about. I mean, he just came outta nowhere and pulled a weapon on me and..."

"Relax, kid, it wasn't about you. Just know that some guys get involved with things they shouldn't. They make bad choices and, before they know it, they're in way too deep for their own good. Eventually, it all catches up to 'em. They find themselves backed into a corner and see no way out. What Mendoza did last week was of his own doing. He backed himself into that corner, understood?"

"Copy that. I hear Billy's funeral is set for next week."

"Yeah, full departmental honors and everything. The mayor and city council's gonna issue a proclamation. There's even talk of naming a park after him. With the way the city neglects its parks, I don't know if that's such a good thing. Anyway, I'm told all the cable news outlets are gonna cover the memorial service as well as the procession."

"No disrespect, but wasn't he already...I mean, weren't you and Detective Kanakina—"

"Richie, don't worry about the details. Just know the right thing is being done." Henry smiled.

"And what about you?"

"What about me?"

"Do you think you're gonna get your job back?"

Henry handed a box of fresh malasadas to one of the two nurses who stopped in to give Taberejo a new bag of saline and check his scheduled medications.

"I think you should focus on getting better. With that said, I best get out of the way so these young ladies can do their job. Make sure you share these goodies with them, kid. I gotta go check in on Detective Kanakina."

****

Respectful of her social standing within Oahu's most prestigious circles, and sensitive to her history of charitable work in the blue-collar communities of the Waianae Coast, the federal, state, and city authorities investigating the claims presented in the materials that had been assembled and forwarded on behalf of the late Nicky Costa, allowed Noelani Mendoza the week to bury her son before presenting herself for questioning by the various agencies.

On the morning she arrived at the federal building for her appointment with the FBI, she waited for the driver to assist her to exit from the limousine, no different than if she had been attending a champagne brunch at the polo club in Waimanalo. But today, instead of a light and airy flowery ensemble, she was dressed in black leather from head to toe—the stiletto-heeled thigh-high boots creating quite the media buzz.

Ignoring the throng of reporters, the lone surviving member of the Mendoza family was greeted by the agent in charge who apologized for the inconvenience before escorting her to his office.

As with the other agencies, the FBI said it found no credible evidence warranting an in-depth investigation into the accusations made against her. For the sake of optics, however, they still had a few cursory questions about Costa's rambling and incoherent diatribe, and his connection to her son. Little did she know that a separate federal investigation into multiple violations of campaign finance laws and money laundering linking

Carmen Ramos-Brown to the Mendozas was gearing up to get underway.

With this day's business concluded and upon exiting the building, she approached the press. Through crocodile tears, she briefly explained her suspicions that Peter had been having significant emotional issues since the loss of his beloved father which had been exacerbated by the stress of his job. The thought that her son had been involved with such an evil man like Costa compounded the regret she now carried for never having said anything to his superiors or encouraging him to seek out professional help.

"I've done a great deal of reflection over this past week," she began her rehearsed summation, "and while my heart aches for not recognizing my son's pain, please know that this experience, what he did, is what I now have to live with. But I pledge to all of you that I will turn this into an opportunity to benefit others. That is why, on behalf of the Ernesto Mendoza charitable trust, a donation will be made to the Queen Emma Mental Health Research Institute at the university. In spite of my poor son's actions, and I do not excuse them, I truly believe his was a cry for help…a cry that fell upon my deaf ears. I can only pray that the good people of Oahu, my *ohana*, my family, can one day find it in their hearts to forgive him and to forgive me. I trust that with this significant contribution, great strides will be made so that all of us will hear and respond to those cries for help before anything like this ever happens again. After all, it is our *kuleana*, our responsibility, to look out for one another. So now, I will take the time to mourn and be with the memories that I hold of my Peter when he was an innocent and happy little boy. *Ka`u* *po`e ipo*, my loved ones, *aloha nui loa a hui hou, a hui hou.*"

****

Like Richie Taberejo, Kaelani Kanakina had tubes and wires going in and coming out of her to monitor vital signs and administer a myriad of medications from antibiotics to opioid pain relievers. Unlike Richie, Kaelani did not receive an abundance of flowers, chocolates, or visitors. Her room was not barren by any stretch of the imagination as media coverage of the events during the past week, which also focused on women in law enforcement, saw the delivery of several floral arrangements along with inquiries about her relationship status.

When she woke from her drug-induced slumber, the blurred vision of Henry slumped in a chair had her wondering through her fog if she was still asleep. He had dozed off from a combination of emotional fatigue, the rhythmic beeping of her heart monitor, and the late afternoon sun heating the small private room.

"If you're not a dream," she slurred, "please get up and turn on the air conditioner. I'm roasting here."

Henry woke, pushed himself to an upright position, yawned, and rubbed his eyes.

"Sorry, didn't mean to nod off like that. Huh, you're alive."

"…air conditioner, please," she repeated.

"Sure thing." He forced himself up and spied the control box by the door.

"…and something to drink, something with…ice," she ordered. "My throat's dry."

"Coming right up. How you feeling?"

"…besides the cotton mouth…" Her words coming

slow, she smiled. "Totally stoned outta my mind."

"That could be a good thing. Maybe I should let you go back to sleep."

"Go...no, wait. On second thought, stay. Let's talk."

"Sure, but are you gonna remember any of it later on?"

"...I doubt it. But if I go back to sleep, the little bunnies...they're gonna return."

"They got you on some powerful meds."

"Yeah, I guess...but it's okay. The bunnies are really, really friendly."

"I see you have a few admirers. I think it's nice."

"...yeah, I think a couple marriage proposals." She laughed.

"So, what do you wanna know? What I can tell you?"

"...I've been thinking about Uncle Billy. I know you guys...you guys had your...problems, yeah? But he was a good man. He really was...you know? He was, um...he had a good heart. He...he looked after us kids when...when Auntie T went away."

"I know. I know all about it. Don't worry, though, I took care of it. I fixed it for him with Tanaka, and the brass signed off on the captain's report. You and Billy are getting all the credit for hunting down Costa, and the media's eating it up like you wouldn't believe. One headline read, 'Two Kanaka Maoli Take Down the West Side Butcher.' Billy's getting his promotion to sergeant and the Warrior Gold Medal for Valor—the department's highest honor. By the way, you and the kid will be getting those medals too."

"...that's crazy. What...what the hell did you tell

him, and why?"

"I only said what needed to be said."

"But why, Hank? You had a...a chance to save your job."

"It's not as if I made anything up; I just left a few details out. It's about time the locals had more than a homegrown athlete to hold up on a pedestal. And who knows, maybe this will instill enough pride to inspire local kids to wanna become cops."

"...and what about you, Hank? You not getting any credit at all?"

"Don't worry about me. I'm just glad I got off that mountain in one piece. I'm glad that you and Taberejo are gonna be okay. I'm glad I got my wife back, and now...now I need to address some of my own issues. I just wanna get my life back."

"...yeah, your wife...she tricked me, she really tricked me."

"She tricked a lot of people, but that was all my doing. It needed to be done."

"...the docs said my hip...my hip was busted up in many pieces."

"I heard."

"Dozens, dozens of pieces. I'm so fucked."

"No, you're not. You're strong; you'll get through this."

"...that's easy for you to say."

"I know."

"...I'm out of a job."

"Nonsense. These guys are miracle workers. They can give you an artificial hip that'll be better than the original. And the best part, it's all paid for. So, no negative talk. Sure, it'll take some hard work on your part to rehab, but you're a badass, and you'll be back to your badassery in no time."

She had fallen back to sleep before Henry could finish. He watched her for a moment longer, quite confident and disappointed that she wouldn't remember his visit.

"You're a good cop, and we would've made a pretty good team. Don't forget to count how many bunnies," he whispered in her ear.

****

When he woke face down in the dirt, the hangover and urine-drenched work pants were familiar companions to Keahi. What was different this time when he fought off the glare of the late morning sun beating down on his weathered face was not just the absence of a hungry dog's tongue stroking him back to consciousness, but the presence of police officers and crime scene investigators swarming over his property.

After several days of imbibing and boasting in a couple local bars, more than one concerned patron had telephoned HPD with their suspicions of the junkman's association with Nicky Costa.

Once he was awake and the search warrant was officially served, a few men armed with hydraulic tools began the task of separating sections of the large metal cube with streaks of bright-yellow paint that sat in the middle of the yard.

The noise from the compressor-powered tools that pounded in his head ceased when Judy Coleman's bloodstained shoe was liberated from the steel and plastic block. His head full of cobwebs, Keahi still remembered the mirror-like finish of the Oldsmobile.

"I shoulda trow da ting in da ocean, mon," he

mumbled.

Detectives turned to Keahi, who pleaded ignorance but offered up his wrists nonetheless.

Chapter 19

There will come a time when we ask ourselves
"So, what now, where do we go from here?
Have either of us satisfied our debt?
Are we even close?"
I have wondered when our souls will be allowed
to dance to the music of the cosmos.
I have often contemplated, I have often asked
knowing full well, answers do not come without query.
Then again, regardless of the rationale for being
impetuous,
I wonder if that day will ever see the sunrise.
Forgive me, but I think it is time.
I have watched you more than I've watched anyone.
You have been a loyal companion through the
centuries.
It is part of why I am inexplicably drawn to you.
The rest cannot be put into words.
I innately know you.
With words expressed only in your eyes,
you are not so silent,
especially when it comes to this.
I share your fatigue.
So, when that day does come,
and I believe it has,
let us face this question,
where do we go from here?

Richard I Levine

We have the ability to ignore the pain
as we have the ability to confront it,
bury it, and move on.
Either way, it becomes part of the past.
And that is where it should stay.

From the vantage point of his outdoor table at Hokulani's Oceanside Café, Henry watched the waves crash along Maili beach while nursing his coffee. The breeze coming across Farrington Highway carried the freshness of a morning cleansed by the pre-dawn rain and with it, the floral bouquet of Maya's favorite perfume. It was her favorite because it had always been his favorite. With his eyes closed, he savored the touch of her toes caressing his lower leg. It reminded him of their earlier years together, when life was simple and the future seemed filled with infinite possibilities. It had been too long since the last time she publicly flirted with him. It had been too long since they had been able to sit alone as a couple. In spite of the solemnness of the day, he was happy, and his smile prompted a playful giggle from her. The sound was music to his ears.

For a moment he hesitated opening his eyes for fear that he'd wake alone in his bed and the past eight months had been nothing but a premonition of what was still to come. He had witnessed things that made other men vomit but had him seeking comfort out of a bottle. Many nights he forced himself to stay awake out of fear for his dreams. But they came anyway. They tortured him nonetheless. Henry knew he had no one to blame but himself. He had taken this case because it was personal and the stakes were too high to fail. He thought he knew what the risks were when he fought so hard to get the assignment. He just never counted on the emotional toll that it would take on him. In retrospect, he felt as though he walked through fire. And now that it was over, now that he made it through that trial, a little singed around the edges perhaps, he felt that maybe there was something more personally rewarding that he was supposed to do with his life.

"Three fried eggs sunny side up, a little crispy on the edges, whole wheat bread toasted no butter, three slices of bacon well done. A little too well done if you ask me," Hokulani said, shaking her head, "but I don't gotta eat it. And you got your coffee *without* that special little splash, am I right?"

"Yes Hoku, you're correct, no more special splashes."

"You're getting help?"

"…yeah." He looked at his wife. "I'm getting help."

"Good, Henry, very good! But still, like your taste in women, your coffee is hot, dark, and sweet, just like Maya. And speaking of Maya, I'll have your special breakfast in a minute. Now that I'm shorthanded, we're running a little behind."

"I can help." She started to get up.

"You sit yourself back in that seat and enjoy your man's company. I can manage."

"I wanted to talk to you about that…if it's okay with you," Maya said, watching her husband nibble on his toast. "Perhaps tonight after the ceremony we can talk story?"

"Um, yeah, sure, absolutely," Hoku said, then turned on a heel at the sound of a bell and the words "order up." "Gotta go!"

Maya looked at Henry and, knowing an explanation was now owed, took his hand and liberated a piece of whole wheat.

"I'm starved." She took a bite. "For the first time in months, I woke up with an appetite."

Henry added another sugar to his coffee, stirred, then took a drink.

"You're thinking of continuing to work here?"

"Maybe. I like it here. Great view of the ocean, it's simple work, and the food is good. Like you, I need simple now, Henry. I need safe, though I'm not quite sure what that means."

"What about a return to teaching?"

"I don't know. I need time to think. The other day I drove to the Kuhio academy in Manoa. Hoku let me use her car. I hadn't been there since…you know. Anyway, I parked across the street and sat there watching for a long time. I saw her. I saw Leilani. She was there, in my imagination maybe, but to me it was real. She was real. To me, her spirit went back there, where she was safe. I saw her waiting in the parking lot for her breakfast; I saw her sitting there eating all by herself, alone, lost. I think if I went back there to teach, I would see her every day. If I stay here, in Hawaii, I think I would want to stay here on the leeward side. If I go back to teaching, I think my journey would be better served, more fulfilling, if I were to serve these children here on the coast, not the ones in a private academy in town. These children here are the ones who need our help so that there are no more Leilanis." She studied his face. "I can see you have many questions."

"I think what you're saying is admirable, and I don't disagree. I need…I want simple as well. But 'if you stay here' has me wondering what that means."

"It's been many years since I've been back to the rez. I've spent many nights dreaming of that other part of me, the part I feel I've abandoned on the plains. Those dreams have haunted me, and please don't think I'm minimizing the nightmare you've been living with. I should at least go back and visit the graves of my parents, to pay my respects. To let my mother know we did our best."

"It's true we each suffer our own internal struggle, but please don't ever think for one moment that I blame mine on you."

"I know you don't."

"What you wanna do, to visit your parents, it's reasonable, and yes, it's long overdue. I never knew your mother, but I knew your dad, and he was good to me. He accepted me and trusted me with your care. We should go, and then maybe do a road trip or look for other places to…"

"No…not we." She bowed her head.

"Alone? Seriously?"

"Alone, Henry."

"Why? Is it because of my drinking?"

"No. Lord knows I'm no angel there."

"Have I done anything wrong?"

"No, of course not. I just need some time alone. In these past months, I was so focused on being Mary, I was so focused on the Mendozas and what happened to my mother, I never gave any thought to what was supposed to have happened to me. I still need to process all of this in my own way and at my own pace."

"I understand, but tell me one thing, Maya…do you still love me?"

"Yes, of course I do."

"Do you still need me?"

"Henry! You shouldn't have to ask me that."

"Yes, I do, because…I'm not proud of some of the things I've done, or the way I've done them, and it haunts me. It haunts me in ways that I never thought possible. So I'm suddenly wondering if you feel any different about me. I'm wondering…what if you decide not to come back, or that you…that you wanna be on your own?"

"I understand what you've been going through. I know that you're critical of your decisions, your actions, and yourself. You've always been that way. I understand that this time it's different because there were lives involved. But their deaths weren't your fault. Leilani's death wasn't your fault. Henry, one of the reasons I love you is because you're willing to reflect on things such as this, to ask the tough questions, to want to atone for whatever sins you feel you've committed. Isn't that part of what having a moral compass is all about? And given all that, I wonder if you really want to stay here too. I've sometimes wondered if it hadn't been for me, your exposure to Hawaii would've been nothing more than a luau at Auntie Lily's and a couple surf lessons in Waikiki."

"I've wondered that myself. Long before we had any serious commitment to one another, I made the decision to follow you here because I wanted to be with you. I don't regret that decision, and never have. And know this: if you decide not to come back here, and unless you tell me otherwise, I'm coming after you. You're always talking about the path we're on and the journey. I know in my heart that our journey together is far from over."

"And you'd quit your job?"

"They were never gonna take me back, so I handed in my resignation yesterday. It actually felt liberating to do it."

"But, Henry, you always wanted to be a cop."

"I always wanted to help people. Besides, the system here is so broken, so corrupt, it's a punchline of a very bad joke."

"And what will you do?"

As he was about to answer, Hoku returned with Maya's breakfast.

"Listen up, you two," she said. "I decided to join you later today, if that's all right."

"You're closing early? Now that's a first," Henry said.

"You'll always be a New York smartass." Hokulani leaned over and kissed his head.

"I think your offer is a beautiful gesture," Maya defended. "We'll be gathering at Pokai Bay. You know the time."

"Yeah. I just need to make a few calls and throw a fresh coat of wax on my board."

"We'll have a lei for you," Henry said holding up an empty cup.

"Coming right up," she said, then ran to seat another customer.

"Henry, you didn't answer my question."

"I've got well over a decade of stories from being on the job. I could write about them. I could write a bunch of novels or a few screenplays about a private detective in paradise."

"Or maybe become one?"

"Following cheating husbands, tracking down a missing person, or get involved in one of those outrageous hard-to-believe cases like in one of those private-eye television shows?"

"Maybe it's better to stick to novel writing."

"That sounds like a plan, Maya."

Chapter 20

I feel your uncertainty,
I knew I would.
But listen—
The universe is deliberate, is it not?
Converging paths are every bit integral
to the physical manifestation of our existence
as is the time spent in solitude.
Welcome it.
There are no accidents,
there are no mistakes.
What ego dismisses as random occurrence,
a chance meeting, a fleeting memory,
has always been predestined by source.
They are the signposts,
the messages, the gentle reminders.
There are no accidents.
Be it good or bad,
the lesson, the encounter,
the experience, remains the requisite energy
that fuels the ongoing journey.
Without it, we are stagnant,
condemned to repeat for as long as it takes to learn.
Eternity is infinite and the universe is patient.
When the day comes that our paths diverge,
promise me this,
continue the adventure without remorse,

for we will meet again.

Of all the beaches, coves, and bays along the Waianae coast, Pokai Bay was by far the most seductive and the place Leilani Kalua spent the majority of her free time. Be it spending her solitude in prayer and deep meditation, paddleboarding, enjoying a homemade lunch under a palm tree artfully sculpted by the trade winds, or giving comfort to the homeless camped out on the Kuilioloa Heiau—the small peninsula-like piece of land once used by ancient Hawaiian navigators and revered as a site of great spiritual significance. Pokai Bay was also the place Maya felt was the most fitting for Leilani's final resting place.

Hopeful for a few close friends to join them for the paddle-out ceremony, Maya and Henry were speechless to see the large turnout from the community coming to pay their respects to a young woman who could have easily been anyone's daughter, niece, grandchild, sister, mother, wife, or best friend.

As she watched people gather on the beach, Maya thought back to a picnic the two women once had here:

****

"I love this place. Of all the places on Oahu, I always felt that this bay and these hills behind us is where I was always meant to be. I remember when I was little, my mother used to bring me here when she wanted to escape a stressful day," Leilani recalled. "There were lots of stressful days back then. Daddy couldn't find steady work, and when he did, there was never enough money to pay all the bills. He always found a way to feed us, though, even when we ended up living out of his truck. I didn't know back then that he spent a lot of his paycheck on his habit. He had it bad. There were many nights I heard him begging to the stars in the sky for his misery to end. But my mom, she was...she never fought with him about it. She knew it wasn't his fault. She knew he got hooked from the drugs given to him after a bad injury. But she also had her own struggle. I remember she would come here to sit at the *heiau*. She'd sit for hours on end, and I would play with the feral cats or build castles in the sand. I'd look out at the water and be so taken by the intensity of the color. I often dreamed that if I were to swim out to the middle of the bay, the water would wrap around me like a blanket and protect me forever. That was right before we moved to Vegas because we just couldn't even afford to be homeless here anymore."

****

Henry placed his surfboard next to Maya's and Hokulani's at the water's edge, then returned to the car to retrieve the small wooden box with Leilani's ashes. He handed it to the *kahu* who came to officiate, then he and the holy man greeted and thanked the people who came to offer condolences and share their love.

He recognized faces from his many encounters over the years—most friendly, some had been adversarial, and some of those faces previously unknown to him. But all of them came together in worship and respect for the deceased as only a culture of aloha and ohana could do.

One by one as the people approached, Maya and Henry greeted them with leis made of white, yellow, or purple plumeria flowers. He couldn't remember the last time he had been physically embraced and kissed by so many. He certainly felt grateful and humbled, and for the first time in all the years he'd lived on this island, he finally understood the spirit of aloha. It made him think of his first meeting with Billy:

****

"So, you're the New Yorker I heard about. I'm Detective Iona, but you can call me Billy."

"Hank Benjamin," he said, looking around the bullpen. "Which desk is mine?"

"Easy there, son. You just got here, yeah?"

"I've been on the job for a few years now."

"Yeah, but you just got here, and you're always in a rush. You're still living in New York, barreling your way through everything. That's not island style, and that's not good."

"How so?"

"I'll give you an example. After just a couple years as a uni, you pushed hard to become a detective, and here you are. While it's admirable, others feel you've jumped to the head of the line."

"Not by special favor and not by cheating. I just know what I want."

"Like I said, you're charging like a bull. One more example. You barely say hello to me, your new partner, and the first thing you say is 'where's my desk?' "

"I'm motivated is all. I just wanna get settled in and get to work."

"Bruddah, you just gotta slow down and relax. The work will be here. You moved here a couple years ago, yeah? You gotta get on island time, my man. You'll live a lot longer, and you'll be a lot happier. Trust me, I know these things. This is my first lesson for you. No need to approach this job like your pants are on fire, okay? That's all I'm saying. So, first things first, brand new detective Hank Benjamin. I'm gonna take you around this place to introduce you to the *ohana*, your new family. You should already know that if you're good to your family, they will always be good to you and have your back. Are you hungry?"

"I could eat."

"Good, because after you meet everybody, we'll go to Oceanside Café for breakfast, and after that we come back and get you your desk."

****

Forty-five people sat upon their surfboards and formed a floating circle just outside the breakwater of Pokai Bay. As tradition dictated, they joined hands to complete the ring. The box with Leilani's ashes was held by the *kahu* as he recited a ceremonial chant. Then he nodded to Maya.

"*Aloha mai kakou, e komo mai, e komo mai.* Hello, my friends, welcome, welcome. Take a look around you. Look at the beauty and the serenity of this holy place. Face the sun and feel its warmth. Turn to the ocean beyond the bay and feel its gentle breeze. Are these things not the hands of our ancestors giving us comfort and letting us know we are loved? Touch the waters, and you touch the source of all life. You've just experienced the heart and the spirit that breathes life into the soul of our mother earth, and what are we if not her children. It is just one more simple reminder that we are of the same source and therefore we are *ohana*, we are family. If you want to know the heart of the beautiful soul we are sending off today, this place is the picture of a thousand words that could easily describe our sister, my friend Leilani Kalua. And how fitting it was that her earthly name described who she was in life. Leilani a beautiful flower, Kalua a companion. Her physical existence in this world was a hard one. She endured more than anyone should have to. But in the short time that her presence blessed my life, I never once heard a complaint; I never once witnessed a moment of bitterness. Just the opposite. She never spoke ill of anyone. In fact, she found beauty in all people, in flowers, in the sand between her toes, and in the sound of the rain. To her the laughter of a young child was a symphony. Perhaps, she learned to cherish that sound because there was not much laughter in her own childhood. I remember she marveled at the gooey texture of poi and took pleasure from the steam rising out of a pot of rice as it washed over her face. She said it was good for her complexion, but I think she did it to remind her of when she was a child and a bowl of rice or a little bit of poi was all she had to eat. If ever I needed a lesson in gratitude and appreciation, she was the perfect teacher. She loved this place and would come here to seek solace because, as much as she wouldn't let the pain of her past make her negative, I believe it was this sacred place that brought peace to her soul. It was this sacred place that allowed her to reconnect with the spirits of her mother and father. And now, she is with them once again, sleeping peacefully and cradled in their arms. I could find no better place for her ashes to rest as her spirit launches back to the heavens from the *heiau* our ancient navigators used to launch their own voyages. It is said that our spirit will continue to return to the physical form until we've learned all of our lessons and pay our karmic debt. I believe this to be true, and I believe in all my heart

Leilani has done just that."

With that, she nodded back to the *kahu* who handed the box to Henry. He opened it, held it out to Maya who helped him pour those ashes into the waters of the Pacific. And without need for a prompt, forty-five colorful plumeria leis were launched into the air followed by cheers and hand splashes that made the floating circle look as if it were a giant lei that had come to life.

As Maya turned a tearful eye to her husband, she felt a small wave lift her board, a warm embrace, smelled the perfume she had once given to Leilani as a Christmas present, and heard her quiet voice whisper on the wind, *Ua lawe mai oe ia u i ka* home, you brought me home. Her eyes lit up as did Henry's, because he heard her too.

Maya thanked the *kahu* and, while the others paddled their way back to the beach, she and Henry stayed behind.

"I've been reading your journal. One page a day, every day since this whole thing started. When I got to the end, I'd start all over from the beginning. It allowed me to believe we would emerge from this mess. It allowed me to believe we would continue our journey together."

"That's why I left it with you. I began writing long before we met because I knew one day, I'd be leaving it for you."

"Does it bother you that so far, Noelani Mendoza walks away from this unscathed?"

"Did she? She lost her one and only son. She knows it's a result of her own actions, and she'll be tortured with that reality for the rest of her days. If that isn't karma, I don't know what is. The question now is are you unscathed? Are your scars too deep to heal? What I asked you to do on my behalf makes me ask if I had that right in the first place."

"Is that why you wanna go back to the rez? Is that why you wanna run off without me? Tell me you're not feeling responsible for all of this, because I know you...and I think you are."

"I know that you're not putting this on my shoulders, but still—"

"Stop right there. This job...this job has affected me in ways that I never imagined. I knew that long before this event today. It's part of the reason why I resigned. Yeah, yeah, I knew I was getting canned, but that's beside the point. Also, I'd be lying if I said that I wasn't afraid that you had become disillusioned with me, and I couldn't live with myself if you were gone. There is one thing you should know. If we stay here, emphasis on 'we,' in addition to doing a little writing, a little private-investigating stuff, I was hoping we could maybe focus on doing a lot more community work. When you said that if you went back to teaching, it was these kids up here that you wanted to serve. That really resonated with me."

"We?"

"Do you really think I would let you go off without me? I've read your journal; I've analyzed those visions of yours, and I think some of your interpretations are a little off."

"Oh?"

"Our mission in this life together is far from over. Our paths are not even close to diverging. What do you think about that?"

"I've been known to misinterpret some of the meanings of my dreams, my visions, my premonitions. After all, it's not an exact science…and even if it was, the science is never settled. So, I guess it's possible."

"Do you remember what you once said to me on a very cold and snowy night?" Henry asked.

"Open-mic poetry night at the rathskeller?"

"That would be the one."

"It was one of our first dates. Of course, I remember."

They turned their boards to face the horizon, took hold of each other's hand, and held them up to catch the setting sun.

Chapter 21

I cannot remember the last time
the voices of my counsel were quiet.
From a constant stream
to a dry riverbed,
there was nothing in between.
It is uncomfortable to say the least.
Save for my intuition,
the silence seems so out of place.
I watch you in your sleep,
spent from a night of passion,
unconscious to the world.
I wish it was that easy,
I wish I could take comfort.
Did I become too reliant on the guidance?
Too addicted to the consultation?
Too expectant of the dialogue?
I recall a message from the very beginning;
"what once was will be again."
And so it is.
So why can't I sleep?

Maya rested her pen and brushed a hand over the newly inked entry—the first addition to those pages in many months—then closed her journal. She had other entries to add that she had kept in a separate tablet during the time she was without her cherished book.

Given the late hour, however, their inclusion would have to come after some much-needed rest. Her fingers caressed the leather cover and couldn't help but notice the worn-out portions of the binder from all the times Henry had tightly grasped it in his sleep—marks from his fingernails now a permanent part of the design. She looked over at him, watching his chest rhythmically rise and fall, unconscious to the world—she was envious of his ability to finally sleep more soundly. Maya smiled, knowing he would tease, that, like a skilled exorcist, it was her wild love-making that purged every ounce of his energy—draining him to exhaustion. Still, she wondered how many exhausted yet sleepless nights he suffered throughout this ordeal. She wondered if he had any regrets, or did he honestly believe that what had happened was predestined and unavoidable? With his silence, she thought him predictably chivalrous in his attempts to bring her comfort.

Restless, she paced the floor, trying to summon help through prayer and a steaming cup of chamomile tea—trying to convince herself that her uneasiness was nothing more than the volume of the silence that was louder than she could remember.

****

Kaelani tossed and turned as the effects of her medication waned. The speed and the intensity of the withdrawal brought her from an opioid-induced euphoric state to a painful and semiconscious confusion that had her ripping away at the bandages. She scratched and pulled at the sutures and staples until both her fingers and bed linens were stained with blood. She faded in and out, repeating the attack several times until the agony was more than she could bear.

311

"Get in here; I need your help," she called to her housemate, then vaguely remembered the woman's panicked exodus after a volley of profanity and a near miss from an empty bottle that had been rifled in her direction. "You're useless anyway, do you hear me? You're useless! I can't believe you ran away and left me here. I wouldn't get mad at you all the time if you knew how to follow directions, damn it! Oh, what's the use? I don't need you. I don't need you at all. I can do this shit myself!"

She reached for the vial of pills on her nightstand and, like before, ignored the label and doubled the dose, which was washed down with the remnants of a very warm lager. She grimaced at the bitter taste but drained the bottle nonetheless.

Bearing down to suppress the pain, Kaelani forced herself out of bed, used a combination of a crutch and the wall for support, and with each step a challenge, she hobbled to the bathroom. With hollowed cheeks and sunken eyes staring back at her, the face in the mirror seemed unfamiliar. "Where the hell did you come from, and who the fuck are you looking at, bitch?" she challenged the image. "Damn it, girl, you look terrible. You should eat something. Go ahead and help yourself to what's in the refrigerator. Lord knows I ain't eating any of it."

She couldn't recall the last time she had an appetite. It was a fleeting thought at best, and she refocused on cleaning her hip before the medication kicked in, causing another ten hours out cold on the linoleum floor.

She bravely suffered the sting of the rubbing alcohol as it splashed over the raw flesh. Daring the reflection to complain about the rough treatment, she always had something to prove—even when alone. Her stomach, empty except for the pills and the couple of ounces of stale beer, began to tighten. She doubled over, then lurched and stumbled her way back to the bedroom. The condition of her bed disgusted her so much she grabbed her phone, her pills, and a small photograph, then set her sights for the lounger in the other room. "You can do this," she said before falling into the chair as her legs gave way. "Just a little more." Using what little upper body strength she had left, Kaelani pulled herself into a seated position, breathed a sigh of satisfaction, then proceeded to check her voicemail: two from the surgeon's office, one from Captain Tanaka, one from Henry, and one from Maya. She listened to Maya's message as the heaviness in her head started to return.

"Hey, Kaelani, it's Maya. Henry tried calling earlier, but we guessed you were sleeping. How's it going? I made some food for you, and we'd like to bring it by if that's okay. Give us a call and let me know if you need anything from the store. Okay then, we'll wait to hear from you. Bye for now."

She stared at the photo stolen from Henry's cottage. "You fucked with me, Mary...Maya, whatever the hell you call yourself. You teased me. You let me believe you had no one in your life. What kind of person does that to someone else? What kind of cold-hearted bitch plays with someone's head like that? Fucking mind games, yeah? You like playing mind games on people? You like hurting people? You fucked with me. You messed with my emotions. I thought you wanted me like I wanted you. Well, guess what? You can't hurt me. You can't hurt me at all, but I'm gonna hurt you. Just you wait. I'll show you what happens to people like you. Malia learned her lesson for betraying me, and you will too."

As Kaelani's vision began to blur and her lids started to falter, she used her remaining energy to crush Maya's photograph.

A word about the author...

Richard I Levine is a native New Yorker raised in the shadows of Yankee Stadium. After dabbling in several occupations and a one-year coast-to-coast wanderlust trip, this one-time volunteer fireman, bartender, and store manager returned to school to become a chiropractor. A twenty-one-year cancer survivor, he's a strong advocate for the natural healing arts. Levine has four Indy-published novels and his fifth work, *To Catch the Setting Sun*, has just been completed. In 2006 he wrote, produced, and was on-air personality of the Dr. Rich Levine show on Seattle's KKNW 1150AM and after a twenty-five-year practice in Bellevue, Washington, he closed up shop in 2017 and moved to Oahu to pursue a dream of acting and being on *Hawaii 5-O*. While briefly working as a ghostwriter/community liaison for a local Honolulu city councilmember, he appeared as a background actor in over twenty-five *5-Os* and *Magnum P.I.s*. Richard can be seen in his first co-star role in the *Magnum P.I.* third-season episode "Easy Money." He presently resides in Hawaii.